Frozen Trail to Merica
Volume Two
Walking to Merica

Frozen Trail to Merica

Volume Two
Walking to Merica

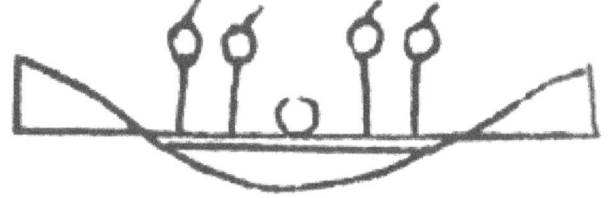

To the [west], in the darkness
they walk and walk all of them.
—Walam Olum 3:18

Myron Paine, Ph.D.
Norwegian Collaborator,
Frode Omdahl

2015
Galde Press, Inc.
Lakeville, Minnesota, U.S.A.

Frozen Trail to Merica: Volume Two, Walking to Merica
© Copyright 2009 by Myron Paine, Ph.D.
Printed in the United States of America

First Edition
Third Printing, 2015

Cover painting by Garret Moore

Galde Press, Inc.
PO Box 460
Lakeville, Minnesota 55044–0460

Contents

Acknowledgments

To my friends in three toastmaster clubs, in an Explorer's group, and in a church group, who have listened patiently to the unbelievable subject of Norse in America. Your willingness to listen allowed me to congeal the hypothesis of this novel. Thanks

To my first editor Julia Youst, who was with me when the "ice" was not yet firm. Julia provided a timely vision to make the novel more readable. Thank you very much.

To Joan Schoellner, TaVee Magner, Richard Moriguchi, Ed Schoemberger, Marcia L. Sydor, John Peeples, George Mendonsa, Virawan Sombutsiri, Paul Paine, and many other supporting readers, who gave me specific feedback on the novel. Your feedback caused me to rewrite the novel—twice! Thank you sincerely.

To Larry Stroud, who also wrote about Sherwin. His interest in reading the draft chapters of the novel was a driving force to keep the re-writing moving along. Larry's interest of ancient artifacts led me to the discovery of the photograph of the härbret that explains the stone columns in the Arctic. Thank you, Larry, for your enthusiastic interest and support.

To Frode Omdahl, a Norwegian, who was also searching in Internet space for Reider T. Sherwin. Together we went on to locate all of Sherwin's eight volumes. Frode collaborated with me by translating the novel into Norwegian. More importantly, he was not shy about suggesting necessary changes. Frode, I am grateful to have you as a collaborator and, more important, a friend.

Finally to my wife Birdie Lou, who watched an interest in history grow into a full time obsession. She discovered her talents for technical proof reading and for unrelenting chopping of excess words. Her loving support made working on the novel possible. Birdie, I am extremely grateful for your talents and support.

Foreword

The Norse in Greenland "vanished" between the years 1340 and 1410. Where did they go?

The Frozen Trail to Merica focuses on this question. The book is written in narration to give human scale to an incredible feat that appears beyond man's ability. Some of the events actually occurred as written. Conjectural prose adds the unknown details of several events. Most characters are fictional, but under the same circumstances the actions of people would have been similar.

Maps are included to provide a scale of the panorama of places. A genealogy is included to provide an understanding of the relationships of people. The Factual Fiction appendix contains information relevant to the story under the heading indicated by the keywords in boldface small capital letters in the text.

In the first book of this set we watched as Talerman grew to be forty-four years old while gaining a reputation as a leader on two continents. The icy circumstances of the Little Ice Age still limited possibilities for normal family life, but Talerman and his friends had learned hard lessons. They knew there was a way out—a long, cold, hard way out. Could they convince the people in Greenland to follow them to a strange land?

When I began to write the *Frozen Trail to Merica* manuscript, my intentions were to explain how the last seven verses of the *Walam Olum* may solve the mystery of the vanishing of the Norse people in Greenland between 1340 and 1410. But the first reviewers all commented, "I do not understand what is going on."

If you have just picked up this book and have volume one, *Talerman*, available, please read it first. Then you will know "what is going on" and you can read this book with understanding.

If you choose to read this volume without the background provided by

Talerman, the following synopsis may help give you a skeleton sketch of the situation and locations.

Synopsis of *Talerman*

Talerman begins with a vignette of Maalan Arum, an old Leni Lenape historian, who learns he will soon die. He wants to record the story of the migration which is in his mind. Two youth, Azon and Pitolo, are selected to help him make pictographs and verses of the migration. Vignettes of the pictograph development alternate with historical information and Maalan Arum's stories.

The historical description begins with the Big People in Ungava Bay before the explosion of Krakatoa in 535. The big people make low stone walls as bases for inverted boats which are used as shelters. Then the Christian Albans of Scotland and Ireland are driven to America by the Vikings.

Maalan Arum tells the Alban side of the big fight, similar to the Norse saga story, where the Vikings are defeated by Albans, who use catapults, war slings, and crossbows. The Vikings in Greenland divide into house builders and hunters. The hunters return to Ungava in small groups and go on to the marsh area on the west side of James Bay to hunt geese for survival.

Christianity drives families, who believe in Odin, to the marsh area. Small groups of Albans and Norse interact as friends because they both recognize the cross symbol worn by the others. King Haakon Haakon IV sails to America and declares it to be "Haakon's man," meaning "Haakon's people." When he gets back to Norway, he sends men back to build a church at Newport, Rhode Island. Haakon's man morphs into Akomen.

Magnus, a fictional character, tries to help King Haakon establish Haakon's Eastern Settlement in Greenland. He fails and flees to the Northern Settlement. King Haakon returns to America and is disappointed by the lack of construction of the church at Newport, but he uses his fleet to impress Greenland and Iceland on the way back to Norway. Greenland and Iceland agree to become Norway colonies. King Haakon dies and civil war returns to Norway.

Then the narration advances to 1300. Most of Northeast America is in chaos because of the deepening cold, because many of the Norse men taking native wives, and because the men who come from Norway fight each other.

In Greenland, Bjarni (Talerman) is born. The Greenland men argue about hunting close to home or traveling long distances to get food in the cold weather. Bjarni's mother dies when neither method gets her food in time. Bjarni's cousin joins men who sail to Merica but walk home on the frozen ocean. Bjarni's cousin makes roundtrips to Merica in the following years.

Bjarni and his cousin help row the Paafa's to the Eastern Settlement in 1315. They meet Bishop Arne, who asks to go across the ice to Merica. They make the trip across the ice two years later. Bjarni becomes the laughing stock when a buffalo hunt results in only one baby bull. Later Bjarni becomes a hero after winning a fight with a bear. At the end of his journey Bjarni becomes a beaver head, a respected man in America.

Bjarni is chosen as the young wise one by the older Norsemen walking back to Greenland. His ability to make wise decisions develops into a recognized reputation. Bjarni returns home to marry Arnora. He turns down chances to go to America for meat. The men who do go miss his ability to make wise decisions. But Bjarni has made a bad decision to stay at home. His son dies of protein poisoning. Because of his own protein poisoning, combined with his son's death, Bjarni goes into a deep depression. Arnora realizes the need to eat fat and threatens Bjarni to go get meat to trade for fat. Bjarni walks to his cousin's house and trades caribou meat for seal fat.

Then Bjarni joins the men going to Merica to get meat and fat at the open water marvels. His reputation as a man who makes wise decisions grows on both sides of Davis Strait. During times when the Norse men are trapped in Merica because of impassible pack ice, Bjarni asks the men to think about how they could use the low stone walls for shelters for families if they migrate.

Bishop Arne observes Bjarni's development as a leader and decides to give him the honorary name of Talerman, the speaker of the people. Bjarni chooses to remain behind in Merica when a period of pack ice prevents boats from getting through. For three years he and his men hunt and visit hunting camps in Akomen.

They begin visiting with a plan to enlist the local people as helpers for a possible migration. By the third year they just try to maintain the good relations with the friends they have made.

Bjarni and his followers believe the cold is coming again. When the cold does come they will try to convince everyone in Greenland to walk to Merica and on to Akomen. Read this book to learn how Bjarni, Arne, and his friends saved the people of Greenland by *Walking to Merica*.

Map of Frozen Trail to Merica

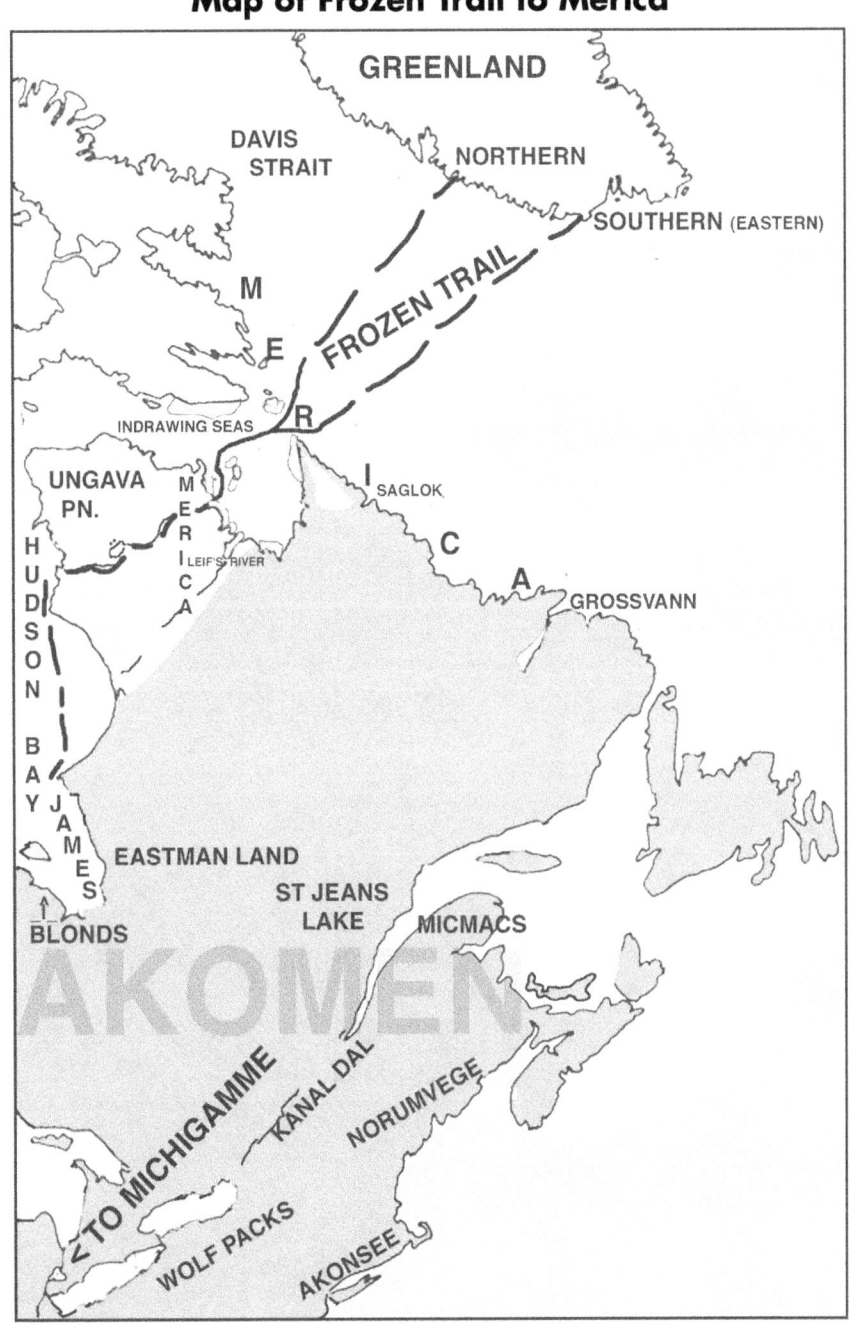

GREENLAND

DAVIS STRAIT

NORTHERN

SOUTHERN (EASTERN)

M

E

FROZEN TRAIL

R

INDRAWING SEAS

UNGAVA PN.

M
E
R
I
C
A

SAGLOK

LEIF'S RIVER

I

C

A

GROSSVANN

H
U
D
S
O
N

B
A
Y

J
A
M
E
S

EASTMAN LAND

ST JEANS LAKE

MICMACS

BLONDS

AKOMEN

TO MICHIGAMME

KANAL DAL

NORUMVEGE

WOLF PACKS

AKONSEE

Stories of Maalan Aarum

Where Should We Go?

Engraved Stick (E.S.) 3:14

Talerman's *Thing*

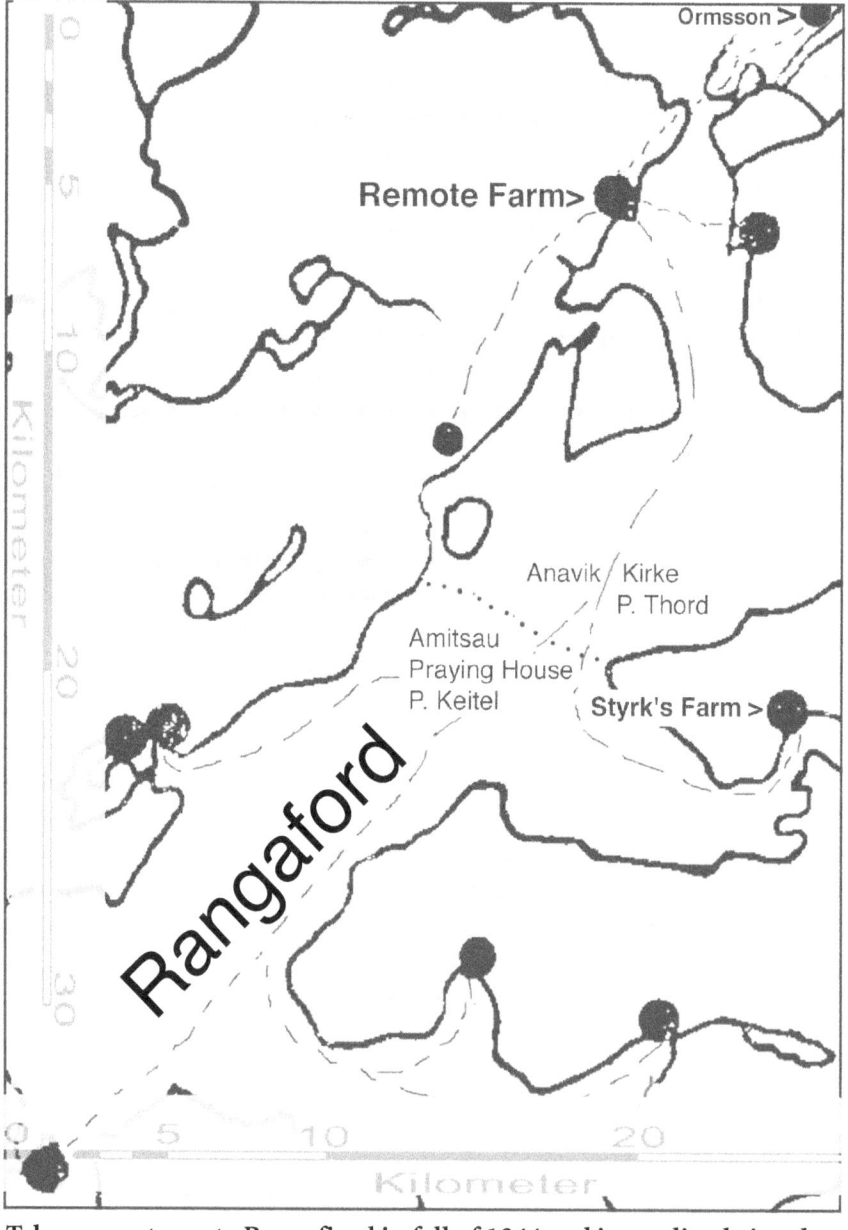

Talerman returns to Rangafjord in fall of 1344 and immediately invokes his power as sakkyndig to call the families in the nearest nine houses to an overnight Thing. He knows the Thing may be the tipping point.

Where Should We Go?

At the remote farm around the peninsula on the northeast end of Ranga Fjord, omens for the future were not good. During the previous winter the livestock had consumed all the forage before they could be put on grass. Some of the animals, including the old bull, starved. In the spring they had borrowed a bull from the neighbors on their small peninsula. But only one of their three cows had settled. She would give birth later in the fall, not in summer when the milk would be better. The animals were now at pasture. Thjodhild, Ingjald, and their four children were camping in a hide tent in the pasture. Thjodhild liked the sense of freedom.

The haying had not gone well. There was about one moon's time less hay than the year before.

The seal harvest had also been small. The cold weather caused the seals to come onto the ice farther south than expected. The delayed scramble to get to the seals resulted in a lower kill than normal. Caribou were not to be seen. The Arctic hares were also scarce, as were the ptarmigans, so the white foxes were not around in great numbers.

Fortunately Bjørn, a mere boy but good with a harpoon, had struck a walrus in the summer. The nine farms in the fjord divided the walrus flesh according to tradition. Bjørn received one tusk, in addition to his share of the meat, as the reward for his skill.

At least there was some meat to be made into pemmican. When the pounding was done and the fat poured over it, the pemmican would go into a natural refrigerator, a hole dug down to permafrost. Turf covered the pemmican in the hole.

The view was still majestic, but the remote farm was not, at the time, a great place to live. The climate of late summer was already chilly. The remote farm in the fall, when Bjarni was forty-four years old, was a poor place at a poor time to continue a story. But that is where Maalan Aarum's story resumed.

Arnora was swinging the rounded mallet with anger.

Thud! "Men!" thud, "All must be," thud, "like stupid," thud, "oxen!" thud.

She laid the mallet on the stone table. She retied the bowknot holding the sealskin covering her fur clothes. Then she skimmed a layer of fat from the simmering kettle and spread a thin layer on the beaten meat. She covered the fat with a scattering of dried berries. She was careful to put on the right amount. Too few berries and teeth began to hurt. Too little fat caused belly pains and made people's feet swell.

The stone table was located outside, beside the food room door, so Arnora could see the glacier, the boat pull-out, and the trail up to the house. She could also see much of the pasture including Thjodhild's tent where her own children Yngvild and Bjørn were visiting.

She had her back to the food-room door and the corner of the house behind her. She felt secure because nobody would think of landing in the birch fjord and climbing over the ridge to the house. Normally she liked solitude. Today, because of her anger, she really enjoyed it. She rolled up the first batch of pemmican and pushed it aside. She lifted a seal-hide sack of dried meat and poured it evenly on the stone working table.

She picked up the mallet. Thud! "All men," thud, "Oxen!" thud, "Bjarni," thud, "is a…" She felt the bow knot slip. The sealskin slipped away.

Her left hand flew to the short lance leaning against the wall. She raised the mallet high. Her right foot hooked back. With a "Hunnah" she turned, intending to drive the lance in an arc toward the neck of the person behind her. As she swirled, she heard, "Is this the house of the hellion?"

"Bjarni!" The lance stopped. It fell to the earth with the mallet. Bjarni had deftly stepped back. He opened his arms. He was holding cloth in one hand and beads in the other. Her arms surrounded his head with an embrace. He clutched her body close.

Bjarni raised his eyes to locate the door to the great room. He lifted Arnora, took a step past the table. He headed toward the door. He squeezed her body tightly to him. He entered.

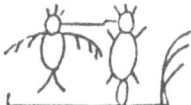

Once more Arnora enjoyed the old sensations. Naked under the bearskin, her body was snuggled close to Bjarni. She felt the blessed sense of togetherness. Her contentment was overwhelming her thoughts. Bjarni seemed to be asleep. She would drift back to sleep herself.

But no! She heard voices. Looking up, she saw the orange light from the other room flickering on the ceiling.

"I better get dressed," she said.

"Why?"

"There are men out there."

"They can take care of themselves. They always do. The men will not be pushy. They are good men. They were with me at the *Althing*."

"Oh, the *Althing*, the annual meeting in the south where everyone goes. Why did you not take me along?"

"I told you this spring. It was too far for you to go to the *Althing*. Besides, I was busy most of the time. Most of the wives from the North Settlement were not there."

"And many of those wives were angry!"

"I sensed your anger as you swung the mallet. I do not understand why you were so angry."

Arnora said, "Bjarni, for more than three years you have been in Merica. At first I missed you terribly. Then, as if I grew numb, I learned to cope. I thought I might be a widow. Many women here are.

"Suddenly, this spring you show up just before the frozen trail breaks up. For two months my hopes were high. I thought we would have a full summer together. A full summer would be nearly half the time as we have been together in the past six years. Then, suddenly, you told me you had to go to the *Althing* because all the important men go there to make decisions about Greenland. You never cared about their decisions before.

"But you left me and one moon's time passes, two moon's time, and now three. Every moon's time I waited, the angrier I got. Our time together is so precious. I know you will have to walk to Merica as soon as the ice freezes. I am angry, really angry at you for wasting my best opportunity in six years to be with you."

Bjarni replied, "Arnora, I walked the frozen trail this spring because, as I told you, getting to the *Althing* this summer was vital to us being together for many years, not moons."

Arnora moved her head away from Bjarni's chest and looked at his face. "I do not see the difference. You were never here during summers for three years when the weather was cold. You were not here at all during three years of warm weather. This time I thought it would be different. But you were not with me this summer even if you were in Greenland. I believe I am married to a snow ghost who only comes to me in the coldest moons."

Bjarni talked at the ceiling as he replied, "Arnora, forgive me. I desperately wanted to be near you also. But there were developments at the *Althing* that will make our future together possible. Events are happening faster than we beaver-heads expected they would. Sometimes the whole plan is scary. Especially when many people suddenly start to think it will work. The beaver-heads say we should not talk about it too much or the evil spirits will find ways to undo us."

She tightened her legs around his left thigh. She pushed her breasts until his chest hair tickled her left nipple. Her lips touched his skin on the neck below the ear.

"Am I an evil spirit?"

"No, but I am sure you are the hellion they talked about."

"What! How dare you! I am not a hussy!"

Bjarni explained, "I did not say hussy. I said hellion. A hellion is a woman who fights like hell to avoid lying with just any man. After I have been away every day for three long years, I am pleased my wife has earned herself a widely known fame as a hellion."

Arnora tried to absorb the words. "Well, I did not—when did you hear about my fame as a hellion?"

"Two men talked to me when we traveled in the Eastern Settlement. Each man spoke to me privately at a different place. They both were ashamed. But they both wanted me to know how fortunate I was to have a very valuable woman. They said you were a strong woman with a well-known fame—as a hellion. I had not heard about your fame before, but I agreed with their thoughts about you being a valuable woman."

Arnora pulled her knees up and swung them under her as she turned her body. She was half sitting on her legs and half lying on Bjarni's chest. She looked intently at his face. "Who were these men?"

"I promised each I would never tell. My promise is good to keep. We men may be in the same boat someday." Bjarni smiled at Arnora, "But I am sure you can guess their names."

"Would one of them be named Vifill?"

"Yes, Vifill had a reddish scar along the front shoulder to a red spot just under his jaw."

Arnora shuddered slightly. She looked at the hair on Bjarni's chest. "What did he say about the hellion?"

"He said he was strongly attracted to the hellion's body until her lance cut off his badge and caused him to bleed. The sight of his blood suddenly made him hungry."

"Just like men. If they cannot force a woman to lie, they always want to fill their belly."

As a playful gesture, Bjarni put his right index finger on Arnora's nose. "He also said he would go with us to Akomen. He told me that he has been to many places in this world. He knows that a man who can live with a hellion is a man to follow to the ends of the ice."

Arnora shook her head, grabbed Bjarni's arm, and pinned it above his head. "Ha! He was assuming you can live with the hellion."

Bjarni did not resist the pinning. Arnora's breasts above his face made the surrender endurable. Then Arnora drew back. She placed both hands on Bjarni's chest. She looked at her hands, took in a deep breath, and then looked into Bjarni's eyes saying quietly, "Would another man be named Gard?"

Bjarni's eyes flashed with surprise. Then came a look of puzzlement. "Not at the *Althing*, but I do know a Gard. A Gard Asvaldson rowed in my canoe for three summers. He is a big man. His parents were Danes. The Eskimos thought he descended from the Tunit. He was a reliable, resourceful companion. A few times he deflected men and weapons coming at me. Is it he?"

Bjarni felt Arnora's involuntary shudder under the robe. She sucked in a short breath. Then a smile spread across her face. She was trying to imagine two men, with one of them having something to hide, rowing in the same canoe. "Did you see his big bare chest?"

"No, he always wore a deerskin coverlet. The few times he washed he preferred to bathe in the stream alone."

Arnora let her robe fall open. She placed one finger on Bjarni's chest and, drawing a slash, she inquired, "So, you never saw the red slash on his chest? What did he have to say about the hellion?"

"He never mentioned a hellion. He was always very quiet. When the other men told stories about women, he would just roll up to sleep. One time the men teased and teased him to say something about women. All he said was: 'A man who has a faithful wife is very, very lucky.' Then he rolled up to sleep."

Arnora leaned back, crossing her arms and tilting her head. "Well, the hellion can tell you that he was a giant man, but he got hungry at the sight of blood too. Still, as you said, he was reliable. After the slashing, Gard did stay in the house for two moon's time. The first night he had come carrying caribou meat. He misunderstood my elation at having enough food for all to eat. By morning, after a night to nurse his wound, he sensed that we were desperate for food, so he stayed to hunt for us. You are right, he is a resourceful hunter. We were weak and sick then, so we relied on him to get the fires started, water in the pots, and other chores. He was also respectful. Maybe I had relaxed too much that first night. A powerful, respectful man, like you, is seductive. But when he started to…What stories did you tell?"

"A few about the robe warmer I knew before we married."

Arnora shook her head violently. "Bjarni! I am a grown woman. You have traveled many years in a land where stories of willing robe warmers are legend. You could hardly avoid the offers. I do not like it. I hope there were few, but do not lie to me."

Bjarni's hands grasped Arnora's shoulders. He held her centered so they looked eye to eye. "If I have learned anything in my travels, it is that no person likes lies. Tjalve was the one who taught me how to refuse politely. I just said, 'It is against my religion.' I think I gained more respect for that action. People around the campfire the next day treated me as if they trusted me more.

"My other action came from your own advice, which I followed. I kept walking from village to village. After many sleeps in the same village, people expect even a man with strong religion to take a woman into his wigwam. As long as my group kept moving, the situation did not come up. So, Arnora, believe me. I am not lying to you."

Arnora used her forearms against his to knock Bjarni's hands from her shoulders. She still looked Bjarni directly in the eyes. "I would be a fool to argue against you, because I want to believe my actions have been rewarded by your loyalty. But I continue to doubt. What would happen, for instance, if you woke up some morning to find a willing woman in your robes?"

Bjarni smiled. His eyes reflected the humor in his voice as he said, "Arnora, I wake up with a willing woman every time I am home. You know what happens."

Arnora tapped her right fist on Bjarni's chest. "No, I meant another willing woman."

Bjarni grabbed Arnora's fist. His eyes narrowed. "I have worried about that too. Arnora, Big Raven Arne is the only saint I know. I am a man. We both know what might happen when a man finds a willing woman in his robes."

Arnora shook her head, and tapped Bjarni's chest with her left hand. "I try to keep thoughts like that out of my mind. If, for some reason, it happens, I do not want to know. But beware, Bjarni; here in Rangafjord hunger drives actions. While you were away, I heard of three cases where young single women had become with child by richer, married men."

Bjarni held both of Arnora's fists. He nodded once. "That practice was happening before I left home. Rangafjord people expect the man to support the woman and her child as well as his own family. When I was a youth, we boys dreamed to become rich enough for young women to trap us."

Arnora snatched her hands free. She planted them on Bjarni's chest nearer to his throat. Her face showed stress. She was hissing as she said, "Bjarni, in the same time period, I have heard about fourteen or fifteen of those 'trappings'. In the three cases I am talking about, the young girls, and their unborn babies, were dead within weeks of moving into the man's house."

Bjarni moved his hands to recover Arnora's hands. His face showed that he was truly puzzled. He asked simply, "How?"

"Bjarni, the polite talk is that one drowned, one froze, and the last one hit her head after falling. The gossip is that, really, the wives killed them."

"Were the wives that jealous?"

Arnora sat straight. She pulled her robes open, saying, "Look at me. Do I look like I am eating enough?" She raked her fingers along her clearly visible ribs. "We have lost one child to hunger. Even now our two children are hungry. Thjodhild's children need food more than ours. We cannot have two more mouths in this house. So, if you are a man with a willing woman, expect me to behave like a jealous, starving woman. Your willing woman, with child, may not live one moon's time after you bring her into this house. She may fall on my lance."

Bjarni saw that their talking had turned very serious. He wanted to change the subject. "In Akomen, when men talked about women, I, like Gard, rolled up to go to sleep. I would lay there thinking how unlucky I was." Bjarni rolled his head sideways. He tried to put on an unlucky face.

"Unlucky?"

"For being so far away from my Arnora, for so long." Bjarni glanced to see if the phrase had improved her mood. It had. Then he remembered, "There is another man?"

Arnora brought the robe closed again. She sucked in a short breath. She turned to look at the dark wall. Her voice trembled as she said, "Runolf is the only other man who would carry any scars."

"Ah, yes, I met him. He had a brown scar low on the left side. He seemed so sad. His friends said he is now happier than he has been in years. His friends said he likes dogs better than women."

Arnora's voice still trembled as she asked, "Will he follow you to the ends of the ice?"

"No, he was embarrassed to tell me how y— the hellion was such an allure. He said closeness to the hellion could be fatal to him. He told me he has chosen to always go in the other direction as far as he can go. He wanted me to tell you there was no hatred in his choice. He wished us the best."

Arnora gave a sigh of relief. Then she was breathing quietly. The talking had been more troubling than Bjarni thought it would be. But he also thought the issue should be finished. So he asked, "Are there other men without scars?"

Arnora said softly, "I… the hellion lived a long way from other houses. People who usually lived in her house were sometimes away. The hellion tried to be helpful to passing strangers in a barren land. She learned men's fancies become queer in the cold dark. The point of a lance helps men re-focus on more practical desires, like eating. Fortunately, many men chose not to test the lance. Only three, who carry scars, were foolish enough to try."

With a shake of her head, sending her hair flying, Arnora showed that the subject was closed. She aimed her right index finger at Bjarni's nose say-ing, "But you have not told me anything about the *Althing*."

Bjarni raised his hands over his head. He was smiling as he said, "All this talk about blood has made me hungry. Besides I sent some beaver-heads to invite the neighbors of Rangafjord over to parley. Let us join them in the great room. Then after they are settled I can talk to everyone at the same time."

Arnora threw off the covers and slid out of bed. "What? You invited the neighbors without telling me? Now I must get my clothes on! My fame as a cook, instead of seals, may be going into the pot. If my cooking fame does not survive this mess, you personally will see the hellion increase her fame with a vengeance."

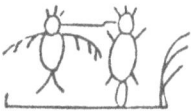

In truth Bjarni, as sakkyndig, had sent a summons instead of an invi-tation to the neighbors of Rangafjord. His beaver-head messengers told all the adults and children above fifteen years that they were expected to come and stay the night. A major group decision was going to be made. As Arnora dressed, all those neighbors were rowing toward the remote house.

Arnora came out of the master bedroom while tying an apron over her best fur dress. She was muttering to herself, "Sixty people. Sixty people are more than our household by, by…"

"A factor of six," said Hallgrim, whom she nearly ran into. "How much seal do you eat every day?"

Arnora answered, "If there are no limits, we eat a seal a day. We plan for that."

"Then we will need at least six seals," said Hallgrim. "We were able to bring two. We found the walrus meat you were turning to pemmican. We can use that."

Arnora said, "There is a seal under the stones on the north side. It has been there five sleeps. The meat should be turned by now."

"Good, that is equal to four," replied Hallgrim. "I asked Tjalve and Styrk to beg for two seals each. If the people have them, we will get more than we need. Do you have anything else?"

"The bundles of caribou bones I save for hunters that drop in."

"How many?"

Arnora held her fingers to her temple, trying to remember, "I tie them in bundles for four men and put them in the cold hole. I think there are thirteen bundles left."

Hallgrim said, "Not quite enough, but close. I know Halldis is bringing the rear legs of a sheep. You can start with that, and then bring out the bones after the mutton is nearly gone from the pot."

Arnora added, "I have enough butter, and dried fish. I think I should serve that in the morning. For good things tonight I have the guts with fat stuffed into them. I know I have guts from eight seals. I also have the roots we get down in the birch thicket. I bundle them for four people. I have more than twenty bundles. I suppose we could get out a sealskin with fermented birds. Some people, especially the youth, are starting to like them."

"Good," said a smiling Hallgrim. "I think you have enough food. We asked others to bring something if they could."

Arnora smiled back, saying, "Now I know why Bjarni calls you his numbers man. But numbers will not get us more cooking pots. We will need at least, at least…"

"Six," replied Hallgrim. "We have four getting warm now. I brought one of ours along. We found your two and the old one in the food room. The crack leaks a little but we smeared heavy grease on the inside and can keep doing that through the night."

Arnora said, "Thjodhild has one out in the tent. The only other one that is close is across the little bay. The sun will be down by the time somebody gets it."

Hallgrim nodded. "When Styrk and his sons arrive, we will send the boys to the pasture to bring Thjodhild and her family home. You will need her boiling pot and her help. Then the boys can row across the bay to go after another boiling pot from the neighbors."

"That is what Bjarni says he likes about you: numbers and quick ideas."

Hallgrim smiled as he turned to adjust a sputtering wick. "Did he tell you that on the trail I can cook almost as well as you?"

Styrk with his wife Halldis and their sons were the first to come into the great hall. They were from the Amitsau praying house nearby, but they lived just as close to Bjarni's great hall. Three other men of Rangafjord left their wives at home with the younger children, but they brought five older boys and two older girls. Paafa Ketil from Styrk's praying house slipped in to stand against the wall. Then Arnora saw Sigrid enter the room. Of the six wives from the far houses, Sigrid was the decision-maker. Arnora thought, *I am pleased Sigrid is here; we will not have twelve undecided people at least.*

A few moments later Paafa Thord, who served Talerman's kirke, entered and went to visit with Paafa Ketil. In time, there were fifty-eight people clustered around the boiling pots eating, sitting cross-legged on the floor, sitting on the benches, or leaning against the wall.

All of the people in the great room were visiting in small groups. They all expected an important meeting. Some of the adults were aware that many of the beaver-heads and the priests had just returned from a prolonged journey through the Eastern Settlement. They had heard from other men, who came back earlier in the summer, that the decision at the *Althing* had been very close. They were anxiously waiting for Talerman to tell of the meetings at the other kirkes.

Because Talerman was in his homeland, he had wanted to open the migration discussions in the Northern Settlement with a good start. The desire for a friendly crowd was the reason he summoned his closest neighbors to the great room.

After entering the great room, Talerman visited with many of the guests as he worked his way around the boiling pots. When he neared his bench in the center of the wall opposite the door, the loud jabbering lowered to a hushed murmur. Several eyes watched the Talerman's every move. When he sat down, the room went quiet.

Talerman looked around. Then he said in a loud voice for all to hear, "I have been surprised to hear many of you, especially the women, ask, 'Where is Akomen?' As you know, all of us call the lands to the west 'Merica'. We get to Merica by sailing or by walking over the frozen ice.

"When we get to Merica, we hunters going to Akomen walk across the land to the west. On the other side of that land is another salty sea. Hunters walk to the shore of that salty sea. From there they go south on the ice. The walk on the ice takes about a moon's time. At the end of the walk is a land called 'Akomen.'

"When we beaver-heads were in Merica and Akomen we often talked around the campfires about the possibility of moving our families to Akomen. We talked about how to make a safe migration for our families. Everyone thought first of sailing. But the people in Einarsfjord and Lysefjord have few big boats. So a migration by water would be much too long. Also the unsure season for safe sailing would make water migration much too risky. Then we realized that nearly every one of us men had walked the frozen trail more than once. Some hunters make two round trips every year.

"So, over many campfires, we schemed. We thought maybe we could convince our families to walk the frozen trail to Akomen with us. If you families walked the frozen trail, life would be so much better for all. We hunters would not have to be away from our families most of the year. If we pulled you to Merica, we would not have to pull pemmican home year after year. Slowly, the migration began to seem possible to us.

"As many of you know, most of us hunters wear beaver hats. The beaver hats help the people in Akomen know which men are familiar with Akomen customs. The Akomen people know that blond, blue-eyed men without beaver hats need watching.

"We hunters in Merica selected experienced beaver-heads who came from each of the kirkes in the fjords of Greenland. Those beaver-heads returned with me. Each beaver-head planned to talk about the migration to the people of his own kirke.

"This spring we beaver-heads walked from Merica to the Northern Settlement just before the frozen trail melted. We went to the Eastern Settlement as soon as we could sail. At the *Althing* in the Eastern Settlement, we talked about the migration. We talked with as many people in the Eastern Settlement as possible. Now we are here to talk to you.

"I know most of you have discussed the idea of migrating at home. Many of the women in this room have made the sled run to Merica. You women know that crossing the ice is hard, but it is possible. The distance from Merica to Akomen is shorter than the distance from Rangafjord to Merica, but some of the walking must be over land. The land is better traveled in the winter when both water and land are frozen. The walk over the land through snow is harder than the walk on the ice, but walking across the soggy ground in the summer with the many flies biting is sheer torture.

We beaver-heads prefer to walk to Akomen in winter. We believe that all of you can make the entire walk in three moon's time.

"Tonight each of you must make a decision affecting all of us. We beaver-heads have been a long time bringing our proposal to you in the Northern Settlement. We waited until we knew the decisions of the *Althing* and the Eastern Settlement before talking to you. We waited because if the Eastern Settlement was opposed to migrating, then we in the Northern Settlement would have had difficult choices to make. Many of the beaver-heads believe the Northern Settlement does not have enough men to make the migration survive in the face of possible enemies. We now know that if the Northern Settlement decides to walk to Akomen, most of the people near Einarsfjord will follow. Their numbers will increase our strength.

"I am hoping you can make a decision here tonight. If we can decide tonight, we beaver-heads will have just enough time to get ready for the migration to Merica next winter. A decision not to decide will be the same as a 'no' decision. By the time you leave tomorrow, everybody will know if we will migrate or not.

"If we are to migrate to Akomen or if we stay here, we need everyone to decide as a group. As we talk tonight, think, will you move your families to Akomen as members of your Kirke or praying house group? When we know your answer, we may change the history of Lysefjord and Einarsfjord."

Hallgrim and Tjalve, seated in a corner, watched the movements of the crowd. Then they put their heads together, talking quietly. They were close in their estimates. The ten youth were a toss up. About twice as many men were in favor than opposed. But eight men did not reveal their position. Ten women did not either. Tjalve and Hallgrim were surprised that four women gave clear nods they would go to Akomen. The crowd seemed to be slightly in favor, but there were about twenty uncommitted people. Hallgrim held his hands flat in front of his chest, crossing them back and forth. Talerman caught the signal. He knew the outcome of a summer's effort was still in balance.

Arnora brought slices of seal meat to add to the stews near the center of the room. When she turned toward the food room, Talerman continued, "We beaver-heads did not go straight to the *Althing*. We went to Big Raven Arne's house first."

Paafa Thord stepped forward from his position near the entrance. He raised his right hand. He pointed over the boiling pots to Bjarni. Paafa Thord said loudly, "I told you before, his title is Bishop Arne and you know it!"

Bjarni put his hands on his hips, glaring at Paafa Thord. He answered, "And you know everyone in Akomen calls him Big Raven Arne. He prefers for most us in the Northern Settlement to do the same."

Then Tjalve stood, shaking his head. Talerman saw Tjalve's move and remembered the purpose for the meeting. They needed the help of the priests to convince the people to migrate. So Talerman extended his hands, palms up, and spoke, "Paafa Thord, I ask your forgiveness. I have been calling Bishop Arne 'Big Raven' most of my life. Allow me to finish what I have to say, then you and Paafa Ketil can talk to us without interruption."

Paafa Thord had put his arms on his own hips. He was swayed more by the tone of respect than the words. He dropped his arms, gave a slight nod to Talerman, and stepped back to the wall.

Talerman continued, "We knew the Greenland people would never leave their homes unless the priests in their kirkes bless the venture. We also knew Big—Bishop Arne was once in favor of going to Akomen, but we were not sure if he was still in favor. Some of the beaver-heads had heard him talking about sailing directly to Akonsee. We thought it necessary to know if Bishop Arne was in favor of our plan."

Styrk rose from his seat next to Talerman. He shifted from foot to foot, obviously wanting to talk. Talerman nodded. Styrk spoke: "How do these priests get so much influence? Halldis says she will walk the frozen trail only if Paafa Ketil is in favor. Why should she listen to him? He has not walked the ice."

Paafa Ketil stepped forward, raised his right hand, palm up, and spoke quietly, "Styrk, I apologize for not meeting you at the *Althing*. I stayed here, in the Northern Settlement, because many families needed comforting.

"Bishop Arne appoints priests to serve in the local kirkes and praying houses. I have baptized all your family. Also I have comforted Halldis and the rest of your family many times, especially when Halldis's parents died. I believe I provided needed support."

Styrk waved his right hand across his face, then responded, "Paafa Ketil, I have known you since we were kids. I could always whip you. I have difficulty believing you gave support that I could not. What have you done to gain so much influence over Halldis?"

Paafa Ketil continued in his quiet manner, "I visited Halldis shortly after each of your children was born. I have been with your family more times than you have. During the first ten years of your oldest son's life, you were home only three years. Most of the other seven years, you came home only for a moon's time at Christmas.

"Instead of running off like you did, I have stayed here with the people in distress. I have suffered with them. I have starved with them. I have prayed with them.

"Because I am one of five people in the Northern Settlement who can write, I was, several times, able to request food and robes from Bishop Arne."

"Paafa Ketil," Styrk exploded, "I pulled many sleds full of pemmican to feed my family. I starved myself to save pemmican for families here. When I arrived here from Merica, the families were starving. They needed all the pemmican we brought. Yet you dare tell me you were responsible for saving them?"

Paafa Ketil, still speaking softly, replied, "I was partly responsible. Four years ago, I wrote Bishop Arne about our lack of food even as summer approached. The hunters did not get across the ice in early spring that year.

"Bishop Arne was able to use his influence to get ships to go to Merica. Those ships brought back enough pemmican to give us food until the next winter when the hunters brought more pemmican."

Styrk was visibly agitated. "But Paafa Ketil, the men in Merica were the people who loaded the boats. We were able to send two shipments of pemmican by boat. By our efforts, we saved many people, including my family."

Paafa Ketil responded, "Styrk, you did save the people, including me, but Bishop Arne was responsible for sending the boats. I was responsible for sending the timely message to Bishop Arne."

Styrk, waving his hand again in disgust, said, "I see we have a standoff right now. I will not follow you even if you pray for me. I believe in the Great Spirit of Akomen instead of your God."

Most people in the great room had never heard an exchange where the words of a priest were questioned. All nineteen women and half of the men sucked in their breath when they heard their God denounced.

Paafa Ketil said quietly, "Bishop Arne told us they are the same spirit, Styrk. The first Big Raven who walked to Eastman Land over two centuries ago taught the Original Ones about God. Because those people were used to thinking of animal spirits, the first Big Raven was more effective when he talked about a Great Spirit than when he tried to tell them about a powerful God. There are many paths to the top of the mountain. At the top, the Great Spirit and God are the same."

There were sighs of audible relief. Several women nodded their heads in agreement. Styrk sensed that the mood of the group was turning toward Paafa Ketil. Halldis moved out of the food room to stand in the doorway. Styrk noticed her movement. He changed the subject slightly: "If your God is so great, why did his most powerful man on earth, the Popa, assign Big— Bishop Arne to serve a country having less than two hundred and eighty farms?"

Paafa Ketil responded quickly. "Bishop Arne says the reason is because someone in Norway wrote the Popa about the great number of people in Merica and Akomen. There are a hundred souls to be saved in Akomen and Merica for every soul in Greenland. The few thousand souls in all of Greenland are like a misty rain over a wide river in Akomen. One of the first bishops to come to Lysefjord went on to Merica as soon as he could. Some say he never returned."

Styrk, in a reflective voice, answered, "I have spent more of my time in Merica and Akomen than I have in Rangafjord. I have heard tales about the Big Raven in Akomen. The Original Ones and the K'nistenaux have beliefs similar to the ones my family is learning from you. Those people even have altars in most tepees. Except over there the pavows do not serve in kirkes. There are no kirkes."

Paafa Ketil, respecting the change in Styrk's tone, smiled and said, "The kirkes in Greenland were built by the leading farm families. Because the farmhouses are permanent, the kirkes are also. We priests have been appointed by Bishop Arne to serve the people who come to the kirkes. Bishop Arne told me the hunters in Eastman Land move their camps three to four times a year, so a permanent kirke is not useful there.

"Bishop Arne also said each village has their own praying man called a 'pavow.' Their word 'pavow' sounds similar to our 'paafa.' From what Bishop Arne could learn, the comforting roles are similar. Bishop Arne said most people visit the pavow's hut for spiritual support, but not at a set time or all at once. He said they have a word for 'cross' that sounds like ours, and many people wear one. He said they also had a word similar to our word for prayer. Do you know what it is?"

Styrk replied, "You must mean the word 'attaboan.' I guessed, correctly, that they were talking about 'ALTERGANG' when I first heard them say 'attaboan.' As a little boy I used the word 'altergang' to mean 'prayer.'"

Paafa Ketil, with a truly friendly smile, replied, "So, even if the people of Akomen have no kirkes, their belief in the Great Spirit may be as strong as our belief in God because the faith is inside each hut and every man. When we get to the top of the mountain, we all will see only one God, even if you, and they, call him the Great Spirit."

The women and youth in the great room were learning about things rarely discussed in the kirke or at home. After the first confrontation, they were relieved to sense the two opponents were engaged in serious but respectful discussion.

Halldis stepped further into the room. Styrk could see her better in the glow of the lamp. Halldis was holding a cloth by both hands. She was listening with a pensive look on her face.

Styrk said to Paafa Ketil, "I ask you to tell Halldis; her health depends on being with a man who can supply food. If my family walks the frozen trail, I can supply food and be with my family all the time."

Paafa Ketil exclaimed, "I can think of nothing more frightening than for your family to be caught on the ice in a blizzard."

Styrk replied, "Actually, the weather is not that bad. During the first three moon's time after the ice freezes there are only about two short snowstorms for each moon's time. When we walk toward Merica, the slight wind is often at our backs. The temperatures are really the same as in Lysefjord. Most men make the walk in a moon's time."

Paafa Ketil replied, "I cannot in truth tell Halldis to go with you if I believe my God is not in favor. She has lived two decades without you being around eleven moons of the year. She may live longer here than over in Akomen near you."

Styrk was looking toward Halldis. Paafa Ketil turned to see where he was looking. Both men saw Halldis raise a single index finger to her lips. Paafa Ketil responded to the signal.

"These people have come to listen to Talerman, not us," he said. "We all will be staying here tonight. We will have time to discuss this matter later. Let us think on it and talk again."

Styrk smiled and replied, "Talk again? With a boy I could always whip?"

The tension was broken. The crowd laughed. But Styrk felt that he had lost the debate. He glanced at Halldis, who had her hands on her hips. Then he knew it was even worse. He was losing her respect, rapidly. He had to stop the loss and, if possible, recover some of her respect. Styrk continued, "But Halldis does want your blessing and I want a willing wife. Without your blessing my wife will not be willing. So I promise you, we will talk later this evening."

There were audible murmurs of approval. Styrk now felt like he was back in the debate. But a glance at Halldis' slight nod told him he was still walking on thin ice.

Paafa Ketil nodded and stepped back toward the wall. Styrk turned to Talerman, lowered his head, and said, "I apologize, Talerman."

Talerman nodded to accept the apology. He said, "Styrk, you know, I like men who ask good questions and listen well. All of us have learned more about the pavows, the priests, the Great Spirit, and God."

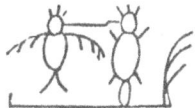

There was a flurry of movement as people readjusted their positions. A few people came forward to the stewpots with their bowls and spoons. They fished slices of meat out of the boiling pot and spooned the broth into their bowls. Arnora, seeing the liquid going down, carried more water from the food room to the boiling pots.

Talerman surveyed the crowd. He was pleased. He had asked his men to summon the leading women, as well as the men, from the nine farms on Rangafjord. He was able to count nineteen of the women and twenty-three men from those nine farms. There were a few elder sons. The young men and several young women were grouped at the end of the room near the food-room door.

Less than half of the families of the Anavik Kirke lived in Rangafjord. He, Paafa Thord, and the other beaver-heads would meet with the rest of the Anavik kirke later. Most of the Rangafjord men were beaver-heads, but many of them were not the migration leaders. Most of the people had known Talerman longer than they had known Paafa Thord.

Talerman waited until the rustle subsided. When he had their attention again, he continued: "I was saying that we beaver-heads went to Bishop Arne's house. Not all beaver-heads stayed overnight. Bishop Arne's house was close to the *Althing* grounds, so many of the beaver-heads went to visit family or friends in the booths.

"Bishop Arne knew we were coming because the beaver-heads from the Eastern Settlement had told him to expect us. So he had instructed all the priests to come to his house. Most priests were already in the area because they had come to the *Althing*.

"As usual when old friends meet, there was chaos at first. Most of the beaver-heads and priests visited about mutual friends. I was not able to talk very long with Bishop Arne. The priests wanted to talk personally with him. So they, by twos or threes all night long, slipped away from the general visiting for their private talks with Bishop Arne.

"They were concerned about the new official from the Popa. This new official, a man named Ivar Bardarsson, has the power to collect the church's ten-percent tithe and also the power to collect taxes for the King in Norway. Also, Bardarsson appears to be using Norway values for the property, which will result in taxes much too high. So, Bishop Arne and the priests were trying to figure out what to do.

"Because Bishop Arne knew we were coming, he had suggested to Ivar Bardarsson that he should visit the court farm at Foss and survey all of the farms there. Bishop Arne was surprised but relieved that Bardarsson took his suggestion and went to Foss.

"As most of you know, we beaver-heads were selected for a purpose. Each one of us beaver-heads grew up in different kirke. We had a beaver-head from all the kirkes in Greenland. At Bishop Arne's great room, our beaver-heads purposely sought out the priest of their childhood kirke. We knew the decision for the people to leave Greenland would be easier if beaver-heads and priests could work as comrades.

"So the first night at Bishop Arne's passed away with small groups of men talking. As you have just learned by listening to Paafa Ketil and Styrk, not every pair became bosom friends. There were a few priests disturbed with our heathen ways. There were a few beaver-heads who were uneasy with priests who wanted to save their souls overnight.

"Bishop Arne's hall is the biggest in Einarsfjord. Even so, the nearly forty men milling around looked like a melee. We were lucky not to have any fights other than playful shoving. The talking, and some shoving, lasted until the sky began to pale again. Then slowly, one by one, we found a spot to sleep.

"When the sun was about two fingers high, I slipped out of the hall for necessary things. Bishop Arne was standing outside. He pointed to the kirke and asked me to visit with him when I returned.

"When I entered the kirke, I told Bishop Arne how pleased I was to talk to him alone. It had been a long time since we last visited together as friends.

"Bishop Arne asked me to call him 'Big Raven.' Then Bishop Arne told me that our trip to Akomen, twenty-five years ago, was the best event in his life since his baptism.

"But Bishop Arne said he was now very sad. He did not know why God was testing the Greenland people so much. He said you people are good people. You work hard. You love your families. Yet you can barely get enough forage to feed the livestock through the winter. The seafood harvest is unpredictable except at the open-water marvels, which are so far away. He said Greenland must have food from both the sea and Merica to survive. Despite valiant efforts during the recent warm years, very little food has been stored up.

"Bishop Arne talked about other bad trends occurring in Einarsfjord, such as the permafrost rising so the grave can only go down knee-deep. He told me that the graveyards look as if there are no men in Einarsfjord. The men die either at sea or over in Merica.

"I told Bishop Arne that we have visited with many of the Einarsfjord families who came to Akomen in previous years. They live in safety in villages where the climate is warmer than ours. The spring and the fall are like our summers. In winter they hunt in the forests where there are many animals to eat and where the trees protect them from the wind. Their men are with their families all year around. We have not yet met an Einarsfjord family in Akomen that wants to come back to Einarsfjord.

"Then Bishop Arne lamented about the troubles people had in Einarsfjord. Men were able to come home from Merica for only one moon a year. But that was time enough for women to get with child. Having only a few men and many women with babies makes survival difficult for all, even if people have enough food, which they do not.

"The Norway ships did not get here last summer. When they last arrived, two years ago, the crews were arrogant. With few of our men around, they had an opportunity to take advantage of the many eager women. The priests tried to shelter the women in remote kirkes until the ships left. But there were some nasty happenings.

"The ships' crews placed high values on goods. The crews said they could get even more value from the people of 'another land.' The crews were referring to Norumvege and Akonsee.

"Finally, Bishop Arne told me about his anger with Ivar Bardarsson, the church ombudsman.

"Bishop Arne wanted me to tell you that we cannot depend on Norway or the Church to the east to help us survive. He thinks the missing Norwegian supplies and a greedy Church are signs of human failure in our world.

"Since he came back to Einarsfjord from his trip to Akomen, Bishop Arne has lived through three very cold periods with a total of ten very, very cold years. He thinks that the numbing cold today is a sign from God. Bishop Arne thinks God, for the past twenty-five summers, has been shaping our people to go to a land prepared for them. This very cold temperature, right now, is God's sign for us to go."

Talerman stood silently, looking at the crowd. Then he continued: "When Bishop Arne said the cold is God's sign for us to go, I asked 'Where should we go?'

"Bishop Arne said without hesitation, 'To Eastman Land in Akomen.'

"I said, 'Some of our men said you were thinking about Akonsee. Have you changed your mind?'

"Bishop Arne said, 'No, I have always been in favor of the Eastman Land.'

"But he said that a wise servant of God must consider options. Akonsee, with its regional kirke, more priests, and warmer temperatures seemed to be a good migration option.

"Once he had Hallgrim figure the number of ships it would take to sail to Akonsee. Hallgrim figured moving four thousand people would take, at least, one hundred and thirty voyages. That is a lot of sailing for ships that should be hunting whales, seals, and other sea animals. But the voyages were not impossible if done over several years.

"So about ten summers ago, Bishop Arne asked two priests who had been to Eastman Land before him to take a look at migrating to Akonsee

"The priests sailed to Akonsee in a warm summer. Their trip took four moon's time. One priest barely returned to Einarsfjord before the sea froze. The other priest died in Akonsee of a disease, which turned him yellow [YELLOW DEATH].

"The returning priest said the food was adequate in Akonsee, but not plentiful. The hunting territories were small. The people of Akonsee would not like four thousand newcomers at all. The people were friendly but were suspicious of people with an accent. The yellow sickness might return as it had in the past

"The priest advised Bishop Arne that the people of Greenland should go to Eastman Land. The recommendation matched Bishop Arne's belief. So he definitely decided he wants the people of Greenland to walk over the ice to Akomen.

"Bishop Arne asked me how the people of Merica and Akomen would react to many people coming to their land.

"I told Bishop Arne that the people of Akomen would help us rather than block us. In Merica the Norse hunters are eager to pull their families west instead of pulling pemmican east.

"I also told Bishop Arne that during the last three years when I was in Akomen, the beaver-heads picked me as the person to speak for all of them. They call me Head Beaver.

"So I, as the Head Beaver, and Bishop Arne, the Big Raven, looked deep into each other's eyes and we agreed. 'Let us go to Akomen.'"

Vignette Sixteen
Head Beaver
and Big Bird

Azon was again seated on his left leg at the bottom of the steps. He wanted to hurry. He said, "Ah, Pitolo, you are so late."

Pitolo grumbled: "I finally gave up. I know how to draw a large group of people in a meeting. But I could not think of how to draw them trying to decide if they should go to another land. Let me see your carving."

"Here you are. It was a difficult concept to show."

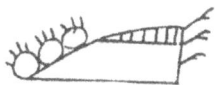

Pitolo studied the engraved stick and said. "Ah, you stacked three heads on the left of the hut, which must be the meeting house. The heads must mean the house is full. They cannot get in. Then you have three wisps of smoke coming from the house toward the right. The wisps might mean talking about the decision."

Azon nodded with a smile, saying, "Something like that. People left out, meeting house full, and talking shown by smoke on the right. I hope Grandfather approves. I could not get a simple set of words for the beaver-head and the Big Raven. I did not know what to say about the hellion."

Pitolo replied, "The hellion is only to make the story interesting and, maybe, to teach some values, similar to most tales. I ignored her."

"What did you say?" Azon asked.

Pitolo paused for a brief while. Then he said, "Head Beaver and Big Bird said, 'Let us go to Akomen.'"

Azon said, "Easy to remember. But so many details are left out."

Pitolo inclined his head and pulled his right hand past his ear, as if he were pulling down thoughts from the night before. "When our grandsons' grandsons tell this story, who is going to care how mad the hellion was? Akomen, this land, will still be here. My uncle went south and east to the salt sea when he was on his quest. He is always jabbering about the STONE TOWER in Akonsee and the many places nearby named Ako-something or other. "

Azon replied, "My uncles, four of them, and grandfather made their quests to learn about Eastman Land. I think the words should say something about those places."

Pitolo shook his head, saying, "I do not. Akomen will be here. Eastman Land or Akonsee may not be known anymore than last year's village."

Azon persisted, asking, "What about the stories Head Beaver was telling? Surely there should be more words to guide our grandsons."

Pitolo shook his head and said, "No, the important thing to say is that Head Beaver and the Big Bird decided to go to Akomen. That was the beginning of the events that brought our ancestors here. Whoever tells that story can make up his own details to hold his audience's attention."

Azon frowned. "I do not think Grandfather will approve. But let us hurry. There was a light covering of snow this morning. My father says we will be leaving as soon as the Big House ceremony ends. Grandfather did not accept food this morning, only water. Grandfather seems to be ready to die."

When they reached the top of the steps, Pitolo swung his leg in a rapid gait as he skipped along the path to the stockade. He said, "I am ready to hear about the *Althing*."

Azon's grandfather had been at the Big House celebration until late in the night. They found him still asleep. He was lying on his side with his knees pulled up.

Pitolo got a bowl of stew from the ever-present pot hung over the fire. Azon found Grandfather's cup and took up water. He touched Grandfather on the shoulder. Grandfather stretched and then rolled on his back before sitting up.

They waited patiently while Grandfather set the soup aside, but took slow sips of water. Then Grandfather extended his hands as a signal to look at the engravings. Only Azon handed him one. Grandfather asked, "What? Only one?"

Pitolo said, "I tried many engravings. The idea sounds simple. The doing is not. I could not finish a good one. Mine were all worse than Azon's."

Grandfather frowned as he looked at Azon's engraving. He shook his head. Then he said, "Let me hear the verses from the last story."

Azon said, "Grandfather, I tried many times. I also knew the engraving must be finished, so I worked on it. I have no verse, but Pitolo's verse is better than any of mine."

Maalan Aarum turned to Pitolo and motioned for him to say the verse. Pitolo said, "Head Beaver and Big Bird said, 'Let us go to Akomen.'"

Grandfather lowered his head into his hands. He stayed there for a time. Azon and Pitolo thought it was a long time. When grandfather raised his head, he said, "Boys, you are getting wiser and your judgment has been good before. But I have only a little time left. Now, I do not know if I am forced to accept the worst or if I am truly getting the best. Please, tomorrow each of you bring an engraving and a verse. You need experience in making both. I will have the satisfaction of choosing the best."

Grandfather added the engraving to his collection. Then he leaned back into the storytelling position. He said, "The story for today is about a meeting at a place called an *Althing*. The meeting was similar to our Big House celebration. The setting was not. Our people will recognize the engraving you made as a meeting, but the *Althing* was held outside in the summertime. The meeting was for the men. They usually stood in a circle. The only women there were servants.

"In that land to the east, the *Althing* controlled human action. If the men of the country agreed to an action, other men who wanted the action could go ahead. If the men of the country were opposed to an action, then men who wanted the action could do nothing.

"Head Beaver and Big Bird wanted all the people to go to Akomen. To do that action, they needed the approval of the *Althing*."

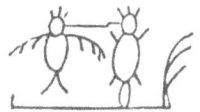

"Head Beaver and Big Bird said:
'Let us go to Akomen.'"

STORIES OF MAALAN AARUM

Will You Go with Us?

E.S. 3:15

The *Manalthing,* 1344

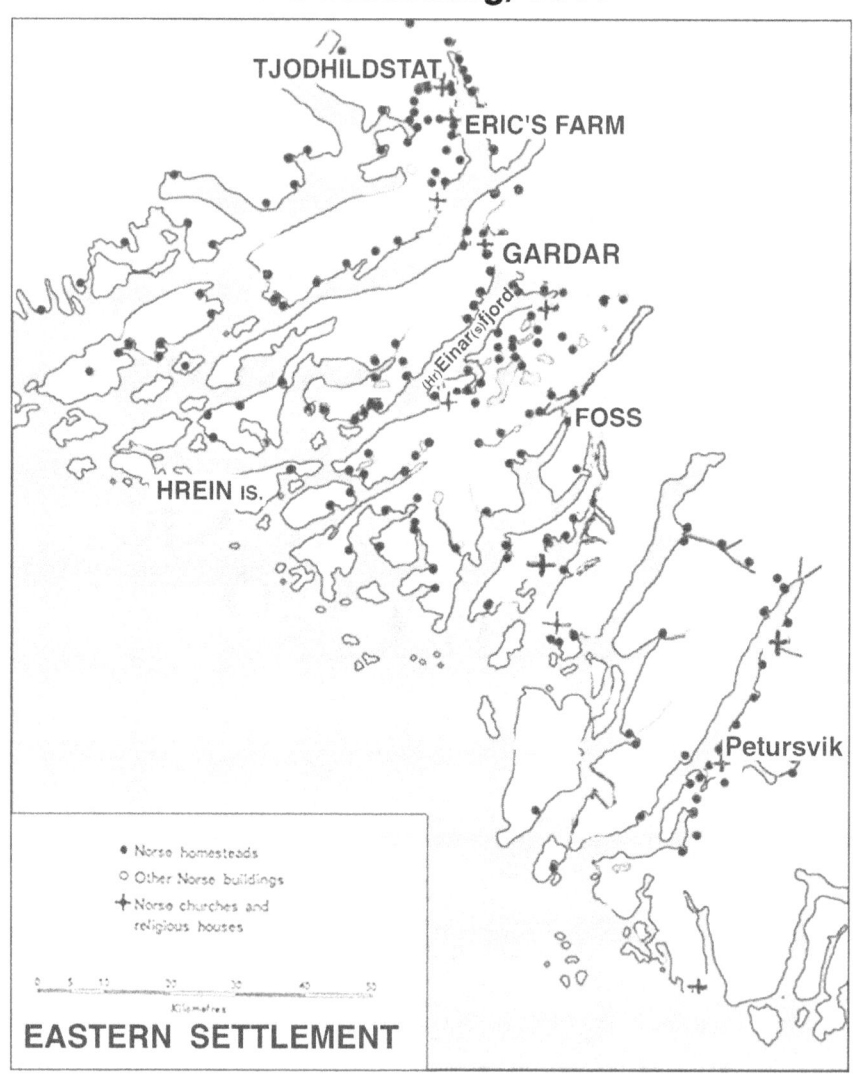

EASTERN SETTLEMENT

Talerman and Bishop Arne presented the proposal to migrate at the *Al-thing* at Gardar. Then Talerman and Paafa Thord debated the proposal in all fourteen kirkes of the Eastern Settlement.

Will You Go with Us?

After telling the people in the house that he and Big Raven Arne had decided that the people of Greenland should go to Akomen, Talerman said, "Let us take a break so you can do necessary things. When we get back together shortly, I will tell you about the meeting at the *Althing*."

The people in the house stirred, stretched, and went outside as necessary. Cold air from the opening door moved into the house, brightening the fires. Smoke curled up to the fire hole. Arnora added more meat to the stews.

Arnora and Thjodhild moved from woman to woman discussing places to sleep. A few couples were planning to sleep under their boats or in small tepees. Those men were outside checking on the bedding. Thjodhild's family was going to sleep in the pasture tent. Bjørn and Yngvild had already planned to stay with them.

Arnora assigned the thirty-two sleeping locations in the great room to twelve couples and their children. She chose extended families and best of friends.

Without making an issue of the situation, Thjodhild showed the guests who were known to be more troublesome to other rooms, including her bedroom. Halldis and Styrk were invited to sleep on the floor in the Arnora's bedroom.

The talking in the great room would continue until the people reached a decision. Then everyone would sleep at the Talerman's farm because tiredness, distance, and darkness would discourage traveling. In the morning when they awoke, families would leave as they were ready. A few people with long distances to row would eat something before leaving.

Arnora checked the food supplies for the morning. Yngvild went around refilling the oil supply in the lamps throughout the house.

Arnora passed through small clusters of visiting guests to slip into her bedroom. She was after spare robes stored under her bed. She noticed her lance was not in the usual location on the block of wood beside her bed. Then she remembered the last threat she had made to Bjarni. She had been far too busy to think about her words.

But now she felt harried. A few of the women had said that they were surprised how well she was coping. So she knew that they had noticed she was coping. She was not surprised that they could see she was coping. Her struggle to be a good cook under the trying conditions was as plain as the nose on her face. Her fame as a cook was being tested to the limit. The verdict was still much in doubt.

After this mob left Arnora thought that she would confront Bjarni with the lance in her hands. Perhaps he would be startled enough to avoid making her cope with big crowds of unexpected guests in the future. She went to her side of the bed to find the lance. She could not see it. She felt on the floor. She could not feel it. The lance was gone.

Returning to the great room, Arnora gave the robes to the guests to sit on until later. Then she went outside the food room door to pick up a small water pail. One of the few blessings of living near mountains of ice was cool water. Then she took the pail and Talerman's cup to him. The men visiting with Talerman sensed her desire to talk to him alone. As they moved away, Talerman turned to take the cup of cool water from Arnora. After a long drink, Talerman whispered, "I hope Paafa Thord's ghost stays away tonight."

Arnora was caught off guard. She whispered, "What are you saying?"

Talerman said softly, "You will soon hear that Paafa Thord and I traveled to each kirke in the Eastern Settlement. There we held meetings, like this one, to decide if the whole kirke was willing to migrate. If the meetings in the Eastern Settlement kirkes appeared to be undecided, Paafa Thord used the deaths in his own family as the clinching argument. He argued that his aunt had said his mother and his sisters died because his father abandoned the family to walk to Merica."

Arnora asked in a normal voice, "Are you talking about Paafa Thord's aunt who raised him after his mother died in childbirth?"

Bjarni glanced around the room. He was thankful the noise level swamped Arnora's question. "Please speak softly. Yes, that aunt. But Paafa Thord says his aunt told him that his mother and sisters starved to death because his father abandoned them and walked to Merica. When he told the story in the meetings, his eyes showed moisture almost as if he would cry. Those moist eyes swayed most women and a few men in every crowd. I know Paafa Thord's story is not true because I learned the truth from his father, long ago, around the campfires in Merica."

Arnora replied softly, "Paafa Thord's mother died the same year as your mother. But he was much younger than you. Paafa Thord's aunt, who raised him, repeated the starvation story to anyone who would listen until the day she died. So most of the younger people here probably believe her story."

Bjarni shook his head slowly. "I could not tactfully tell the people in the other meetings that Paafa Thord was not telling the truth. People believe a tearful priest talking about his family."

"Why did you not tell the truth that Paafa Thord's father gave you? He was closer to the matter than the aunt."

Bjarni lowered his head, talking to the floor. Arnora could hardly hear him. "The one time I told the truth about the matter, the people thought I was lying. The truth weakened my other arguments. That time, almost all of the kirke people voted to stay in Greenland. In the other meetings where the vote was close, all the earnest talking about going to Akomen seemed wasted because the final decision often hinged on Paafa Thord's emotional argument."

Arnora tapped her right foot lightly. "The issues are different. Why should a story of a man going to Merica and starving his family concern the wives when most men here in Greenland are now pleading for their families to come along?"

Bjarni continued to look at the floor. He very slowly shook his head. "I used that logic at every meeting, but life is not a chess game. Emotions swamp truth. Paafa Thord's strong emotions tying Merica to starvation overrode my mere statements that there is more, not less, food in Merica."

Talerman raised his head, took another sip of the cool water, gave a shrug of his shoulders, and said, "I was thankful that eight of fourteen kirkes finally chose to say they would go. But five of those decisions had been right on the edge of the ice. Three of the opposing kirkes might have been persuaded to go if Paafa Thord had not used his aunt's ghost."

Arnora poured more water into the cup. She whispered to Talerman, "Why not counter with your own experience. You stayed home and hunted well, but our son still died."

Talerman bit his lip and said, "That is something I never want to talk about."

Arnora responded with a soft voice. "You could have moist eyes, too."

Then she saw the sad look in his eyes and said quickly, "You are right. The decision to walk to Merica should be made only on the basis of the best arguments." They both knew that people would accept moist eyes on a priest, but not on a beaver-head.

Arnora looked around and thought that this roomful of people was going to be very difficult to persuade if the ghost of Paafa Thord's aunt did return. That aunt had told her lies over decades. Most of the people in the Northern Settlement had comforted her without learning the true facts.

Arnora whispered to Talerman, "Try to avoid the subject. Do not argue with ghosts." She turned to go back to the food room for more bva, when she suddenly remembered why she had carried the water to Talerman. She turned back. She leaned close to his face.

"What did you do with the lance?" she hissed in a low whisper.

"It is safely hidden. I will give it to you later. The sight of blood would make me hungry."

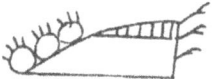

Paafa Ketil returned to the great room from the doorway of the live-stock family. Styrk followed him. Halldis stopped visiting with the other women and went to Styrk. They returned to their bench.

Paafa Ketil moved to meet Paafa Thord, who had returned from out-side. Arnora carried a mixture of warm bva to them. They held out their drinking cups as she poured. Then they returned to a corner away from the door. Arnora left them talking in low voices and went to the food storage room to pour the warmed water and blood into a large serving bowl and to refill the vessel over the lamp with cool water and blood.

When she returned to the great room, the three men from the farthest houses down the fjord had come back inside. They were shedding their outer furs and wiping off their cups. Their sons and daughters had remained inside, visiting with the young group. Arnora realized that there were now ten young people in the room.

Two beaver-heads came back inside. With them was Bjørn, who had two birds dressed for the pots. Bjørn's face was flushed red from the cool-ness, but his eyes revealed his internal pleasure. Once again Bjarni's eyes flickered with surprise. He had not yet realized Bjørn could hunt.

Bjørn responded to a young woman's question. "I got the first one with an arrow and the second one with the harpoon—in the air!" Bjarni's eyes opened wide. Bjørn must be joking. Bjarni could never harpoon anything except a seal lying on the ice. Still, Bjørn was smiling with pleasure, not with humor as if he were joking.

Paafas Thord and Ketil rose and began to mingle with the reassembling crowd. The younger people congregated at the other end of the room. The volume of talking became louder.

Valthjof Ormsson with his two daughters, Grimhild and Thurid, had just arrived. They shed their furs and held out cups for bva. Valthjof had lost his wife four years ago. Before she died, women of the settlement spread rumors of cruelties he had inflicted upon her. After her death, even desperate single women with children had avoided Valthjof's advances. Now Grimhild, his oldest daughter, kept his robes warm.

Arnora had served as the midwife when Grimhild gave birth. Thankfully, the child appeared to be normal. Arnora told Grimhild about the dangers of incest. She also explained to her about methods to avoid having more children.

She had used those methods herself after Bjørn was born. She had realized then that more mouths to feed in Greenland would not be wise, especially with Bjarni away from home for eleven moons' time a year.

Arnora took a good look. Grimhild's coverlet was stretched firm over her breasts. She was still nursing and so probably not pregnant. Grimhild nodded to Arnora with a sly smile and followed Valthjof to a bench against the wall. Thurid's eyes sparkled as two of the older boys moved apart to give her a spot between them.

Bjarni switched to his public role as Talerman by making his traditional circle around the room and visiting with as many people as possible. Then he moved back to his bench and sat down. The crowd was more animated than earlier but slowly the room became quiet.

Talerman smiled as he spoke. "Paafa Ketil and Styrk, you left us with an opportunity to create many rumors. Most of the people here say they want to hear about the *Althing*. But the first question they ask me is, 'What have Paafa Ketil and Styrk said to each other?' So Paafa Ketil, would you enlighten us?"

Paafa Ketil stepped nearer Talerman's bench and addressed the group: "Styrk and I did have a short, private discussion. I appreciated learning why he thinks hunting in Merica is best for his family's survival. He does provide four more moons' time of food for his children than he would if he hunted here.

"I had thought that his sending pemmican home instead of coming home himself on the summer boats from Merica was abandonment of his family. Now I understand that if he had put his weight in the boat that meant thirty sleeps of pemmican for the family had to stay behind. I also now know about his feelings of loneliness after each boat pulled away. Styrk very much loves his family. He is making great sacrifices for them to survive."

Styrk leaped to his feet and spoke: "I also can understand Paafa Ketil's concern for my family. [He baptized all of my children. He came to care for them when illness afflicted Halldis. He arranged for other families to help feed my children until my sons grew enough to become hunters. Paafa Ketil truly desires to help my family make the best choices for the future."

Talerman asked, "Paafe Ketil, are you ready to recommend walking the Frozen Trail?"

Paafa Ketil looked at the floor for a moment. Then, raising his head and turning to the people he said, "I am trying to discern what God is saying. Bishop Arne taught me to collect all the information possible before becoming a messenger of God's will. I was not at the *Althing*. I want to hear what was said there."

Talerman responded, "Very well, then. I had told you how we beaverheads had gone to convince Bishop Arne that the people of Greenland should move to Eastman Land in Akomen. I also told you I was surprised to learn that he had already decided that a move to Eastman Land in Akomen would be best for the people of Greenland.

"So the next step was for Bishop Arne and me to convince the *Althing* that the people of Greenland should walk to Eastman Land.

"Before we went to the *Althing*, the beaver-heads and the priests talked things over in Bishop Arne's great room. Naturally the beaver-heads were all in favor. Despite Bishop Arne's exhortations, five priests, including our own Paafa Thord, were opposed. Three priests were undecided. Six priests in favor of the move themselves expressed extreme concern because they thought their people would not accept the idea. Four priests were in favor and thought their people were also in favor.

"Then we all, beaver-heads, priests, Bishop Arne, and myself, went to the *Althing* grounds.

"During the spring the priests had announced to their kirkes that Bishop Arne would present an important motion at the *Althing*. They had encouraged the men to come if they could. So more men than usual were at the *Althing*. Most of the sakkyndigs were there and many of them had large followings. The *Althing* grounds were packed with men.

"Almost immediately the priests opposed to the plan began talking to people throughout the *Althing* grounds. I appealed to Bishop Arne to silence them. Bishop Arne said, 'As far as I can tell, they are not spreading false rumors. They are telling the men that there are valid questions, which must be answered. If we cannot prevail, then God is not for our plan.'

"Now, Paafas Thord and Ketil are here tonight and are still asking those valid questions. I will tell you what happened at the *Althing*. Then I will allow Paafa Thord, who was in opposition at the *Althing*, to correct any statements I make. After that, Paafas Thord and Ketil can say what they think and ask us, beaver-heads, questions. The rest of you can ask questions also. Then we all, especially the women and young people, must make a decision. We beaver-heads want you to decide if your family will be willing to leave Greenland and walk the Frozen Trail, never to return. That is the plan for tonight. Is the plan all right with everybody?"

Talerman slowly scanned the room. The beaver-heads nodded readily. The wives who had walked the ice before also nodded reluctantly. Six wives held their heads rigidly with lips pressed into firm lines. A few of the youth nodded, the rest acted confused. Valthjof and a few others sat in stony silence. Three men from the far houses checked each other and then nodded together. Their wives looked at the men, then at Sigrid, and nodded when she did. Paafas Thord and Ketil saw that no one was shaking his head. With stern expressions, they slowly nodded also.

Talerman continued: "Good. One of the first actions was to name the *Althing*. By acclamation the people there called the meeting the '*Manalthing*,' meaning the people's *Althing*.

"Bishop Arne had asked for the chance to introduce the first major business. Because he was bishop, he was granted his request. I will shorten Bishop Arne's words, because many of you have already heard about them. Bishop Arne spoke something like this:

"'People of Greenland. I do not need to tell you the troubles we are facing here in Greenland. If I did, most of you would think I am just repeating words you have often said to your own families.

"'Today, I stand here with a new hope. I believe that I see God's plan for us to take action to get a better life for our children.

"'Most of you, I am sure, have been praying for a way, short of death, to escape this freezing cold of Hel that we call Greenland. Most of you have heard the beaver-heads tell of the mild, cool lands with many deer and buffaloes. Most of you have prayed to be delivered into those lands before you enter paradise.

"'Now, God is telling us to go to those lands. We can do it the same way as the followers of Moses in my prayer book did—by crossing a sea. Those who followed Moses walked on a sea bottom without getting wet. God is making it possible for us to walk across on top of sea without getting our feet wet. God wants us to go to a better land that he will give us to possess.

"'We can do God's will, but doing it requires the effort of all the Greenland people. In the land God wants us to possess, we must have the combined forces of all the men to protect our families from savage attack. All the wives and children must be there to support the men. Our men will strive to possess land only where their families live. So, the business I want us to discuss is: Will you join together to move all of Greenland's people to Merica?'

"The crowd was silent during the first words of Bishop Arne, but at this point they began to speak out. Some shouted, 'Yes, yes, let us go!' Many more shouted, 'What are you talking about?' Bishop Arne raised his arms holding up his robe as if he spread his mighty black wings. The crowd quieted. Then he said, 'Please listen as Talerman explains to you how the people of the Eastman Land and Merica can help the people of Greenland walk across the sea without getting their feet wet. Please listen to Talerman.'

"I arose to stand beside Bishop Arne and I told them: 'As most of you know, most men and many women have walked the Frozen Trail to Merica during the very cold years. Many of you know that beyond Merica there is a better land called Akomen. Some Greenland families have already gone to stay in Akomen. During past centuries many young men have gone there. They have not returned to Greenland because their life in Akomen is much better than here. There are trees all around. The trees shield the people from the driving cold wind. There are many animals to eat. The climate is warmer. The spring and fall feels like summer here. The whole summer feels like the hottest day of summer here. There is open land for us to settle. You and your children would have a better life in Akomen.

"'The beaver-heads you see at this *Manalthing* have walked from Akomen to Greenland this spring. We came because all of us believe we can guide your families safely to warmer lands in Akomen.

"'Our plan is this: If you agree to go, the beaver-heads will return to Akomen. We, with the peoples of Merica and Akomen, will prepare for your coming. Then next summer they will help us prepare shelters and food for you. The shelters will be built in Merica on the seacoast facing Greenland. The low walls for the shelters are already there. The people helping the beaver-heads will dig pemmican storage pits beside the shelters. They will fill the pits with pemmican. They will provide caribou hides for the roofs of the new shelters.

"'Meanwhile here in Greenland, you will be preparing. Each family who is willing to go will prepare pemmican. You will take enough pemmican to last two moons' time. You should be able to walk the Frozen Trail to Merica in a moon's time. We beaver-heads have sometimes walked the distance in half a moon's time.

"'You will also make sleds to be pulled on the ice. The sled should be long enough so that two people, feet to feet, can lie down on the pemmican. Two people will be sleeping on the sled, while four people will be pulling it. The sled load will be the same as having four people on a sled.

"'Then in the winter beyond this coming one, we beaver-heads will walk east on the Frozen Trail. We will come from Merica to Greenland to test the ice. At least sixteen beaver-heads will walk as fast as we can to get to Greenland as soon as the Frozen Trail is solid.

"'When we beaver-heads arrive in Greenland, the people must be prepared to leave. It is important for the people to be ready, because we will have only a short time to start everyone walking across the Frozen Trail toward Merica.

"'On the other side of the Frozen Trail, when you walk off the ice, you will recover your energy in the shelters we will have prepared. You will also make snowshoes and learn to walk on them. Then, you will take some of the stored pemmican along for the rest of the walk to Akomen. You will walk over a short stretch of land to reach the frozen ice of another sea. Then you will use sleds as before to walk on to Akomen.

"'At Akomen the people there will show you how to build a house very fast. You will cover it with the caribou hides that have kept you warm during the walk across the ice.

"'There is only enough shelter in Merica for about a thousand people at one time. We plan for about a thousand people to walk to Akomen the first year. If things work out well, we will make additional trips in each of the following three years. This cold spell that we are in now should last about seven more years. So we think four trips in the next four years will get everyone safely to Akomen.

"'We must go together as a group. The land available for us to possess is empty because vicious men, who behave like wolf packs, have killed or driven out the people in that land of Akomen. But the wolf packs have not settled the land. So it is empty. There is great danger if we try to settle the land without having enough fighting strength to repel the wolf packs. The people of Akomen tell us the wolf packs avoid villages with many fighting men. We will have more than two hundred fighting men in each migration of a thousand people. But all of the people in each kirke must commit to going to Akomen at the same time. A small group of families could not resist the wolf packs.

"'So the decision to move requires the full commitment of all of us: men, women, and children, in every kirke in all of Greenland. If most of you decide to stay in Greenland, we are all condemned to live and quickly die in this frozen land of Hel. If we all choose to migrate we can reach a land God has given us to possess in three moons' time or less. Please join those of us wanting to move our families to Akomen.'

"Then our Paafa Thord and three other priests led the resisters with a series of heated questions and scathing comments. Tonight, I will give Paafa Thord, Paafa Ketil, and others a chance to speak later. First I want to tell you more of Bishop Arne's comments. He stood up to speak again after the arguments of the resisters had been heard.

"Bishop Arne told the *Manalthing*: 'If the people of Greenland agree to this plan, I suggest the people of the Northern Settlement walk the Frozen Trail first. I make this suggestion because the Pope's and King's Agent, His Eminence Ivar Bardarsson, is now in Greenland. He would do anything possible to stop us from moving beyond Greenland. Fortunately, at my suggestion, he has chosen this time to survey the farmhouses in the south. The less he knows about our decisions today, the better it will be for all of us.

But he will surely want to see the Northern Settlement someday. If God and time are in our favor, there will be no one there when he does visit.

"'When Ivar Bardarsson has convinced himself there is no one in the Northern Settlement, he will probably return to Foss to continue to record data for tithe and fee collections. With Ivar Bardarsson back in Foss, the people in the northern kirkes of the Eastern Settlement can prepare to go over the Frozen Trail in the following winters. In five years all of us should be able to walk the Frozen Trail.'

"After Bishop Arne finished his statement, the *Manalthing* recessed for two sleeps. There was much discussion during that day of recess. Priests and beaver-heads moved from booth to booth explaining details. In some cases, for example, with Paafa Thord and myself, we discussed opposite viewpoints. Sometimes the discussions led to minor fights. In other cases, where the priest and the beaver-head were in agreement, only positive arguments for walking over the Frozen Trail were heard. The arguments were so intense and the issues so contested that the sakkyndig of the *Manalthing* decided the talks within small groups should go on yet another sleep. He hoped more discussion would get a visible majority large enough to prevent an outbreak of total rioting.

"Finally we met together again on the fourth day of the *Manalthing*. What an assembly! First there was an immediate motion, by those opposed to migration, that the people of Greenland should concentrate on improving farming and stop wasting time on other things, such as talking about walking to Akomen. The issue failed because the powerful men of Greenland, the southern farmers, felt insulted. They were already doing the best farming they knew how. Many of them stood up to say so.

"Then a motion about taking more sea mammals was shouted down without much discussion. All of the available boats were already stressed to the limit and most people knew it.

"Finally Bishop Arne's motion, 'Will you join together to move all of Greenland's people to Akomen?' was brought before the assembly. The arguments lasted from a little after midday until the sun approached the horizon. Because the summer sun would just dip below the horizon and arise in a short time, Bishop Arne recommended everyone take the dark time to take care of necessary things. Then when the sun rose above the horizon, those standing would be counted as in favor of going; those sitting would be counted as not in favor of going. If those standing were many more than those sitting, everyone would be expected to walk the Frozen Trail.

"A man of the powerful Eriksson family in the south stood to protest. He did not want to be forced to go. He was bound by commitments to his relatives in Iceland. If he had to leave Greenland, he would go to Iceland. Both Bishop Arne and I agreed that people who are not truly free to go should not be forced to go. We suggested the motion should be reworded to be: 'Will all say they will go along, all who are free to go, to move Greenland's people to Akomen?' By voice acclamation the new wording was accepted.

"The next morning, the nine standing priests moved through the crowd taking the count. The people for six kirkes, all in southern Greenland, were almost all seated. Another six kirkes in the Eastern Settlement had almost all of their people standing. Two kirkes were almost evenly divided. One kirke had slightly more than half standing. There were slightly less than half of the people standing in the other. In the groups for our northern kirkes, Paafa Thord sat with slightly more than half of his people. Paafa Ketil was not there, but slightly less than half of his people stood. The priests and the people from the other two northern kirkes were solidly on their feet.

"When every head was counted, three times, the motion passed by a very slim majority. Thus the sakkyndig ruled that the *Manalthing* agreed, 'All say they will go along, all who are free to go, to Akomen.' But considering the large number of people still sitting, nearly half of Greenland felt they would not be free to go.

"Bishop Arne met with the priests after the *Manalthing* vote. He asked if any priests wanted to exchange assignments to kirkes so they could minister to people who thought the same as they did. Three priests decided they would prefer changing. So three more priests in favor of the move are now with kirkes where people are also in favor of the move.

"Our Paafa Thord, who is committed to staying in Greenland, has decided to remain with his kirke even if we, in his kirke, decide to walk the Frozen Trail. Paafa Ketil was not at the *Manalthing*. As you have heard tonight, he appears to be committed to remaining in Greenland. Also slightly less than half of his people said they were willing to walk the Frozen Trail.

"As you can conclude, this *Thing* tonight is important for all of Greenland. If we in this house decide to walk the Frozen Trail, we tip the balance in the Northern Settlement. Then the Northern Settlement priests must report to Bishop Arne that the Northern Settlement is willing to go. If the Northern Settlement goes, the Eastern Settlement will go.

"Our decision tonight is truly up to a few wives here. Many of the men here are beaver-heads. You men have already gone on to Akomen at least once. I think there are eleven other men who have made the pull to Merica and back. I see here fourteen wives who have pulled sleds to Merica. So most of you know that walking the Frozen Trail to Merica can be done. It is difficult but, with care, it is not deadly.

"You women, especially those of you who have not been on the ice, hold our fate in your hands. If most of you decide you are not free to go because you think you must live in your farmhouse for the rest of your lives, then the whole community will have to live with that decision. If you can decide that you, too, can live in the world without the shelter of an earthen farmhouse, please say you are willing to go. Then the whole community will work together to enable everyone to go to a land that God has prepared for us to possess.

"I hope, for my family's sake, that you will decide you are willing to take your family to Akomen. You will need to decide before you start home tomorrow. I want you to respond 'yes' to the *Manalthing* motion that 'all say they will go along, all who are free to go.'"

Talerman's voice had risen gradually as he talked. His voice was loudest, and he punctuated the "Yes" with a fist raised high in the air. When he finished "free to go," he stood silently with both hands raised, moving his fingers slowly as if he were drawing the crowd to himself. He was silent. The room was silent. The spell lasted until a woman blew her nose.

Then Talerman quietly said, "Now is the time for Paafas Thord and Ketil to speak. Then we, the priests and the beaver-heads, will answer all the questions you have."

Vignette Seventeen
All Will Go

Azon did not need to look up to know Pitolo was approaching. The "swish, whoosh" sound of Pitolo's stick through the orange leaves on the ground clearly announced Pitolo's walk. Azon swiftly drew two horizontal lines on his engraved stick. Then he looked up to watch Pitolo lower himself down the north steps.

When he reached the bottom of the steps, Pitolo began to complain: "It is bad enough having to spend most of the day sitting in a dark tepee with a dying man. I think it is even worse trying to make an engraved stick of the curious requests made by his deranged mind.

"Picturing a decision made at a council meeting was difficult. But I think it is impossible to show the people of the North and the people of the East agreeing to cross a frozen sea. I have a star, the North Star, and a sunrise with stick people beside them. But I do not know how to show a frozen sea. Let me see if you have anything, Azon."

Azon held up his engraved stick.

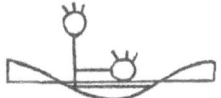

Pitolo squinted at it and exclaimed, "I do not believe it. You have done it again. Circles with three hairs must mean people in the land to the east. The highest circle must mean north. If I face north, this circle to the right must mean the people of the east. This curve is similar to the bottom of the ocean from one land to another. Then these two lines must be ice on the surface. The lines connecting the two circles indicate they are on the 'from' side of the water. We agreed, by convention, that 'from' would be on our left, 'to' on our right. Azon, you amaze me. I wish I had half as many arrows in my intelligence quiver."

"Pitolo, do not belittle your arrow supply. I had a difficult time to put all those names and the complicated plan into a simple verse that our descendants will remember. I trust you have one better than mine."

Pitolo handed back Azon's engraved stick. "Azon, you can be so creative with direct, but silly, instructions and so incapable of boiling a story down to bones. When our grandsons have grandsons, who will care what the story was? For that matter, anyone can think of a plan for the people to cross on the ice. Maalan Aarum told us, and then he repeated the main stone of the story, the stone our descendants must remember."

"I do not remember any stone."

"Oh, you see only the swirling waters, not the stones at the bottom. Maalan Aarum told us, 'All say they will go along, all who are free to go.' The sentence says it all.

"Our descendants can remember the saying because it is easy and catchy. They will know the people were at a meeting. They will know their ancestors agreed, as a group, to go somewhere. They will know a few were not free to go. When we tell about it, maybe you and I can pass along the rest of the story and the complex plans. If we cannot do it, they will still remember, 'All say they will go along, all who are free to go.' Then our descendants will make up their own stories to enrich the important idea that our ancestors were free to choose their fate."

"I am not sure of your reasoning, but we will see what Grandfather thinks. He took no food after we left yesterday and none this morning. Mother is sad. She told me she would go for a walk as soon as we start to visit with him. She said, 'Do not try to serve him food, unless he asks.'"

"My father says Maalan Aarum is deciding his own fate. If I remember correctly, there is today's engraved stick and then, according to Maalan Aarum, only four more.

"The decision of our ancestors must have been a very important event. Maalan Aarum is using up three engraved sticks to tell about the decision. He has only four more to tell about the actual crossing. The decisions happened in a few moons' time. The crossing must have taken years."

"The way we live," Azon said, "we are used to moving. We rip up our houses and move nearly every third moon. We enjoy the excitement of the move to new hunting grounds or to the summer camps. Think how difficult moving would be if we had grown to be as old as we are living in just this valley since we can remember."

"I have thought about their decision. The vision to live on the other side of the water must have shone brightly or they must have sensed the shadow of certain death creeping up on them where they lived. They were pulled or driven by great forces."

A brief while later Pitolo and Azon ducked through the doorway of the tepee. When their eyes adjusted they moved along one side of the tepee until they were near Maalan Aarum in the back. Maalan Aarum was seated resting against his backrest. His legs were extended along the ground. He smiled feebly as they sat down.

Maalan Aarum listened to Pitolo's verse. He said, "I am pleased you caught the essence of the story. Although I would have been disappointed if you had not. I repeated the words twice."

Azon admitted sheepishly, "Grandfather, you must be disappointed in me. I could not think of a short saying to describe your story of yesterday. My story is much longer."

Grandfather said, "Let me be the judge. Please say your story." Azon did.

When he had finished Grandfather said, "You have done well, Azon. There are many people and the story is complicated. And now, both of you, please show me your engraved sticks."

After Grandfather carefully studied both engraved sticks by holding them close to his eyes and moving them from side to side, he said, "Good. Pitolo and Azon, in a few sleeps, you two will each have to do the engraving and compose memory verses of the important events for your own village. Now I am satisfied to know that each of you can do both the engraving and the memory saying. You have both done well, but today I must choose the better engraved stick and verse. So I will choose the saying, 'All say they will go along, all who are free to go' for the verse to go with yesterday's engraved stick.

"For today's engraved stick I will chose the one with two heads, each having three strands of hair. The tall head is the people of the north and the lower head to the right is the people of the east.

"Yesterday the engraved stick and today's verse told us all the men, who were free to go, said they would go. But life is not that simple, especially if the people have been living in one place for many, many grandfathers. The real decision to go was much more difficult. The men were inclined to walk the Frozen Trail, but were the women and children willing to go?"

All say they will go along,
All who are free to go.

Stories of
Maalan Aarum
c. Fall 1344

Are You
Ready To Go ?

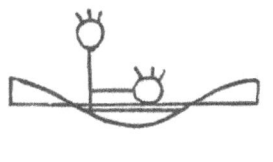

E.S. 3:16

Are You Ready to Go?

Although the people in the great room had listened quietly to Talerman, they were beginning to stir. They could sense the coming confrontation. Talerman paused. He took a drink of cool water. Then Talerman turned to Paafa Thord and said, "I know I have omitted many words, but I think I have been honest to talk about the major details. Do you agree?"

Paafa Thord with a serious expression stepped forward to say, "Talerman, you have been honest in the details you mentioned, but you have not talked about all the major details. For example you have not told what happened after the vote at sunrise. May I tell of those events?"

Talerman smiled. "I expected you would want the honor. Please proceed."

Paafa Thord made a mocking bow. "Thank you. As you heard from Talerman, the vote of the *Manalthing* slightly favored migration to Akomen. But myself, other priests, and many farm owners realized that the men voting at the *Manalthing* actually spoke for only about one out of every eight people in Greenland.

"This year more men then usual gathered at the *Althing*. But even if we called it a people's assembly, the *Manalthing* was still only a meeting of our chosen representatives and a few other men who could take time to come. They were making life-and-death decisions for the other seven out of eight people who could not come.

"Those people, seven of every eight, should be heard, because the decision of the *Manalthing* may cause many of them to die before they should in the years to come. The edict of the *Manalthing* means we will all abandon farms where our ancestors have lived for over three centuries. Then we will march onto the frozen sea with its unknown dangers. If we survive the march, we will arrive, starved, in a land where we do not know how to get food or shelter. There are no farm animals there. A horde of wild men behaving like wolf packs will be looking for any weakness so they can destroy us.

"Some of the other priests, many farm owners, and I were, and still are, concerned. So after the vote we asked to speak to the *Manalthing* before everybody left.

"I served as spokesman. I told the *Manalthing*, 'We, in opposition, accept the vote of the assembly, but we insist that the issue involves everyone. The resolution, "all say they will go along, all who are free to go," implies everyone, including women and children, should say for themselves if they are free to go.'

"Bishop Arne understood our position. So he helped form a plan of action. We finally reached an agreement that all the people in each kirke would be asked to decide for themselves. If more than half of the people voted to walk the Frozen Trail, the rest of the people would plan to go also unless they had very, very serious commitments requiring them to stay. If a migration happens, those people in each kirke who really cannot migrate can move to an abandoned farmhouse near a kirke where the people are planning to stay in Greenland."

Talerman raised his arm. He waited until Paafa Thord nodded. Then he said, "Paafa Thord and I have been through this discussion many times. Yet, it seems, we both forget to be fair to the other's viewpoint.

"My memory is that Bishop Arne and I both helped to form this plan of action. I know from personal experience that a person on the Frozen Trail must choose to be there. A person not choosing the trail becomes a troublemaker, risking his own life and endangering the life of others. It is better if those people who do not want to walk the trail are left on a farm in Greenland. It is also better for the people remaining in Greenland to be as close to each other as the food supply will allow."

Paafa Thord gave a slight nod toward Talerman. "I apologize. Yes, it is true. Bishop Arne and Talerman stood side by side and spoke as one person. The assembly agreed only personal decisions should commit those who really wanted to walk the Frozen Trail.

"The powerful men of the *Manalthing* proposed that Talerman and I visit each kirke to present our arguments for each person's decision. The crowd yelled in approval. Then they began scrambling for the boats to go home.

"So this past summer after the *Manalthing*, Talerman and I visited each of the fourteen kirkes in the Eastern Settlement. He presented the reasons for moving everyone over the Frozen Trail just as he has done tonight. I presented the arguments against migration. Then we had the local priest and sakkyndig moderate as the people discussed the issue. Finally we had a 'stand or sit' vote."

Talerman interrupted, "The voting was interesting. In each of the fourteen kirkes, there were two or three men who remained seated while their wives and children stood to show they were willing to walk over the Frozen Trail."

Paafa Thord responded, "I talked with many of those families. Several of the women had long periods of being sick because there was no fat in the meat. But it was also true that many had long, long periods of hunger waiting for the men to return with seals from the sea or across the ice from Merica. Still, most of the people around the six southern kirkes in Ketilsfjord and Siglufjord desired to stay in Greenland."

Again Talerman interrupted: "There are reasons for their choice. Most of those farms are larger and in good locations because their ancestors were powerful men when the people first came to Greenland. Also, many of the southern people have maintained family ties with Iceland. They keep hoping the pack ice will go away so normal sailing to Iceland can return."

Paafa Thord continued: "The people of the other eight kirkes did vote to walk the Frozen Trail. But an interesting trend developed. The people of the Eastern Settlement began to say to us, 'Bishop Arne suggested that the people of the North should walk the trail first. Fine, we are willing to walk the trail if the people of the North do it first.'

Once more Talerman interjected: "The people of the east were eager to walk the trail, but they thought the people of the North, who had more experience, might be better able to make the best decision about the safety of the Frozen Trail. So, in many cases, they said, 'We want to go, but we will go only if the people of the North go first.'

"That is why we are here tonight. We want you to ask us questions. Then, at the end of the night we too will take a 'stand or sit' vote. Paafa Thord and I have a pretty good idea how the other kirkes of the North will vote. We watched their representatives at the *Manalthing*. Ketil, your praying house appears to be just slightly opposed to walking the trail.

"The people of the other two kirkes in the Northern Settlement have always been very independent, but also many of their men have been over the Frozen Trail. Most of their representatives stood for going. I think most of their people are already making preparations to go.

"Paafa Thord is respected by most of you and appears to have influenced the vote of your representatives at the *Manalthing*. I regret that he has not been as supportive to me as Bishop Arne, but I accepted the challenge to debate him. The final decision is yours.

"Paafa Thord, a while ago you said I had not talked about all the major details. What other details have I left out?"

Paafa Thord responded, "One example is the danger of wild animals. Last winter a white bear killed two boys in a family trying to cross the Frozen Trail. If we put a hundred and eighty families with children on the ice, they will draw white bears as if they were flies around fresh meat in the summer."

"White bears are indeed animals to avoid," replied Talerman. "Those two young boys who died tried to stalk the white bear. It was a mother bear protecting a small cub. Boys doing such a foolish thing have died right here in Greenland.

"But in our case, at least one beaver-head will be with each group of ten sleds. There will also be men from Greenland who know how to hunt on the ice. They can spot and avoid white bears, or kill them if necessary. The rest of the people—women, young boys, and elderly men—should avoid all bears, white or brown.

"Bears want to snoop around but, usually, they will not pursue when we move away. I do not believe a large group of humans draws them closer. My experience is contrary."

Paafa Ketil said, "Styrk has explained the dangers of crossing the ice to me. I am comfortable to face them except for the fog that forms in Merica in the month before the ice goes away. The last of our people to leave Greenland may be trapped in the fog as the ice breaks up."

"Paafa Ketil," replied Talerman, "you have the talent to identify the most serious worries. Yes, the fog at the Merica end is a very dangerous situation. Hunting groups who have been trapped in the fog have never been seen again. We have found their tracks in the snow on the ice. Even good hunters made tracks that went in big, wandering circles.

"We now show everyone how to set ice pointers after every two hundred paces if they are separated and lost. An ice pointer is a slice of ice one mitten wide and three mittens long. Men, and women too, can chisel the ice rapidly with a knife held at a slant. Two men working together can do it real fast. Then we cut a groove in one end of the hole. We push the pointer up into the groove until it is about a mitten above the ice. Then we pack the loose ice and snow back into the groove. Ice pointers can be seen from a long distance away and have led rescue parties to many people.

"The moisture makes the air feel colder. Even a slight wind drives the coldness into bodies. The ice breaks up with cracking sounds all around. When a fog-bound traveler is able to see again, he may not be where he was when the fog came because the ice has moved.

"The best thing to do is to sit and wait until the fog lifts. But the supply of food may be gone before visibility returns. Running out of food may happen every so often. So, if for some reason a group tries to move, they try to go along a line kept straight by observing the sleds just visible behind and ahead and they should set ice pointers.

"The beaver-heads in Merica will have a fire on tall timbers as a guiding beacon to guide you during the last days of the walk. They will have similar guiding fires on Bjarni and Akpatok Islands.

"Also, the beaver-heads in Merica will be counting the sled groups who arrive, so they will know how many sleds are still on the ice. If some sleds are missing, they will search for them along the path. While they search, they will carry fire and pound a drum.

"The fog is dangerous, but if we leave Greenland as soon as we can, and if we keep our wits when we reach the other end, things will work out."

Paafa Thord asked, "Why not have the Merica beaver-heads build ice towers along the trail as they wait for Greenland people?"

Talerman realized Paafa Thord's question was the first indication since the *Manalthing* that he was starting to solve the problems of the Frozen Trail rather than resist the entire idea. He replied as gently as he could.

"Paafa Thord, your suggestion seems practical. I truly wish we could make it work. The beaver-heads in Merica discussed that action for a long time. Some of us were concerned about the movement of the ice. One group of beaver-heads walked ten days east and stayed there on the ice for a moon's time. They came back with discouraging information. The ice moves southward at a rate of one notch every moon.

"A food cache left on the ice would move south at least a notch before the people of Greenland found it. If the people from the Northern Settlement went after the food, they would travel extra sleeps. They might not find the food, and they might not get back north before the fog catches them."

Paafa Thord responded in a civil, but serious tone. "Talerman, my understanding is that the people of the Eastman Land want us to move into the empty lands south of them. The wolf pack people have devastated those lands. Moving into those lands would put our people into danger from the wolf packs. Is that wise?"

Talerman took a few seconds to gauge the effect of the question on the people in the great room. Hallgrim and Tjalve did also. Once again Hallgrim signaled with hands held horizontal and crossing over one another. The concern of the people in the room could not be judged. Talerman responded, looking at Paafa Thord, "Paafa Thord, you always try to stick me with that question."

Then Talerman turned to face the wives who came from the farthest houses because he knew their decision was going to be vital to the outcome. He said, "The people of Eastman Land gave us these beaver hats as an sign of brotherhood. All of us who wear the beaver hats have lived in Eastman Land and learned to be like them. I, personally, could not lead you to possess land of the people of the Eastman Land. That would be like fighting my own family. In Hallgrim's case and for a few other men in the Northern Settlement, my statement is really true.

"But the wolf packs continue to threaten the Eastman Land. They have made the southern lands empty of people. The people of Eastman Land tell us that the men in the wolf packs are vicious and cruel. But when confronted by a superior force of fighting men, they behave similar to wolves. They preserve their own lives by retreating. The Eastman Land sakkyndigs told me that the people in Akonsee, very much further south in Akomen, were able to resist the wolf packs by concentrating superior forces. So we will have to organize our own people to enable us to concentrate a large number of fighting men when needed. We have worked together before, in bear and walrus hunts, harpooning whales, and in harvesting caribou. We can work together when our lives depend on it. Our kirke groupings are a basis for establishing strong villages in Akomen."

Talerman noted, with relief, the affirming nods from most of the beaver-heads and the lack of alarm on the faces of the women. He nodded to Paafa Ketil, who was signaling. Paafa Ketil said, "I am not speaking to awaken the bad spirits, Talerman. I am trying to understand the long-range effects of moving all the people of my praying house to another land. Styrk told me many of the details of making the move. At the final settlement in East-man's Land, Styrk says the families will live in small houses called wigwams. Are they cramped and are they colder than our earthen houses?"

"Ketil," responded Talerman, "I cannot explain how, but a wigwam, a framework of branches covered with hides, seems to be more comfortable than our sod houses. Many evenings the men sit and visit without shirts on. I have often undressed to the skin on my chest in a wigwam, but I usu-ally cover my shoulders with an extra fur here in this sod house. The wood fire in the wigwam is small but warm. Many people have told me that the name 'wigwam' comes from our own words meaning 'stronghold nook.' Yes, the wigwam is cramped, but in Akomen we will use it mostly to store food and tools, to tell stories, and to sleep. In Akomen, people live outside as much as possible.

"Besides, when the camp area gets dirty and smells, the people move on to a new hunting area. The wigwam needs to be small enough for the women and the children to carry it to the new site. I promise you, Ketil, most of the women here will be glad to change their cold, freezing, dirty, smelly home in this icy land for a warm, small, movable, repairable home in a sweet-smelling forest. In the evening with the family around, the wig-wam does seem like a stronghold nook."

Paafa Thord, raising his fist, whirled toward Talerman.

"Talerman, I told you. You should not use that argument. You may know what beaver-heads think, but priests are more in touch with the thoughts of the women who want to stay in Greenland. Here, the women know their homes are secure against all weather and animals. They are able to make

their earthen homes comfortable. They appreciate their location near do-
mesticated animals, which produce food and wool."

Then moisture began to form around Paafa Thord's eyes. There was a
catch in his voice as he continued.

"My aunt never allowed my uncle to walk the Frozen Trail. She always
spoke about my father, who did, as an example of the Frozen Trail fever
gone wrong. She used to say, 'Going away on the Frozen Trail allows men
to commit sins without feeling guilty.' She said my father walked the Frozen
Trail because he could not accept his duties as a father. He left my mother,
my sisters, and me behind to starve to death. My aunt insisted that if my
father had stayed home, my mother and my sisters would be alive today.
My aunt always said my father killed my mother and my sisters as sure as
if he hit them with an axe, but he never suffered guilt because he was away
in Merica.

"I say God wants us to grow where we are. God wants men to stay near
their families. We all, especially the men, should stay in Greenland. With
God's help and with our men staying at home to raise animals and to hunt
wisely, we can make Greenland a better place for all to live."

Bjarni turned with hands on his hips to face Paafa Thord. Anger was
clearly visible in his face. His arm lashed out, finger pointing, "Paafa Thord,
I have asked you, many times, not to use your emotional story in these de-
bates. I regret the death of your mother and sisters, but your story is not
true. I have talked to a few women…"

Arnora, carrying a tray of blubber cubes for the children, heard the
anger in Bjarni's voice and turned to watch. Arnora knew instinctively that
Bjarni's anger was the wrong answer to Paafa Thord's emotional ploy, but
what could be done? Then she saw Sigrid stand up in the far corner of the
room. She thought, *There were other voices!*

"Bjarni, quiet!" The voice of Arnora rang out.

Bjarni, still angry, turned to face the new attack. Everyone swung to
look at Arnora. Arnora was pointing to Sigrid. Arnora said loudly, "Taler-

man, Sigrid has something to say. Please listen to a woman who is well respected by all women."

Sigrid did not wait for approval. She stepped closer to a boiling pot so that the firelight lit her face. She turned toward Paafa Thord.

"Paafa Thord, I was the attending woman when your mother died trying to give birth. I can assure you, your father stayed beside your mother through those terrible days of agony. Your father's family, including you, was starving. The difficulty of getting seafood and making hay was as bad as now. The death of your mother, her unborn child, and your two sisters happened because they were not healthy enough to overcome the coughs, loose bowels, the cold, and other illnesses. Your father was only skin and bones. He had starved himself to save food for your mother and you children.

"After your mother and two of your sisters died, your father became so listless that your aunt and uncle took you and your other surviving sister into their home. Then your aunt began to talk against your father. She said he killed your mother by making her pregnant.

"All the community thought he would surely die of sorrow before he died of hunger. One day Styrk, returned from Merica, took pemmican to your father. Styrk talked your father into pulling on a sled team going back to Merica. Your father accepted only because he thought he would die faster on the Frozen Trail. Styrk told me that when your father did finally die in Merica, he had a wide fame as a caribou man. Caribou men from a large region gathered for his death feast. I sincerely believe your mother would still be alive if your father had walked the Frozen Trail earlier."

Paafa Thord shouted, "No! No! Stop, you old hag! Talerman tried to tell me the same slop. He is lying. Now he has seduced you to lie for him. My aunt told me over and over, 'Your father walked the Frozen Trail and deserted his own family.'"

Sigrid was not about to be intimidated by a mere priest. She scowled and clenched her raised fist. She leaned onto her forward foot and continued: "Your aunt hated your father because she believed, at first, he killed your mother by making her pregnant. Pregnant women die. That is a sad truth of life, but no one blames a man who loves his wife. Nobody would accept your aunt's ranting. Her mind became confused. As the years passed many things that she said were not straight. Nobody, even your uncle, could stop her from twisting happenings of the past. When we tried to tell her differently, she would just repeat her words louder and longer."

Paafa Thord exploded again. "I do not know how Talerman has cast a spell on you. Maybe both of you are lovers. My aunt never lied. She taught me lying is a great sin. She also taught me walking the Frozen Trail causes unnecessary death."

Halldis was on her feet. She raised an arm and said, "Listen to me." As the crowd swung to gaze on her, she said, "There is no other woman more faithful to her husband than my sister Sigrid. What she is telling you is true. Paafa Thord's mother died. Then, and only then, did his father walk the Frozen Trail."

Halldis swung and pointed at Paafa Ketil. "Paafa Ketil, why are you so silent?"

Paafa Ketil appeared embarrassed as he responded with less than full conviction, "I have been very, very prudent to never criticize the dead nor repeat a confession made to me."

Halldis stamped her foot. She said, "I am not talking about the dead! A woman in your praying house has been insulted. She has been accused of lying. She has been accused of sin against her husband. Yet, you, you stand silent! You! You, who preach about the support that your God will deliver if we stay in Greenland. Speak to the living!"

For a moment Paafa Ketil and Paafa Thord locked eyes. Then Paafa Ketil stepped back and looked down. He slowly raised his face toward Halldis. He said, "I regret the insults. I pray Sigrid will receive an apology when emotions subside. Sigrid is very faithful to her husband. I have never heard a rumor otherwise. In all the years I have known Sigrid, I have never known her to lie."

Paafa Ketil gained renewed conviction. His gaze turned to Paafa Thord. He said with strength in his words, "Sigrid is not lying now!"

Paafa Thord's face flushed red. Beads of sweat stood out on his bald head. Suddenly the left side of his face sagged. [See **BELL'S PALSY**.] The flesh on the cheek dropped. The left side of his mouth sagged downward. The left eyelid drooped closed. Paafa Thord's left hand came up to shield his face. He hunched over to hide his face. He stumbled around the boiling pot and then barged his way out the door.

Paafa Ketil called out, "He needs help!" He grabbed furs from the doorway pegs and also left the great room.

Talerman allowed the conversations to subside. Then he said, "We all need to do our necessary things before we take a vote. I pray the priests will return."

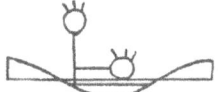

The subdued murmur in the great room rose to a higher level when the two priests entered the passageway from the outside door. Paafa Thord slumped down against the passageway wall, keeping his hood over his face.

The murmur reduced as Paafa Ketil worked his way around the boiling pots to Talerman. Paafa Ketil and Talerman conversed for a few minutes. Then Talerman held up his hands to quiet the room. Paafa Ketil stepped in front and said in a loud voice, "Paafa Thord will be well after some time. I have seen his affliction twice before. It seems to occur when a man is tired. Usually after two or three months the ill person recovers to almost normal. But, right now, Paafa Thord does not speak very clearly. He wishes me to speak for him.

"First, Paafa Thord begs forgiveness. He has listened to his aunt for too much of his life and not enough to God. He does apologize to Sigrid and to Talerman. He regrets he did not listen closely to many others who informed him correctly.

"Both Paafa Thord and I have not been listening closely to God. We have heard many, many mothers tell of limited food, of sickness from eating lean meat, and of the lack of husbands. We thought that the latter caused the former. We supported each other's thoughts, believing that more food could be harvested if the husbands stayed near the farmhouse. But Styrk disturbed my thinking when he convinced me, with strong words, that his absence was worth four months of food for his family.

"Until now Paafa Thord's strong belief about the deadly effects of walking the Frozen Trail convinced me that we were following the true word of God.

"Now both Paafa Thord and I admit we have not been listening to the word of God as spoken by most of you. We now realize that having more men near the farmhouse does not increase the yield if the crops and the animals are not there.

"Our praying book begins with a story of the sorrow of the original people leaving paradise. But this land is not paradise. Later in the same praying book, people walked across the bottom of a sea to a land God gave them to possess. The land that lies in Akomen for us to possess sounds much better than here. Let us walk across the sea!"

The great room resounded with a roar. The young people leaped to their feet. Many men were already on their feet. Their wives reached up for a hand and pulled themselves to their feet. Paafa Thord in the passageway struggled to rise. Two beaver-heads lifted him to his feet.

When Talerman was finally able to silence the crowd, he said, "Those of the north agreed."

Paafa Ketil sang out, "So, those of the east agreed."

The young people began to chant, "Over the water, over the frozen sea."

Men turned to their wives to promise, "We are going to enjoy it."

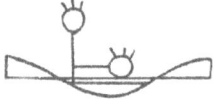

Arnora lay snuggled under Bjarni's arm, her head lying on his chest. She could see daylight through the hole in the roof. The design on her wall hanging was becoming distinct. It was late in the morning.

Bjarni coughed, then raised his head again. His head lay down again, but his breathing indicated he was awake.

"We fell asleep again," Arnora said softly.

Bjarni said, "It was a long night."

"And a good morning."

"Ah, yes," Bjarni reflected with a smile, "I suppose you are going to turn into a hostess again?"

"Soon, but they must be as tired as we were last night. I can lie here for a while. Now that the decision-making is done, what are you going to do?

"The first thing I have to do is pick a man to stay in Greenland and keep people working on the vital arrangements. I need a man who can plan and who can talk people into doing things. I need someone who can keep calm when people begin to complain. I need someone who can be an accepted leader without question."

Arnora rolled further onto Bjarni's chest and pushed herself up saying, "How about Valthjof?"

Bjarni's head snapped up so he could look at Arnora's face. "It is a good thing you are smiling."

Bjarni pulled the rolled robe up under his head so he could continue to see Arnora's face. He continued, "I have waited a long time to see my woman smile."

Arnora looked at the wall hanging as if she were thinking. "I think Paafa Thord with Paafa Ketil as his assistant is the only choice you have."

Bjarni used his left hand to turn Arnora's head toward him again. "You are not smiling now."

"Think about it."

Bjarni lay his head on his hands behind his head. "I think Paafa Thord is organized and very persistent. He can read and write."

"And do numbers."

Bjarni continued thinking out loud. "Paafa Ketil is a dynamic leader. He is passionate. Somehow people just seem to like him. He can persuade them to do things a man with a big club cannot. Maybe you are right."

"Can there be any doubt?"

Bjarni was silent for a moment. Then he said, "Yes, Paafa Thord lost his composure last evening."

"Suppose Sigrid, a mere women, had proven your arguments baseless. How would you behave?"

"I would never talk to her a... It took a lot of courage for Paafa Thord to return and to apologize to everyone. Paafa Ketil has assured me that Paafa Thord will rapidly improve and soon his affliction will not be noticed by many."

"I think no one who was there will ever accuse Paafa Thord of failing to stand by his convictions."

Bjarni took another close look at Arnora's face. "You still are not smiling. I will think about them. Aha, now I see a slight smile."

"I am smiling at my big gruff bear, Bjarni. But I should not be. You will probably go somewhere too soon."

"I would like to make a trip to the mouth of Ranga Fjord,where we will set up the departure camp," said Bjarni. "The shore ice should be strong enough to travel in about a moon's time. Meantime, I have to have many planning meetings, but they can all be here in the Northern Settlement. I will take you along.

"The beaver-heads for each kirke in the Eastern Settlement will go back to tell them our decision. From each kirke, they will bring back a stone-mason and woodworking man to go to Merica with us."

"Why do you want a stonemason and a woodworking man from each kirke?"

"To build the shelter houses in Merica for when we walk off the ice."

"But, if I heard correctly, only the people in this settlement are going to cross the first time."

"True," Bjarni continued, "but it would be a difficult task for our stonemasons and woodworking men to build enough shelters for our people. The people from the Eastern Settlement will also be using the shelters in the following years. They should help with building them. If the eastern men assist, we can be assured of shelters on time, and the Eastern Settlement will have experienced men to guide their people to the shelters during the coming years."

Arnora looked Bjarni in the eyes. "Sounds much too complicated for my brain. I had better become a hostess again. If you will show me where you hid the lance, I will put it away."

Bjarni blinked his eyes and said, "Lance? That reminds me. Who taught Bjørn to use a harpoon?"

Arnora wrinkled her nose and hesitated before saying, "Iqquk."

"Iqquk? Isn't he the meat-eater living north of the thicket?"

Arnora nodded tentatively. She remained quiet.

Bjarni rose on his elbows with an insistent tone as he asked, "How did Iqquk do anything with Bjørn?"

Arnora replied, "It started about four years ago, when Iqquk observed Bjørn having difficulties catching fish. He signaled a better spot. Then he showed Bjørn a better way to throw the net. Since that time Iqquk has remained in our region. They often hunt and fish together.

"Bjørn says Iqquk talks about a son who drowned in a chase after a whale. He thinks Iqquk likes teaching a boy again. I think it is good that someone is teaching Bjørn the things he needs to know."

Bjarni's tone was still insistent. "That is my role!"

Arnora met the firm voice with her own. "You are never here."

"But a meat-eater…?"

"Yes, a meat-eater. Thanks to him, I can still play at being a hellion."

Bjarni shook his head, then asked slowly, "What are you saying?"

Arnora signaled calm as she said, "One night two years ago, Iqquk, his wife, and Kuptana, his daughter, burst into our great room. Kuptana and her mother grabbed Yngvild. They rushed her into our room. Iqquk talked swiftly to Bjørn. Bjørn has learned Iqquk's tongue. I can only understand a few words. Then Bjørn said to me, 'Mother, four mean men who have landed in kayaks are coming toward our house. Behave as if you are Iqquk's woman.'"

Bjarni's face showed alarm. He hissed through his lips, "You knew how to behave as Iqquk's woman?"

Arnora put her hands up, palm outward to signal patience. Then she continued: "I have watched Iqquk and his wife many times. When people are visiting, they never touch. They hardly look at each other. Now and then they make eye contact with a sly glance. She seems to anticipate his needs and tends to them. Once in a while she smiles slightly. She sits near, but slightly behind him when she is not serving. I behaved like that.

"Bjørn had gotten his harpoon. Iqquk and he were cleaning their harpoons when the four big, ugly meat-eaters came through the door. Their faces showed a flash of surprise. Iqquk waved toward the stools near the boiling pot. Bjørn told me, 'Bva, Mother.'

"I served bva. The men leaned their harpoons against the wall and came to the boiling pot facing Iqquk and Bjørn. Iqquk's eyes and mine met in a sly glance. I thought his glance said, 'You are doing well.' I hope my eyes read, 'I am thankful you came.' Iqquk said later it was my slight smile that convinced the men I was his woman. They visited while drinking three or four cups of bva and eating many mouths of food from the pot. Then they left.

"Later Bjørn told me, 'Mother, no one made any threats. Iqquk did tell a story about his father killing a man who tried to steal Iqquk's mother. The man had too much of a load on a broken sled. He could not carry Iqquk's mother away fast enough. The men understood. To them you, Mother, are now Iqquk's woman. If they harm you, or your family, Iqquk will hunt them down to kill them.'"

Arnora lowered her hands to Bjarni's chest, nodded, and said, "After you, I will trust and depend on Iqquk."

Bjarni's face was limp with unbelief. "Why would a meat-eater do a thing like that? He must want something very much."

"I think he was just returning a favor."

"What favor?"

"About three years ago, Bjørn went to visit Iqquk. He came right back with the news that maybe they all would die. When Bjørn, Yngvild, and I went to their ice cave, we found them very weak. I thought the symptoms seemed to be of eating meat without fat. Iqquk was almost too weak to talk but was able to tell Bjørn that he had hurt his knee three moons' time before. Their meat-eater friends had moved north for the foxhunt. Iqquk's family became so desperate for food they traded two walrus tusks to Valthjof, near the ice, for pemmican."

"Valthjof! The meat-eater sure made a bad choice there. Nothing goes right near that man."

"You are right. Valthjof's second wife, his own daughter, probably did not know how to prepare the pemmican correctly. Her mother may not have known either because she was so young when they married. We quickly gave Iqquk and his family meat with fat. In two days they were better. In two weeks, they were restored to life."

Bjarni's slight smile reminded her to ask again, "Now, where is the lance? I will put it away."

"Why would you put it away?"

"With a gruff old bear around, the hellion can rest for a while."

Vignette Eighteen
The Frozen Sea

A zon was waiting at the waterway. He looked up to watch Pitolo making his way along the path. He thought, *There is no spring in his step. He is not skipping as usual.*

Last night until the stars indicated the coming dawn, they had both stayed in the Big House listening to the young men tell of their quests. Azon pushed himself to his feet. He went to meet Pitolo at the waterway.

"Azon," said Pitolo, "I am getting tired. This ordeal is worse than a quest. I hate spending all afternoon in a tepee with a dying man. On the other hand, I sure do not want to eat Maalan Aarum's final feast. Somehow I do not feel worthy to carry his knowledge."

"Pitolo," responded Azon, "you are not alone. I think it is good there are two of us. Let us try to concentrate on the immediate things. How did your carving come out?"

"Fair, but not good. Maalan Aarum asked us to show people from four praying houses crossing the ice and going into many shelters. Also, he wanted us to show that other people were along.

"I used your engraving of the land, water, and ice. Maalan Aarum seemed to like that yesterday. Then I put four circles with three hairs each representing the people from four praying houses headed to many shelters that I show as tepees on the 'to' shore. I think the shelters look too cluttered. I used a small circle with no hair for the other people. Let me see yours, Azon."

Azon gave his engraved stick to Pitolo.

"Here you are," said Azon. "Look, I used the same land, water, and ice engraving. Also I used circles to represent people from four praying houses and another circle to represent other people."

"He will still choose yours," replied Pitolo. "I did not think of putting the heads on a line to show they were walking."

Azon placed an arm around Pitolo, pushing him gently toward the south steps. When they were on the path to the palisade, Azon said, "We will accept whichever engraving he picks. My verse was:

'The beavers-heads and the paafas agreed
'The people of North and East agreed
'They all would cross the frozen sea.'"

Pitolo responded, "You have used good words, but I believe Maalan Aarum knows the end is coming. He also knows the words he wants and he is telling them to us directly."

"What words did he say directly?" Azon asked.

At the entrance to the palisade Pitolo turned to face Azon, saying,

"Those of the North agreed.
Those of the East agreed.
Over the water, the frozen sea,
They went to enjoy it."

Azon nodded his head in agreement. "If you are correct, he will still choose your words."

Silently, Azon and Pitolo walked the path to Azon's tepee. Inside the tepee, Azon's mother was holding a water gourd to Grandfather's mouth. Grandfather saw them come in the entrance and pushed the gourd away. Azon's mother swiftly slid around the fire. Avoiding looking at them, she left the tepee. As Gee Hiz came through the doorway to fall on her face, Azon noticed a tear streak on her cheek.

Grandfather whispered with a raspy voice, "I am pleased you came early today. I may need a nap before I can finish this next story. Let me see what you have made."

Grandfather looked at the two carvings. For several cycles he looked at one and then the other. He appeared confused. Azon asked, "Is there something wrong?"

"Is my guess correct that you chose to use only one hair on each head pointing to the 'to' shore because you wanted to emphasize that the people left the land to the east and are headed to the land of the Great Spirit?"

Azon replied, "Yes, Grandfather."

Grandfather nodded and said, "Also does the opening on the head on the ice imply the other people had no Great Spirit?"

Azon simply nodded. Grandfather nodded in reply.

Then Grandfather said, "If only we could combine your drawings. If we could make the four walking praying houses appear to go into many shelters, the picture would be best. But I do see the many shelters get confusing. I do not know which engraving to chose."

Pitolo asked, "Which is the most important to tell our grandsons?"

Grandfather answered, "There were four praying houses in the first move, but they walked in two groups. The first group went into the many shelters in Merica where they prepared snowshoes and after five sleeps they walked on. Then the second group came to the shelters. Some other people walked between the two groups."

Azon suggested, "The four praying houses going to the land of the Great Spirit would seem more important to remember than temporary shelters. I could move the little circle to be between two pairs of praying-house symbols to illustrate the two groups"

"Let us do it that way. Now let me hear your verses. You first, Azon."

Pitolo's verse was selected rapidly. Pitolo was correct. Maalan Aarum had been putting the words he wanted into the story.

Grandfather asked for another drink. After he sipped, he signaled the boys to come closer. He started the story by saying, "The people of the North and the people in the East accepted the decision to migrate to Merica. In the following days, the cold continued and most people realized they had little hope to live a long life unless the plan of the beaver-heads and the Big Raven worked. Their thoughts and actions began to move toward their own role in the adventure. A year in the freezing cold was a long, long time to prepare and the Frozen Trail went a long, long way over icy waters. Still the thought of being alive to experience the adventure and to have plenty of food overcame the thought of death from cold, open leads in the ice, or wolf packs."

Those of the north agreed.
Those of the east agreed.

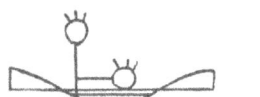

Over the waters
Over the frozen sea
They went to enjoy it.

Stories of Maalan Aarum

C. 1344, Five or Six Days Later

The Bishop's Gambit

E.S. 3:17

Way of the Women's Boat

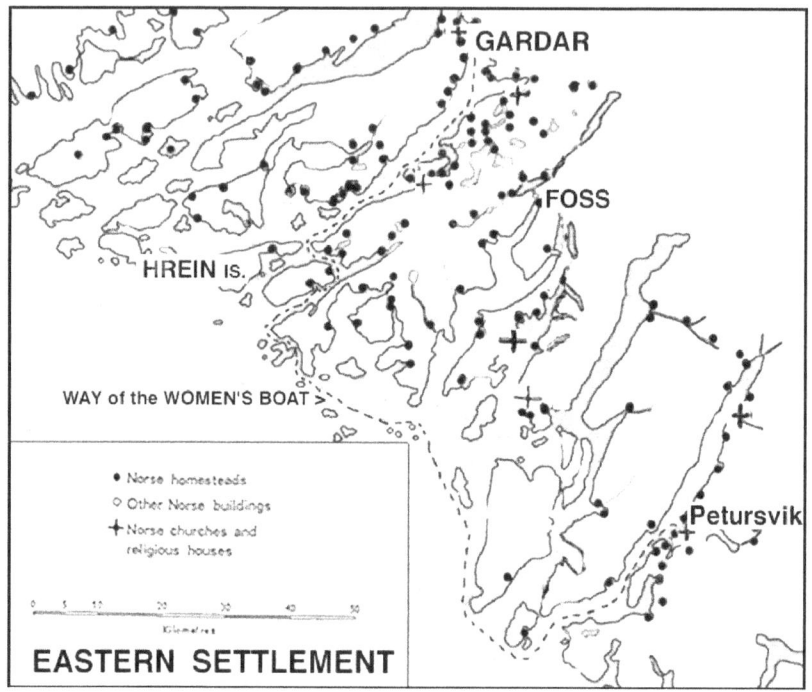

EASTERN SETTLEMENT

The Women's boat carried Bishop Arne and Ketil from Gardar past Hrein Island to the kirkes in the southern section of the Eastern Settlement. Bishop Arne began to set up his gambit at the Petursvik kirke.

The Bishop's Gambit

Paafa Ketil swung his bare feet over the railing. He lowered himself gingerly onto the robes piled in the rear of the skin boat. He was seated facing forward. His bare feet found the first rib ahead of the robes. He hurried to pull on his fur boots. Then he looked up at the six fur-clad women with oars who turned to smile at him.

He looked forward and shouted to ask Styrk, "Will this thing really work?" Styrk was sitting on robes at the other end of the boat facing backwards. Because Styrk boarded first and took the less enjoyable seat, Ketil's respect of Styrk increased.

Styrk smiled and said, "The last one I rode did."

Paafa Ketil looked out at Iqquk, the meat-eater, and Bjørn in the one-man skinned boats and commented, "Those two men do not seem to think so."

Styrk was still smiling. "The women's boat's biggest trouble is high wind and waves. If they occur the men in the kayaks will lash to the front side of the boat where necessary to hold us into the water. Meanwhile they will be hunting and fishing to provide food."

Iqquk's wife in the left front rowing spot said a soft word. Then the women started to chant. They began pulling with rhythmic strokes. They straightened up with every pulling stroke. They steered as close to shore as possible to stay away from the opposing current pushing icebergs northward. They followed along the shores of bays, but cut across inlets of fjords.

Some old-timers still insist the boat made the trip in four sleeps. Others insist the feat could not be possible. They say five, maybe, but not four sleeps. Still, tales of the astonishing speed with which the Northern Settlement's decision became known in the Eastern Settlement were often repeated around boiling pots all over Greenland and Merica.

So four or five days after the Northern Settlement's decision, Bishop Arne looked out his open doorway into the morning light and saw Paafa Ketil racing up the path. Bishop Arne bowed his head with sadness because he thought Paafa Ketil was the spokesman for the people wanting to stay in Rangafjord. Paafa Ketil's excitement appeared to mean that the decision of the Northern Settlement was to stay in Rangafjord. Bishop Arne closed the door and sat down at the table with his head in his hands.

Paafa Ketil burst into the room with a shout: "We are going!"

Bishop Arne had not expected those words. He sat numbed with blank eyes. Only when Paafa Ketil repeated, "We are going!" did he leap to his feet and grab Paafa Ketil's arms. The two men grabbed each other's forearms and began to turn slowly in a circle, laughing together.

"Who's going? Where?" Ivar Bardarsson's chilly voice cut through the air. Bishop Arne and Paafa Ketil backed away from each other.

"We are going, going…" Bishop Arne stammered.

Paafa Ketil caught the unspoken signals and said, "Falcon hunting. They have come to the rocks. They are only three days north by skin boat. Do you want to join us?"

Sir Ivar pointed at Paafa Ketil and snapped, "You address me as 'Your Eminence.' No! Men perish in those deathtraps. Bishop Arne should not go, either."

As Bishop Arne bundled his clothes and nets together, he reminded His Eminence of the value the king and the archbishop placed on white falcons. Besides, he had traveled in skin boats before. Perhaps the falcons were a blessing sent from God. His Eminence was uttering yet another argument when Bishop Arne pulled the outside door shut.

At the skin boat out of His Eminence's hearing, they held a quick conference. Styrk would stay behind to round up the beaver-heads, the woodmen, and the stonemasons from the eight kirkes in the Gardar region that had voted to walk the Frozen Trail. Bishop Arne would go with Paafa Ketil to get a brief respite from His Eminence.

A little after midday the tide was running outbound. The boat leaving Einarsfjord seemed to be moving very rapidly along the shore. Ahead was Hrein Island at the southwestern end of the fjord. Bishop Arne shouted to Paafa Ketil, "Hrein Island is ahead."

Paafa Ketil twisted around to study the low blob of the island oozing out of the haze. He turned back to Bishop Arne and said in a loud voice, "We lived two fjords north of here. We were always skeptical of all the travelers that proudly said they 'Hrein-aa-byy.' Surely they did not mean they were proud to abide on that island, even though its name means 'decent'?"

Bishop Arne shouted back, "It is not the island. The whole fjord was named 'Hrein.' The bishop's church is at the head of the fjord. The most powerful sakkyndig lives there. The *Althing* meets there. The ships from Norway trade along the shores of Hrein. So the major men of power in this region are in this fjord.

"Naturally everybody who can likes to say they 'Hrein-aa-byy.' The educated, like us, who must deal with Iceland or Norway, use the name 'Greenland' in our writings to them, but the ordinary men who live in this fjord are proud to say they 'Hrein-aa-byy' to other people in Greenland and Akomen."

Paafa Ketil shouted back, "The fjord is called Einarsfjord."

Bishop Arne responded, "Over the years 'Hrein' changed into 'Einar.' I will explain later."

Just then Bjørn paddled alongside the women's boat to shout, "Which way?" A decision was needed. Bishop Arne shouted back, "Left, to the south. We are going to Petsurvik Kirke."

Paafa Ketil smiled because he already knew the answer, but he asked anyway, "What about—the falcons?"

Bishop Arne pointed to two nearly invisible specks flying north. "We found them, but we could not get close enough."

The families in the house near the sea on the island just south of Hrein Island were nearly overwhelmed to have Bishop Arne, Paafa Ketil, and Bjørn as overnight guests. The six fur-clad women inverted their boat on the smooth earth of the boat pullout area. They prepared fish from Iqquk's catch. They gladly accepted an offer of water from the farmhouse but, otherwise, they ate quietly and retired early.

In the earthen house, Bishop Arne reassured the families that his haste to sleep and his desire to leave as the sky lightened was not a bad reflection on the cook's skill.

When the boat slid from the shore, as the dark sky grew paler, gift baskets of warm meat were stashed on the boat ribs between the rowers. That same night, a tired boat crew reached the Petsurvik Kirke as the chilling darkness fell.

During the next four days, Bishop Arne visited all six southern kirkes, meeting with eleven groups. He met with the priests and as many of the people as they could get together in midweek. The kernel of his message was, "I know you decided to stay in Greenland. I will pray for your good fortune and good weather. I am here to ask your help for the people of the North and those of the Eastern Settlement who have chosen to leave.

"As you know, His Eminence, Ivar Bardarsson, is at Gardar listing kirke property. He is supposed to list kirke property in the Western Settlement also. But he does not know where the Western Settlement is."

At that statement the groups usually snickered or laughed outright. Bishop Arne had to repeat many times that he was serious. His Eminence, Ivar Bardarsson, really did not know where the Western Settlement was. His Eminence believed the Western Settlement could be reached by sailing along the Greenland coast.

Then Bishop Arne continued, "All he has been told is that the Western settlement is six to eight days sailing to the west. I regret that we in the Eastern Settlement are afflicted with His Eminence. The Western Settlement in Akomen has done very little to aid us. Our western friends have been distant, but they have not been bad neighbors. Pirates may not have ravaged our shores because the richer lands are in the Western Settlement in Akomen.

"Also, many of our Northern Settlement people will soon be in Akomen. If His Eminence goes to the Western Settlement, he will continue his thorough listing similar to his efforts here. His Eminence tells me that as soon as his registration is complete, he will ask for soldiers from Norway to enforce the collection of the king's fees. Then the big kirke in Rome will also collect its tithe from our kirkes plus an additional levy for the crusades. These cold years may benefit us. The cold hampers the ships bringing demands from the leaders in Europe.

"Meanwhile, I do not want His Eminence to find out where the Western Settlement really is. Also, I do not want him to know where the people leaving Greenland are really going."

At this point in the discussions, one of the leading men would usually ask, "Other than keeping our mouths closed, what do you want us to do?"

Bishop Arne would smile and say, "Keeping your mouths closed is a good first step. I know you all are good at that. I have been thinking. His Eminence knows only that the Western Settlement is six to eight sailing days away. I, too, have been able to keep my mouth shut. So he does not know about the Northern Settlement. If all goes well, there will be no one in the Northern Settlement after fifteen moons' time from now. It takes six days to row to the Northern Settlement."

Many of the men in the audiences were good chess players. In every group, one or two faces showed immediate recognition of Bishop Arne's gambit. Someone usually asked, "You want us to keep quiet until the people in the Northern Settlement leave? Then you want His Eminence to visit the Northern Settlement and find no one there. But you also want him to think he has seen the Western Settlement?"

The crowds murmured. Smiles flickered on faces. Heads nodded. Paafa Ketil insisted, later, that eyes sparkled with the same gleams of expectation seen in the eyes of cunning chess players.

Bishop Arne waited for a pause in the murmuring and then continued, "The longer we keep His Eminence from returning to Norway, the longer we all avoid paying the penalty of having him here. If he thinks that he lost the people of the Western Settlement, he may find reasons, himself, to stay longer in Greenland.

"His Eminence has shown us other ways to slow his return. For one thing, he is very proud of his role to serve two of the most powerful men on earth, the Norway King and the Popa. He expects you to treat him as the third most powerful man on earth. If you say 'Mister Ivar,' he will scold you. If you do not immediately respond correctly, he will insist that your sakkyndig punish you. A sakkyndig can use up hours hearing both sides of the accusation. A creative sakkyndig can take days.

"His Eminence is persistent and finicky. Two farms shared rocky land between their pastures. His Eminence listed the rocky land for the first farm. He would not accept the tradition that the rocky land was used by all. The first farmer said, 'No, none of the rocky land is mine.' The sakkyndig ruled in favor of the farmer. So His Eminence listed the rocky land for the second farm. Once more the sakkyndig had to hold a meeting. His Eminence insisted someone owned the rocky land, but neither farmer wanted to pay taxes for the rocks. Finally, after much haggling, each farmer was listed as owner of one-half the rocky land. The time for His Eminence to list a pile of rocks stretched over four sleeps. The event is not finished. Not listing rocks will be an item at next year's *Althing*."

The sakkyndigs and the leading men nodded their heads. One old wise sakkyndig's words were repeated often in every kirke in the months to come: "We will treat His Eminence with respect. But we will politely disagree with details in his lists. The longer he takes to finish his lists, the less likely his lists will cause us to pay the king's fee."

Then Bishop Arne always asked for a favor: "Now, I will suggest that His Eminence start listing property at the southern tip of Greenland. When he comes here, make him feel at home for as long as you can stand him. If he asks, 'Where is the Western Settlement?' face out to sea but hold your right arm up, pointing along the shore. Nod your head and tell him the Western Settlement is six to eight days by boat in 'that' direction.

Then Bishop Arne said a parting prayer. As they left the meeting houses, Paafa Ketil saw gleams in some eyes and a smile on many faces.

Eight days after he had left, Bishop Arne returned to His Eminence with several freshly killed geese but no falcons. For two days he listened to His Eminence rant about the foolish "waste of time." During those two days Bishop Arne let other verbal abuse go by without making a response.

On the evening of the third day, His Eminence and Bishop Arne sat before the boiling pot after they had eaten one of Bishop Arne's best soups. Both men felt the chill. His Eminence remarked, "I feel as chilled as if a farmer were watching me count cattle."

Bishop Arne responded with, "I did not find the houses at the king's court farms at Foss to be better than mine, but they are located in the warmer region to the southeast."

His Eminence sat upright. "The king has a farm here? Why have you been keeping the secret from me?"

Bishop Arne replied, "I have not. I thought you were here for kirke business. I am not interested in the king's tax nor his property."

His Eminence shouted, "I am! You thick skull! I am the king's ombudsman. If I were located on a king's farm, I could employ a decent housekeeper and a good cook."

Bishop Arne was, by now, accustomed to repeated insults. He said with a smile, "If you went to Foss, you would be closer to the tip of Greenland. Then you could list the kirkes from the tip of Greenland in the southeast all the way to the Western Settlement. You could do a very complete job."

His Eminence became aroused. He wanted to know how soon a seaworthy boat could be arranged. Bishop Arne said there was a boat just now going to the Northern Settlement, and that he would go down, right away, to arrange for it to carry His Eminence to Foss. If the captain hurried the crew, the boat could be back before a moon's time to make the trip south-east before the final freeze-up.

His Eminence's eyes sparkled with delight. He said, "Finally, we are getting somewhere."

The knarr was loaded with people. Besides eight stone workers and eight woodmen, there were eight beaver-heads on board. Knarrs were used primarily for cargo hauling. They had a big sail. They had enclosed cabins fore and aft. Usually they had eight oars, four at each end, but other oars could be used if needed. This knarr was smaller than an ocean-crossing knarr. Its primary function was to haul cargo between the Eastern Settlement and the Northern Settlement. On this trip, the passengers would take turns manning the extra oars.

While the crew was preparing to shove off, the beaver-heads in the rear of the knarr were watching with amusement as six fur-clad women carried the skin boat to the water's edge and loaded it. A meat-eater man was preparing two kayaks. Then at the top of the boat pullout, Paafa Ketil, Styrk, and Bjørn said goodbyes to Bishop Arne. They walked toward the skin boat.

One of the beaver-heads shouted, "Styrk, are you out of your mind? We have enough room for all of you. Join us."

Styrk looked at Paafa Ketil. He detected a slight shake of the head and a smile. Styrk shouted back to the knarr, "I promised Paafa Ketil I would always be by his side on this trip."

Then Paafa Ketil cupped his hands to shout, "I made a solemn vow to these people so they would bring us here. If I leave them without a Norse spokesman, something bad could happen to them. I must go with them."

The crew of the knarr made the push to launch. The beaver-head shouted back, "Good luck Styrk. I hope your swim is short." More good-natured insults were hurled from the knarr and many in the crowded vessel enjoyed a good laugh.

The knarr crew swung the bow to head the boat down the fjord. The sail filled limply. All sixteen oars were out. The knarr began to move down the fjord.

With bare legs the women had finished loading their boat in the water. They climbed in, two at a time, on opposite sides of the boat. They slipped on boots. As the last two boarded, the others held the boat in position by the oars. The small sail was lowered. It hung limply. Paafa Ketil and Styrk, also with bare legs, walked quickly to the front and rear of the boat. They swung themselves in at the same time. Iqquk barked a command. The boat began to follow the knarr.

Paafa Ketil, slipping on his boots, asked, "What did he say?"

Styrk responded, "I think he said, 'slowly.' See. The women are not raising all the way straight."

The parade of knarr, skin boat, and kayaks angled toward the center of the fjord. The hooting and hallooing from the beaver-heads at the rear of the knarr continued without letup. A puff of air snapped both sails taut. The beaver-heads felt the surge forward and waved goodbye with jeering laughter.

Iqquk barked, "Steady." The women's song increased in beat. They straightened up and pulled back with every stroke. As the skin boat pulled beside the knarr, Paafa Ketil said, "Ah, now let us wave goodbye to them."

Styrk replied, "I think it would be wiser if we did not. In a moon's time I will be on the ice with those men. Any extra resentment could be troublesome. You will get enough enjoyment retelling the story of this trip all winter."

The woman's boat pulled ahead and then, sooner than the beaver-heads on the knarr would ever admit, out of sight.

Halldis was thankful for the extra two days she and Styrk had together before the knarr with beaver-heads arrived at Lysefjord. The feast at the Sandnes kirke to welcome the beaver heads, the stonemasons, and wood-men from the south was also enjoyed by many people of the Northern Set-tlement who rowed through icy waters for the festivities. Then began days of instruction about sled building, measuring rations, preparing warm fur robes, and hunting the water veins in the ice for seals.

All too soon the moon had completed one cycle. For over seven sleeps the ice along the shore had been firm enough for walking. The air was cold enough to make Styrk and Hallgrim believe that the sea ice would soon be frozen enough to walk upon.

Then the dawn of the day of departure came clear and cold. At the first pale light, the twenty-four men from the south shouldered their packs. They pulled four sleds onto the ice and down Ameragdla Fjord in the direction of Lysefjord. They would keep walking west to Merica.

The men from the four north kirkes, including Talerman, Styrk, Hall-grim, and Tjalve, stood next to their families until the pack of sleds ahead were small dots in the distance. Although these were tough men, who were used to hunger, blood, numbing cold, and death, more than a few had mois-ture in their eyes as their own sleds pulled away.

Their walk on the ice to Merica was difficult. They climbed more pres-sure ridges than usual. The icebergs from the river of ice stalked them. They walked for nearly two moons' time.

As Styrk said, "We walked one day. Then we climbed over ice the next day." Later around the boiling pots inside the low stone walls in Merica, the hunters told each other stories of open water, long detours, long waits for the ice to freeze, and other harrowing adventures.

But even the new men had no problem seeing the tall härbret bases on the Ungava coast. When they approached the north open-water marvel, Hallgrim used his kimal to determine that they were a half-notch north of their target, so they turned left and walked south along the open-water marvel until they found the beacons for Pamiok Island. They followed the solid ice inland to the cluster of low walls.

They had walked on the ice because it was much faster than struggling along on the land. But they did have to be alert for the blowholes and thin, jumbled ice.

The moon of the suckers, the time when fish move upriver, was nearly over when the first of the thirty-six men reached Pamiok Island. When they arrived in Merica, the beaver-heads arriving from Greenland located Gard, the other beaver-heads, and other men who had over-wintered in Merica. These men were encamped in one of the smaller of the low walls on Pamiok Island. The encamped men had put up a caribou-hide tent with center poles to hold the hide roof up and rocks stacked on the rock walls to hold the edges down. [See POSTHOLES.] During the summer the sailors working on a boat stationed to sail in Merica had made a trip to bring poles to them from the inlet on the KOKSOAK River. Unfortunately, the roof sagged and looked ragged. The roof had behaved even worse because rain or mist seeped through the seams nearly every other day until the freezing weather came.

The men already staying in the low stone walls were delighted to see the stonemasons and woodmen coming off the ice. They were even more pleased to learn that the people of Greenland had committed themselves to walking the ice. But they behaved as if they were especially pleased to have nineteen new rookies to tease.

During the next couple of days, the workmen's camp was set up. The workmen scraped away the ice and snow from between the long set of low walls. They followed the beaver-heads' advice about how to make an arched house. After a few trials they set up crude arches and secured caribou robes onto purloins lashed between them. They were all pleasantly surprised at how easy it was to put up the arched house. The workmen from Greenland began to appreciate why the beaver-heads had kept telling them that making houses in Merica was women's work.

The Greenland men had discussed their roles many times around boiling pots. The woodmen knew they were going to walk farther south, cross over Leif's River, and turn southeast until they found the härbret base guiding them up the timber river called Koksoak. Three of the beaver-heads would accompany them to hunt for food. One of the beaver-heads could talk with the local people.

Three of the beaver-heads, who were also the best fishermen, would stay with the stonemasons. In some locations, similar to Pamiok, four stonemasons could work on two low walls at the same time. The stonemasons were to restore the scattered stones to the walls. Some of the stones weighed more than two men and took the combined effort of several men to move into place. Two of the beaver-heads would trade for food with the meat-eating people by using words and signs. They would also trade for blubber to mix with caribou meat to make pemmican.

Styrk and two of the best negotiators would go to Eastman Land before the ice melt occurred. Their assignment was to ask for food caches, house frames, and canoes and to arrange for winter hunters to come to the shore to meet the travelers next spring. There were enough Norsemen in Eastman Land to guide hunting families to the sixteen sites that Hallgrim had calculated would be needed.

Talerman, Gard, and two of the best livestock men among the beaver-heads would accompany Styrk's group to Payne Lake. Talerman's group would stay at Payne Lake to arrange for the caribou hunts. Talerman knew that they had little time to spare.

The caribou would begin to come onto the ice during the moon of the snow crust. The caribou would be moving north in the moon for breaking snowshoes. If the caribou behaved normally, there would be four migrations. The first migration would be to the north in the spring. Then the caribou would return to the woods in the south in the middle of the summer. The caribou would again return north with a slower migration in the early fall. Finally, in late fall, the caribou would form large herds and move south to over-winter in the timber.

Usually the Tunit did not struggle with massive caribou killing in the spring, because the meat had little fat and the shedding hides were in poor condition. The Tunit harvested what they needed for food and waited for the fall caribou migration. But the beaver-heads knew that there would be a thousand more mouths in the area in the coming winter. An extra hunting effort in the spring would help provide caribou hides for the shelters at the low walls and pemmican in the winter.

Talerman had planned to stay on the stone foundations he had seen before on the south side of Payne Lake. He was hoping to find some Tunit people in the area who would help the Norse prepare for the caribou migrations.

Two sleeps after the last group of men arrived, the work camp at Pamiok was reduced to a few stonemasons and their beaver-head support. The woodmen had walked onto the sea ice and turned south around the large open-water marvel. A group of stonemasons walked onto the ice and headed north. Talerman, Styrk, Hallgrim, and the hunters with them walked west up Armaud River.

When Styrk's gang saw the härbret bases south of Payne Lake, they angled southwest and walked on the ice of the Kogaluc River to the sea in the west. Then they turned south on the ice toward Eastman Land.

Talerman and his companions walked along the south shore of Payne Lake to the stone walls they remembered. When the walls came into sight, a slim wisp of smoke rose from a hide cover spanning a corner of the low stone walls. Someone was already occupying the site. Because the sun was low, Talerman decided to test the friendliness of the people under the robes. He yelled a greeting.

Lifting the robe flap, an old Tunit man with a sparse white beard and white hair eyed them silently. Talerman used his left hand to pull his small knife from his waist. He offered it, handle first, to the white-haired man. He had intended only to show he was coming in peace. He was as surprised as his comrades to hear himself saying, "It is yours." The eyes under the white eyebrows sparkled as a hand with wrinkled skin grasped the knife handle. With a flip of the knife tip the man invited them to enter.

The man with the white hair was called Naigu. Talerman recognized this as a meat-eater's name and asked about it. Naigu said he was a Norse-Tunit but he took the name when he lived with meat-eaters for many years. He had taken a wife, a big woman, who lived among them. They accepted him, so he stayed. He and the big Eskimo women, who may have had a Tunit parent, raised several children. One set of children had grown when they had a second set of children. It was like having two families. He pointed to the big woman tending the lamp under the boiling pot. Nokla, he said, was the youngest child of the second family. His wife, an old woman, had died shortly after Nokla's birth.

Talerman was startled as he took a look at Nokla's face in profile in the lamplight. At a glance he thought she was Arnora. But when Nokla turned to face him he saw the black eyes instead of blue, the straight black hair instead of the blond, and, most of all, her size. Nokla must have been at least a head taller than Arnora, and bigger too. He thought to himself, *This wishful thinking cannot be happening yet. I left home less than three moons' time ago. What is happening to me?*

Naigu's father had been half-Norse. The grandfather used to Hrein-aa-byy as a young man. Naigu's mother was mostly Tunit with just a little Norse blood. Naigu spoke with words Talerman thought were primitive Norse. By using very short sentences and speaking slowly with childish words,

Talerman and his companions were able to speak to Naigu and get responses they understood.

Naigu did not say so directly, but Talerman and his friends came to understand that Naigu was the leader of a band of Tunit people. Talerman asked, "Why are the rest of your people camped in the willows beside the stone walls?"

Old Naigu cackled and said, "Most of the other families are afraid of the spirits walking about the stones. They are cranky old spirits—just like family."

Experience cautioned Talerman to wait to talk about the caribou needs of the people who would be coming from the Northern Settlement. If the Tunit were going to help the Norse, the Great Spirit would provide a good time to ask for help. If the Tunit heard the request at the right time, the idea would grow naturally.

The next day Talerman realized with surprise that the right time had come already. Naigu mentioned that his scouts had told him of the many blond men who had just come to Merica and wondered if Talerman would tell him what the blond men were doing here. Talerman told Naigu about the desperation of the people in the Northern Settlement. Talerman explained that many Norse in Greenland were thinking of bringing their families to Merica instead of dragging food for months to feed the families in Greenland.

He explained that if the families could make it to Merica, they would be just passing through the Tunit area. They would try to cross over Ungava in the same winter when traveling was easier. There may be up to a thousand people, but they would come and go during the same winter. He had come to talk to the Tunit because the Norse would need caribou hides and caribou meat. Perhaps, Talerman suggested, the Tunit would help the Norse in exchange for useful things they needed. The Norse would be bringing axes, steel-tipped arrows, iron tools, soapstone cooking pots, needles, and beads. The Norse would trade those items for caribou meat and hides. There were more than enough caribou to feed everybody. The Norse would remember forever any help they could get from the Tunit.

Then Naigu began to talk: "The Tunit people feel more closely related to the Norse than to the meat-eaters. Most Tunit can name at least one Norse man in their ancestry. The activity to prepare for a thousand guests would be a change in the yearly struggle. It is true there is plenty of meat. But the Norse need to learn much to survive here."

Naigu stopped and smiled. "Tunit are good teachers; we have taught you Norse people how to live here for three centuries. That, and a few other reasons, is why most of us have Norse ancestors."

The next day Naigu called a council. As the people assembled, Naigu sat beside Talerman. Naigu softly told Talerman of the lineage of many of the men. All of them one way or another had Norse ancestors. The council went as councils usually do. Talerman presented his case and asked for the help from Tunit people who had common ancestors with the Norse.

There were three men in strong vocal opposition to giving help to intruders. They began a harangue based more on their feelings than facts. Eventually the harangue subsided and intelligent questions were asked. Talerman gave honest, concise answers. Finally, late in the night, a man with sophisticated bearing asked, "Of these thousand Norse, will there be any grown women without husbands?"

Talerman did a quick mental calculation. Thinking of two single women old enough to be a wife in nearly every farmhouse and ninety farmhouses in the Northern Settlement, he answered, "Nearly two hundred."

"Are these castoffs, sick, ugly, mean, or idiots?"

"There are a few of those, but mostly these women are capable and willing. Most are wishing they could find a man. All would be grateful for a man that could bring home caribou meat."

The man kept his stoic face but said quietly, "Enough." The word was repeated both ways around the council circle.

Naigu waited patiently. No more loud comments were heard. Naigu turned to Talerman and said, "My friend, we will be waiting to help our Norse relatives when they walk off the ice next year. Right now we have not finished the caribou ribs for today."

As the weeks passed while they awaited the spring caribou migration, Talerman and his comrades used Naigu's house as a base camp. Gard had surveyed the nearly flat hide covering the corner of the stone walls. Without much thought he called the house the Walls Hut. The name caught on. Within a week, even Naigu was calling his own house the Walls Hut. He said, "Walls Hut gives the place a certain charm."

Most of the time the beaver-heads were in the field helping the Tunit prepare caribou traps. When the work allowed, Talerman, Gard, and the other two beaver-heads were always pleased to return to Naigu's story-telling and Nokla's cooking.

Before the ice in Ungava Bay broke apart, the woodmen had walked on snowshoes past Leif's River. When they came to the Koksoak River, the härbret base was in sight about four hundred paces upriver. They walked to the härbret base. There they were impressed with an area that would be a campsite and a nearby area that would be useful for working with the logs. The ice was still in the river, but the roughness and fall of the ice meant the logs would have to be floated to the mouth of the river. After setting up camp, the woodmen went into the forests. They were seeking treetops that could be cut to lengths longer than four man-spans. The woodmen climbed up the pine trees until the fingers of their two hands could touch around the trunk. Then they cut off the top at that point.

When the moon of the snow crust arrived, two thousand pieces of timber had been lashed together in bundles of two to four logs. The bundles had been dragged to the streambed.

When the moon of breaking snowshoes was half over, the timbers were fed into the roaring waters of the stream. Many times the woodmen had to pry timber jams apart with poles. Sometimes they had to pull apart a jam one log at a time. Just as the floating task was becoming routine, it was over. Two thousand pieces of timber lay floating in the catch basin near the ocean.

Back at the low-stone-wall sites, the stonemasons were finally able to start moving rock. They started first to restore the exterior stone walls to the original height, about chest high. From day to day, they had many little victories as rock after rock went back into the jigsaw puzzle of the walls.

Upon the plains of Ungava near the Indrawing Seas, the caribou harvest was going better than Talerman expected. He had gotten directly involved in the caribou harvest. With the increased length of sunlight, he was staying awake longer and working harder. Talerman found himself enjoying the group dynamics needed to drive a caribou herd to a killing point.

At the killing point, where the caribou had to cross a waterway, the courage and skill of the Tunit spearmen fascinated him. They would paddle their kayak close to a caribou, plunge their spear deep enough into the neck to kill it, pull out the spear, and paddle away before being swamped by the caribou behind. He shared the task of snagging the dead caribou in the flowing stream and hauling it to shore. He found it was a physical and mental challenge, leaving a man exhausted but satisfied.

When the main caribou herds moved north, Talerman followed with a band of Tunit. Gard and the other two beaver-heads followed other Tunit bands trailing other herds.

Two moon's time ago, the Walls Hut had become the place where leaders met. The Tunit from Merica, the beaver-heads from the low walls, and the sakhims from the blond area came to talk about the plans for the Frozen Trail. Sometimes isolated groups of people would come to the Walls Hut to ask what they should do to help. Talerman had needed someone who could remember the plans and the last known intentions of the various people. Talerman had wanted the man to stay near the Walls Hut. But he had really wanted to go with the caribou groups himself. So he had asked Naigu to stay at the Walls Hut to serve as the contact man. Naigu did a good job of listening, remembering, and telling. He became a coordinator of the massive caribou harvesting that spring without walking away from the Walls Hut.

One day the herd of caribou in Talerman's region had moved on beyond good trapping sites. Then Talerman realized he had been out of touch with events for many, many sleeps. He began to wonder what the other beaver-heads were doing. Talerman asked a young Tunit to accompany him on the two-day hike back to Naigu at Walls Hut.

Talerman and the Tunit each packed sleeping robes and two handfuls of pemmican. They began to walk south when the southeast sky lightened. They noticed but ignored the clouds to the southwest. In the sky, the breaking-snowshoes moon was waning. The sun was halfway to its height when the southwest clouds covered it. A misting rain began falling, wetting them and freezing on the ground.

About midday they passed at a distance three hide tents with smoke rising from the highest end. The Tunit wanted to go to the tents to eat. Talerman did not want to take time visiting, as was expected of guests. So standing with their back to the driven mist, they ate half the pemmican. Then they moved on.

When the sun should have been half down, the rain fell with larger drops. Occasionally an icy pellet hit them. After a heavy burst of rain, the Tunit stopped. By gestures and short sentences, the Tunit said he wanted to return to the hide camp. Talerman gestured that he wanted to go to the Walls Hut and, if need be, he could do it alone. The Tunit smiled, turned downwind, and walked away.

Bjarni continued to walk head down into the rain and icy pellets until darkness forced him to stop. He found a few rocks piled together, possibly a caribou diversion. Bjarni put his robe on the side away from the wind. He lay down and pulled the top of the robe, skin side out, over his walking house, including his head. He ate the rest of the pemmican.

The robe provided some comfort as Bjarni slept, but by morning it was drenched and heavy. He had to break ice off the skin side before he could roll it up. The rain had stopped. Now snow was falling. The wind was now hitting him on the right side of his back. The chill drove into his body. The ice-laden robe grew heavy to carry. Bjarni carried the robe until he made it to the last härbret base before the Walls Hut. He knew that he could make it to Walls Hut from the härbret base without having to sleep. So to lighten his load, he lay the robe at the base of the härbret base where he could re-cover it later.

The caribou hoofs had shattered the ice over the stream out of Payne Lake when they had passed a half moon ago. With sunlight fading Bjarni walked to the lakeshore and looked at the lake ice. The caribou had been there too. They had broken the shore ice loose. The solid lake ice had been blown to the other shore. So Bjarni thought his best chance was to wade the ford where the caribou crossed. He had seen that the water had come up to only the mid-body on the caribou. Half a caribou high is over a man's waist but not too risky. Bjarni decided to wade the stream. When the slow moving water was chest high, he thought everything would work out fine, but then his tired feet hit rocks. Three times he stumbled forward, only to catch himself with flailing arms.

Fortunately the clouds drifted away just as he reached solid ground, but the wind was frigid. Bjarni could see the ground well enough to walk to the Walls Hut long after the sun was gone. The clear air was even colder. He arrived at Walls Hut looking like a frozen muskrat.

As Naigu and Nokla stripped Bjarni's clothes off, his tremors started. The top robe from Nokla's bed was put on his shoulders. Nokla filled a cup and lifted it to his lips. Bjarni took a few sips. Then he tried to hold the cup himself, but his tremors caused the liquid to spill. Nokla took the cup back. Bjarni crawled onto Nokla's bed robe. He curled up holding his knees and shaking. Nokla arranged the top robe tightly against his body. She added a robe from Naigu's bed. The shaking was still visible through the robes.

Naigu filled his own cup. Then he said to Nokla, "He needs warmth." Naigu turned his back and gazed at the small flame under the boiling pot while sipping his tea.

Nokla kicked off her boots, slid her britches down, and swung her legs under the robes covering Bjarni. She peeled off her coverlet before disappearing under the robes. Her strong arm wrapped around Bjarni's chest as her large breasts flattened against his back. She tucked her legs up to meet the back of his thighs. Bjarni shuddered and sighed. The tremors continued.

Daylight was filtering through the smoke rising toward the hole in the Walls Hut roof when Bjarni opened his eyes. He was lying on his back. Bjarni's thoughts must have been something like this: *Where am I? Oh, good. I am in the Walls Hut. I thought I made it. I remember now. I got the shakes. I have never had them so bad that I could not move. What crazy dreams! I thought Arnora was here. I saw her blue eyes and blonde hair. But, no, I must be in the Walls Hut. There is the hole in the roof. Or maybe I am still dreaming. I feel Arnora's legs wrapped around mine. I feel her breasts against my ribs. I feel her head on my shoulder.*

Meanwhile the woodmen had been busy too. As they had shed clothes in the spring air, they saw that flowers were peaking through the debris on the forest floor. The flower moon was rising when the first knarr arrived at the timber pond.

The knarr had sailed up to the ropes that held back the timber. Men in kayaks had put loops on the big end of a timber bundle. The crew had pulled the timbers into the knarr. After loading, the knarr crew had eaten and slept. They knew that if the winds were good, they could reach the low-wall sites before the next Arctic day ended.

The ice sheet had been far enough north to allow the knarr to swing around northeast of Pamiok Island. When the captain of the boat sensed the tide rising, the crew had dropped down full sail. The northeast wind had driven the boat toward Pamiok, up a causeway cleared of rocks, and onto the sand at high tide.

Soon three woodmen and three stonemasons pulled the poles from the knarr. One of the crew lifting the poles over the side said, "Why do they want to build a shelter here? This place is like being at the gates of Hel." At that moment another crewman looked up, pointed toward the rock formations above the low walls, and said, "Oh—my—God!"

All eyes turned to where he was pointing. Big men in caribou hide, fur side out, were filing past the big rock along the rock wall. Like a slithering giant worm they came straight toward the ship. At first only their bodies, arms, and legs were seen. Then the individual faces under the hoods became visible. The stonemasons, woodmen, and sailors stopped in their tracks. The sailors in the knarr reached for harpoons and knives.

Talerman, at the head of the human "worm," threw back his hood and shouted, "Keep unloading. The Tunit just want to see what is going on." Unloading resumed amid greetings, questions, answers, and bantering.

The evening meal was a festive event for the Tunit caribou people, the beaver-heads, stonemasons, woodmen, and sailors. Tjalve summed up the event the next morning: "Most of the Tunits have a Norse ancestor. Our Norse forefathers really got around. The feast was just a big family gathering."

The next afternoon the knarr rose on the rising tide and was rowing outbound as the tide fell. The Tunit exchanged caribou hides and pemmican for shelter poles and wood for tools. They began to walk back to the tundra. Several younger Tunit eager for something new to do picked up packs of caribou hides and followed beaver-heads onto the tundra to walk to the low-wall sites farther north.

At Pamiok Island, the woodmen selected two poles and cut off the slender tip one man-span from the small end. The poles were overlapped by one arm length at the narrow ends and the overlap was wrapped with wet walrus rope.

After the rope dried, the poles were placed across the stone walls. A gang of men drove small stakes in the ground near the center of the poles between the walls. They held the stakes in place as the rest of the men pushed the outside ends toward an end of the low walls. Other men tied ropes onto the pole ends. They stood outside the walls on the opposite sides from where the rope was tied.

The wooden poles were pushed and then pulled into a *U* shape. The pulling men continued until the butt of the pole could be dropped inside the rock wall. When both ends were dropped inside the rock wall, the *U* was lifted and then pulled upright to make an overhead arch. A second arch was made so that it was spaced about an arm's length away from the first one.

The two arches were held in place while two pairs of men moved to the arches. Each pair of men carried the small pole created when the longer poles were trimmed. Each pair raised the small pole about head high and lashed it to the two arches. They took a second pole and lashed it into place just above the rock wall. The men let go of the arches. They admired their handiwork for a few moments. Then they started on the next arch.

Meanwhile Styrk and his comrades had reached Eastman's village. They set up camp at a main place for summer gatherings in Eastman Land. They visited with the families near the shore to get the latest news and information. They went hunting on short trips to pass the time until the moon of flowers when summer encampments would come to life.

Then Styrk and his comrades began to visit the summer camps, patiently waiting for a time to speak up at the fireplace councils. During the day Styrk used the hunting language to talk in the sakhim's houses when he had the chance. The people of Eastman Land who had Norse ancestors were pleased to hear their relatives would be coming. The younger men and women were especially pleased to learn about more chances for blond companions. But the sakhims were fearful of a thousand new people at once and the thought of three thousand more to come in the following years.

Styrk explained that the beaver-heads had considered their friends in Eastman Land as they made plans. The beaver-heads thought it best for the people from Greenland to paddle past Eastman Land and go west up the Albany River.

As the flower moon passed, Styrk grew anxious. The people in the summer camps acted as if they were not the least interested in helping their Norse brothers. They ate, they danced, they told stories, they flirted, and sometimes they fought. When Styrk and the beaver-heads spoke before their council fires, the people sat politely, often appearing to be interested, sometimes looking at the earth, the forest, or the sky, and usually nodding in the correct places. Styrk had sat around enough campfires in Akomen to know that polite listening was not commitment to his cause. He was also very careful to avoid saying, "I want to know your answer now." He knew the answer would come in private where the personal trading talk also occurred.

Styrk expected no public talk of support, but one man spoke up. He was an old beaver-head who had been so long in Eastman's Land that his friends forgot he was Norse. But he still remembered his Norse roots. He stood and offered to row two of his canoes to the furthest north camp next spring. The other men of the Eastman Land sat stone-faced.

Styrk and his two companion beaver-heads had carried gifts. They had sixteen annealed copper knives and six metal axes. Hallgrim had informed Styrk about the decision-making process within a wigwam. So Styrk and his comrades also carried twenty-four long strings of beads and they had 160 narrow red-cloth bands an arm's length long. Each band had a cross stitched at the mid-point. Tjalve had told Styrk that the red cloth had worked for the Vikings in the past. Styrk had had the pleasure of telling Tjalve, many times, that the Vikings who traded red cloth were driven away from Merica for seven grandfathers' time. In a more serious tone of voice, Styrk pointed out that the people of Greenland could not afford to wait for seven grandfathers' time. They needed acceptance now.

But Tjalve was correct. A day after the old Norse beaver-head spoke at the council fire, the people in the summer camp saw the old beaver-head's wife wearing the red cloth on her forehead with the cross located above her nose. Then the gossip groups passed the word that every man who offered to build a wigwam at the north shore of James Bay next spring would get a similar gift for his woman. Faster than he thought it would happen, Styrk was having private talks with some men of Eastman Land while other men, waiting their turn, sat outside.

The gist of the talks went something like this: The Eastman man would say, "I was thinking of hunting toward the north this winter. We are planning to send some men with our canoes up to where we think we will come out in the spring. Maybe we could help you by taking along an old canoe that still floats." Styrk would say, "If you could, I would accept your gift. Would your wife like to wear a cross?"

Later that evening when the man gave the red band to his wife, they both knew they were committed to deliver a canoe and help build an extra wigwam in the spring. They also expected the Norse would be bringing another gift, maybe a bag of beads.

Styrk had planned to visit the Blond Area but a wise old sakhim told him, "One of your beaver-heads and Hallgrim can talk to the Blond Area. They will want their Norse relatives to come. So you will have little resistance there. It is far more important that you talk to the gathering of the tribes at St. Jean's Lake. Many of the people there will not be able to help the Norse because they are too far east or south. On the other hand, they could hinder the plan if they come out of the woods in the spring and find an unexpected Norse armada floating down the shoreline."

The overland journey to St. Jean's Lake was much more difficult in the summer than a hunt through the woods would have been in winter. But the sakhim was so passionate that Styrk eventually decided to go. He took one other beaver-head with him. They went up the Nemiskou River in a canoe paddled with four other men from the Eastman Land. Then they crossed through a region of lakes and streams. They portaged the canoe often. They came to a lake lying in the folds of the land. They paddled to the southernmost point of the lake. After a long portage they were on the river to St. Jean's Lake. They began to meet and to join other canoes heading to the lake.

When the group of canoes, including Styrk's, paddled toward the beach of the plain chosen for the summer meeting, he was impressed. On the beach lay canoe beside canoe for as far as Styrk could see to the left and to the right. On the plain stood the tepees of seventeen tribes, each with their own cluster of family clans. From left to right the tepees dominated the horizon. The guides were headed toward the one open stretch of beach in front of a big tepee with a mammoth roof. Styrk saw that the roof was lifted off the ground by a pole wall to about the height of a man. After they pulled the canoe ashore, he estimated the size of the big tepee to be at least three man-spans across at head height. A St. Jean's host came running up. He said, "The sakhim wants you to stay in the mamateek. [See **MAMMOTH ROOF.**] It is the…"

Styrk, who had already picked up his pack, cut him off, saying, "I know where it is." He had no trouble seeing the mammoth roof straight ahead.

The next morning Styrk met with the major sakhim, who then invited Styrk to move into his own tepee. The next evening Styrk attended the big campfire and waited for his time to speak. The obviously important men sat around the big campfire in double rows and another circle of men stood behind the seated rows.

After four campfires and four sleeps, the sakhim gave Styrk a long introduction. Styrk stood and told of the difficulties their Norse brothers were having. The circle of men listened to Styrk politely. He could sense the lack of interest, especially when most of them realized they would have little to do with the coming of the Norse and it would not affect them much. Styrk finished his talk in a pleasant manner. He did not want or need a response. At least the people around Lake Saint Jean would be aware that a Norse armada would pass through Eastman Land going south and west. He sat down in silence.

Then a short, erect man stepped into the firelight. He was wearing black pants and a black jacket with gold stitches edging the cuffs, bottom, and front of the jacket. Styrk thought the design looked as if it were made of crosses without tops alternating with crosses with tops. The man asked the sakhim for permission to speak. The sakhim nodded. The man turned toward Styrk. He said in a low but commanding voice, "My name is Haki. My ancient ancestor was just starting to sew on this very jacket when your ancestors tried to invade this land a long, long time ago. Many grandfathers have come and gone since then. But we still tell the stories about how my ancestors drove your ancestors away. I am named after my great ancient ancestor. Today, I am troubled that I, too, must face the same enemy."

Bringing his left arm from behind his back, Haki held up a red band with a cross on it. Haki continued, "One of the tricks your ancestors pulled on mine long, long ago was to trade red ribbons like this for valuable furs. My ancestors desperately wanted these red ribbons."

Haki's voice increased in loudness and a tremor crept in as he continued, "It will not work today because our grandmothers have adapted your fashions. Long ago this gold trim was all red. But making good red dye was a custom lost when our ancestors came to this land. That is why they were so eager to get the red ribbons from your ancient ancestors. Then the Norsemen, like you, came to our villages wearing coats trimmed in double stripes of yellow with designs of flowers between the stripes. Yellow dye is abundant to find in this country. Our grandmothers replaced the red with the yellow design. They changed the designs too. The cross without a top is more precious than flowers. We do not need red anymore."

Then Haki threw the ribbon down and ground it into the earth with his heel. He continued in a much louder voice, "The red cloth did not work then. It will not work now."

Styrk felt the tenseness in his shoulders come with his rising anger. He could feel his heartbeat grow stronger. He unfolded his legs, ready to stand up. Haki held out his hands, palms down, a signal for Styrk to stay seated.

Haki paused. The tension around the circle of men increased. Then Haki began again in his low voice, "I have listened to the words of the men who have heard you in Eastman Land. I understand the difficulty your people have finding food. I even understand that you hope to come to this land peacefully. I also understand that many of us have similar ancestor blood as yours. There are a couple of men with Norse ancestors in my own village. They are good men.

"But," said Haki with a louder voice as he jabbed a finger at Styrk, "we cannot allow four thousand Norse people into our lands! We have lived here since my grandfather's grandfather. You may think the forests from here to the Kanal Dal are empty, but they provide just enough meat for our people. We hunt the forests in winter when the wolf packs do not hunt humans."

Haki was gesturing with every sentence as he nearly shouted, "Even going west will not work. Those are lands of our brothers, too. They have been there for many grandfathers. Some of our brothers have been out west as far as the high mountains. They are so far west that the earth they walk on is black. The people there walk with black feet, but they speak our language, too. We cannot stand by and watch your people overrun them!"

Haki was shouting at the end of the talk. His arms flailed through the air to make a big *X* in front of Styrk. This time there was a vocal response of approval around the circle. Several men stood up with hands moving to their knives. Haki stepped back and stood with his hands on his hips. The sakhim waited. Haki nodded. The sakhim turned to Styrk, raised a hand palm up, and nodded.

Styrk understood the signal to rise and speak. He rose very slowly, fighting to subdue his anger, and thinking to himself, *Oh, how I need Tjalve now! What would Tjalve do? I know. He would ask a question. He would just ask a question.*

Styrk stood and faced Haki across the firelight. He paused as long as Haki had paused. The crowd went silent, listening for the answer to Haki. Raising his hand, palm up, Styrk asked, "Where can four thousand peaceful Christians who must leave their land go?"

Haki blinked. He had not expected the question. He seemed to be hunting for the answer. He stayed silent. Styrk also stayed silent, his teeth clenched so he would not say anything more. He was trying hard to follow Tjalve's advice: "No threats. No apology. No explanation. No pleading."

The two powerful men faced each other in the circle. The crowd began to murmur, making a low, jumbled noise. Then Styrk began to distinctly hear words as they were repeated around the circle. The jumbled words were *gumme, mi,* and *sjøe.*

Haki inclined his head as though he were trying to understand the words too. He turned his head sideways to hear better. Then he looked straight into Styrk's eyes, raised his right hand, palm up, and said, "You can go to Michigamme. There is plenty of room in Michigamme."

Suspicious, Styrk asked, "Why is there plenty of room in Michigamme?"

Haki said, "The wolf packs ate the people or drove them away. The forests and fields are vacant. The only people there now are outcasts. They are hunters who have little. They run away from the wolf packs. But the wolf packs are not always there anymore. Still, they are nearby. The wolf packs sometimes pass through Michigamme to attack our people.

"One thing you Norse can still do is fight if you have to. Besides, I have heard that your people would make four villages next year. The four villages in the same area would have over two hundred fighting men. That number of warriors would be able to defeat the wolf packs. The wolf packs rarely attack a big village with many fighters. They are really cowards.

"If your people are between the wolf packs and us, we can continue peaceful hunting and fishing. That blessing will make all of us eager to help your people move."

Haki turned slowly with his right hand, palm up, extended toward the men in the circle. As he turned in a complete circle, Styrk saw heads nod, heard affirmative grunts, and watched the standing men return knifes to the waistband before raising a hand of friendship. Haki knew how to compel the crowd to his thinking.

When Haki faced Styrk again, he said, "If you would move your people to Michigamme in the coming years, we would consider it a gift."

Styrk glanced around the circle. The sakhim's head and the heads of other leading men were nodding. Styrk said, "I will tell my leader we must move to Michigamme. But I have one problem. Our scouts have been south and they have been west. We know where to go to the south or the west. We have not scouted southwest to Michigamme and do not have time before our people come. I do not want to move wives and children into a land we have not scouted."

Haki said, "By next spring, we will gather for you a group of the scouts that know Michigamme best. I myself will go with you to prove our scouts can be trusted."

Styrk said, "I accept your promise as a gift."

There was a moment of silence. Then the murmur that arose from the circle of men seemed to be one of relief. A little humor was heard. The sakhim nodded to the drummer. The slow, steady beat of the round dance began.

Haki stepped out of the circle and over to talk to the sakhim. Styrk stepped out of the circle to meet his companion beaver-head, who had watched the exchange from the outer row. Both men nodded with a sense of relief, but they did not speak because there were too many ears around.

Styrk was watching the dancers and feeling his repressed anger drain down when Haki stepped up beside him. Styrk swung around, ready to face the threat again. Haki said, "I invite you to stay the night in my tepee. The sakhim agrees to it. You have been to places that I have not seen. I would like to hear of them."

At the beginning of the moon of the wild rice, Talerman caught a ride on the knarr headed to the low walls located furthest north. As the knarr sailed north, he could see the activity at every low-wall site. More than half the arches were in place in the low walls in the region near Pamiok. Further north most of the low-walls sites had some arches up.

Captain Gunnbjørn told Talerman that the knarr cargo included enough poles for the rest of the low walls on the site farthest north. Gunnbjørn also said the three boat crews had recently met and exchanged sailors. All of the sailors wanting to return to Lysefjord and Einarsfjord for the winter were now on board his ship. They intended to unload the poles and the gift items for the last site. Then they were going to take on all the caribou hides they could carry. From the last site, the knarr had to sail less than a half day to catch the Indrawing Seas on an outgoing tide.

Talerman gave Captain Gunnbjørn three messages. Gunnbjørn repeated each message as he pointed to one of three fingers. At the landing site on the second day, Talerman checked the memory of Gunnbjørn. He found it to be good. Talerman took charge of the beads and knives to be used as gifts for the Tunit. Because the site was only about half completed, he gave the gifts to the beaver-head in charge of the site to be distributed later.

For two days, Talerman worked alongside the woodmen setting up the arches. Then the ship carrying small poles as gifts for the Tunit came into the landing site. Talerman went aboard. The ship was returning to the Koksoak River, but Talerman got off at a barren island located on the center eastern edge of the open-water marvel between the north low-wall site and Pamiok Island. Already the stonemasons had struggled to maneuver several huge stones to restore the small circle of big stones. [See FIRE TOWER.]

The woodmen were laying out three of the biggest poles they had cut. The poles were eight man-spans long. At an arm-span from the small end of the three poles, the woodmen lashed the poles together.

The stonemasons had selected the biggest rock in the ring. They had directed a gang of men to shift the rocks across the ring from the biggest rock until there was a gap between the rocks. Then the gang slid the three lashed timbers so that one slid through the rock gap and butted against the biggest rock. The other two timbers passed on the outside of the rock ring, one on each side.

Talerman helped the gang lift, block with wooden timbers, lift, and block again until the three timbers were raised enough to enable the men to take hold of the ropes tied to the upper end and pull. Finally the three poles were standing upright with men hanging onto leather ropes to hold the timbers in place. The two outside poles were then moved into the stone circle and the butt of the poles wedged against big rocks by smaller ones. Finally the leather ropes were relaxed. The tripod of timbers was in place.

The youngest woodman scampered up a timber. He cut small footholds as he went. He pulled up small poles and lashed them to make a platform at the very top end of the timbers. Within two days a lookout platform with provisions for a fire lamp were in place.

Talerman was pleased. Things were working out better than he had thought. There would be shelter for eighty-eight families. Pemmican for fifteen days for a thousand people was already in the ground. The winter caribou migration was coming. The Tunit promised to deliver more pemmican and more hides. Hopefully, Styrk would return with favorable word from the Eastman Land.

Well, thought Talerman, *we are in God's hands now. I hope they are cold. We need solid ice.*

In the moon of the falling leaves, several clusters of canoes paddled north along the shore of James Bay. Styrk and his companions had enlisted the best people into the adventure. The people of Akomen included several beaver-heads and many local men from Eastman Land. Another group of beaver-heads and several men came with Hallgrim from the Blond Area. Many young women, sisters or wives without children, joined the Akomen men in the adventure. The Akomen group rowed north until they found fast ice about two sleeps north of the North Twin Island.

The people of the canoe flotilla set up an encampment. The next dawn, one or two young men in each canoe paddled some of the canoes south. They were going south for only a sleep or two. There they would store the canoes and start the winter hunt. They planned to meet their main hunting camps and lead them back to the canoes.

When the fast ice had built far enough from shore, the Akomen people walked north. They arrived at Merica when the caribou started to migrate south. The Tunit men guided the Akomen men to the right spots so they could channel the caribou down the chutes into the water where the Tunit in their kayaks did the killing. The Tunit and the Akomen men worked long hours to harvest as many caribou as possible. The Tunit and Akomen women set up pemmican and hide-processing camps. Working together on important activities for half a moon's time increased the friendship bond between the Tunit and Akomen. When the caribou herd had moved on south, the women rolled up the caribou hides and packed up the pemmican. Then the Akomen women went into the rushes near Payne Lake. They harvested the rushes and showed the Tunit women how to weave rush panels an arm's length wide and a man-span long. Then, carrying as much as they could, the women began the first of many treks to Pamiok Island and the other low-wall sites.

Upon arriving at Pamiok, the first women dropped their loads inside the longest low walls where the arches were set up. Then they began to roof the arches.

The women started by standing on the wall and lashing a cross purloin in place an arm's length above the purloin already in place. Then they lashed other purloins in place an arm's length higher. They repeated the lashing until they reached the top of the arch. Then they did the other side.

They lashed the rush panels into place. They started at the low walls of rock and worked upward. They worked fast because they wanted the roof up for their own comfort. In the days to come, they would carefully lace caribou hides, fur down, to the rush panels to make the house warmer and more rain resistant.

Two man-spans along the walls on one side of the center fire pit would serve a family of seven. Another family would have the space on the other side of the fire. So, normally, a space two man-spans along the wall and three to four man-spans across the floor would provide shelter for two families. Big families with eight or more children and relatives would get two spots. Small families would have to share a spot.

Hallgrim had calculated that the sets of low walls in five locations could provide shelter for eighty-eight families. There were ninety farmhouses in the northern settlement with an average of two families per farmhouse. Those people went to four kirkes. So all of the sites in Merica would provide shelter for all the people of only two kirkes at a time.

Talerman, Hallgrim, Paafa Orm, and Paafa Ketil had talked about the calculations many nights. They all agreed the people coming off the ice should not stop on the Merica coast for long. The reason the people should not stop long was because the low walls were only halfway to the summer camps in James Bay. Every day wasted by sitting in at the low walls was one day closer to the ice melting before the people reached the summer camps. The best plan for using the shelters was to eat well, repair clothes, reorganize sleds loads to backpacks, make snowshoes, learn snow shoeing, get some good sleeps on solid ground, and then leave before getting too comfortable. Only the very sick might stay longer to get well.

So they agreed five nights of good food and sleep should restore the spirits of people coming off the ice and prepare them for the snowshoe walk. The first wave of people should be moving out of the low walls toward James Bay as the second wave came off the ice at Merica. They decided that departure from Rangafjord should be in two waves, with a five-sleep interval from the last people of the first wave to the first people of the second wave.

Vignette Nineteen
The Interlude

Azon and Pitolo sat on the embankment beside the steps. Azon's sister and the quiet maiden had brought them a meal of venison and berries. The maidens had visited with them as they ate. Gee Hiz was well into his descent. When the maidens saw the other women of the villages walk toward the Big House, they too left to help prepare the food for the evening.

Pitolo said, "That was some of the best venison I have eaten. I could get used to being an aarum-tid."

Azon replied, "I have not gotten used to having food brought to me. I wonder if it wise to flaunt special treatment?"

Pitolo looked at Azon. "You may be right, but there is a difference between accepting the special treatment with grace and flaunting it. We will have to try to find the best arrangement. Gee Hiz is coming down rapidly. Maalan Aarum told us to come back when Gee Hiz was halfway down."

Azon said, "Grandfather told us a long, complex story about building the original Big House. He said he wants to tell us about the migration next. We will have to tell both stories this evening. Our ancestors sure had a difficult task to get ready for the people to cross the ice. Yet Grandfather did not have us make an engraved stick for it. The engraving we have is of people crossing the ice. I wonder why?"

Pitolo sat silently for a moment. Then he replied, "Maalan Aarum stopped me to say something as you were leaving. I think it was, 'Big House, big engraving.' Do you think he meant the Big House is the same as an engraving?"

Azon looked at the Big House in the distance. After some thought he answered, "It might be, and the Big House ceremony could be like a verse."

Azon took a second look at the big house. "I want to be the one telling the first part of the story tonight. I think I can prepare the people to accept the fact that the walls of the first Big House were made of stone.

"Ah, Gee Hiz has touched the branches of the tall tree near the palisade. That means he is halfway to the sky-boat. Let us go hear what Grandfather has to say about the migration."

Stories of
Maalan Aarum

Leaving Home

E.S. 3:17

The Starting Point

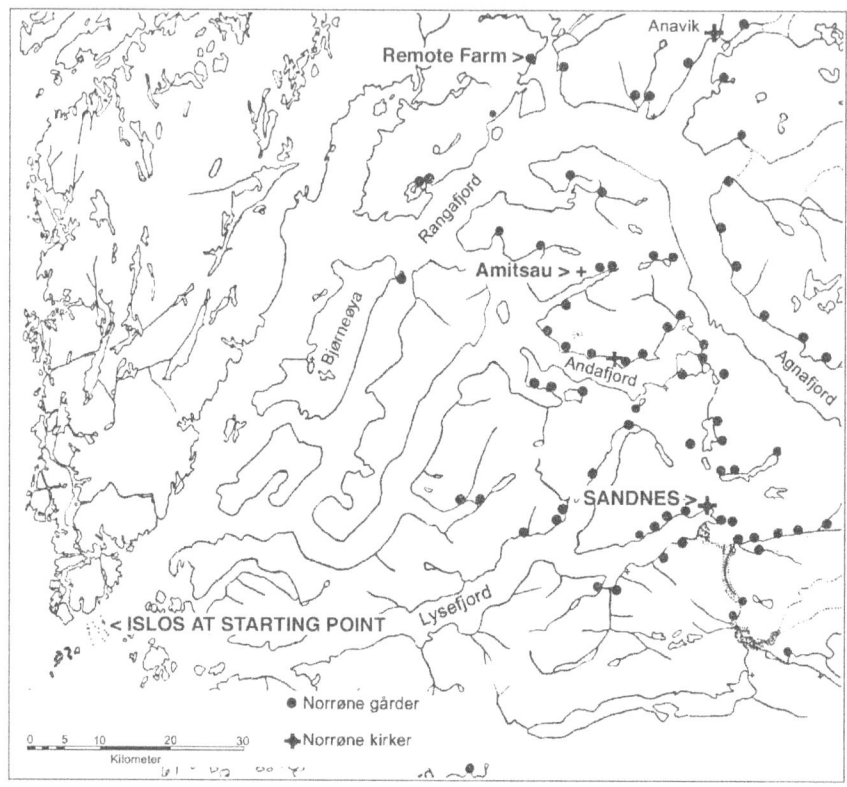

While waiting for the beaver-heads to return, the men of the Northern Settlement practiced making Islos at the starting point of the migration.

Leaving Home

Eight sleeps after leaving Talerman at Merica, Captain Gunnbjørn decided against breaking the ice up to the Magnusson's farmhouse. He chose to pull up at the house before the little peninsula sticking into the bay at the end of the fjord. While his crew enjoyed the farmhouse hospitality, Captain Gunnbjørn walked the inland path to the Magnusson farm.

Arnora was feeding the outside animals. She saw the figure coming toward the house. She hid the point of her lance in her right armpit while she watched. The figure turned into someone she recognized.

"Lose your boat, Captain?"

Gunnbjørn turned and looked back. "No, I cannot see it, but I doubt the crew has moved it. Good home cooking makes them stick like flies."

Arnora smiled and said, "We have home cooking also. The hour is late. Would you accept an invitation to stay the night?"

Captain Gunnbjørn seemed somewhat embarrassed. He scuffled his toe as he said, "I do not really know. I have heard of your fame."

"My fame as a hellion or a cook?"

"Uh, the first."

"I will make a deal, captain. If you do not test the first, you can challenge the second to your stomach's content."

"Deal."

Captain Gunnbjørn ate to his stomach's content first. Then he told the assembled household what he could of Talerman's activities. He expressed his amazement at the effort put forth by the people of Akomen and Merica. He thought that, without their help, many Greenland people might die during the migration. But he could see that the migration was becoming more feasible with each sleep.

Late in the evening when he and Arnora were alone, he had a chance to present the real reason for his long walk. He passed a rolled-up bundle of skins to Arnora saying, "This is the message Bjarni sent for you. Mind you, these are Bjarni's words, 'I love you, I have sent special furs for the hood to keep your face warm until I can kiss it.'"

Arnora undid the strings around the caribou hide. Inside was enough martin fur to make face edging for the hoods of all the people in the house.

"Whew!" exclaimed the captain. "Good thing I did not peek. When the weather is very cold, martin fur keeps the ice from forming on the hood near the face. I need new martin fur myself and a man can exchange those furs for many, many things."

The following morning Captain Gunnbjørn hiked away before pale light. Later in the day, the knarr turned into Agnafjord. That evening, the knarr crew visited the farmhouse at the head of a small inlet. The captain, once again, hiked overland to the Anavik kirke. Paafa Thord was there, just as the people in the farmhouse had said he would be.

"I have a message from Talerman," Captain Gunnbjørn said as he peeled off his outer jacket. "He says, 'Greetings, preparations in Merica are going better than hoped. There will be space for eighty-eight families, or about six hundred people. So the plan to come in two waves is to be followed.'"

During the meal that followed, Captain Gunnbjørn also mentioned: "Talerman says there are twelve sets of low walls with arched roofs in five sites. Some shelters are longer than others. He suggests you organize the people so that each kirke goes into a set of shelters close together. Only the people of two kirkes should walk in the first wave of sleds. The first kirke should go to the north shelters. The second kirke should go to the shelters south of the first group. They should vacate the shelters in five sleeps.

"The last two kirkes of the Northern Settlement should come in the second wave, five sleeps later. They should go into the shelters using the same pattern and stay only five sleeps."

Paafa Thord said that he had not thought about assignments to the shelters, but he thought it was a good idea. He could easily work it into the planning.

Paafa Thord gave information for the captain to take to Bishop Arne. He said the physical preparations in the Northern Settlement were slightly behind what he had hoped. The summer had been cold. Many people were sick or weak. There had been no real hay harvest. Men and women worked many hours trying to find forage for the animals. Yet because of the cold summer, the resolve to walk to Merica seemed stronger than ever. Farmers were already starting to feed the remaining food to the livestock. Many intended to feed full ration until the moon before Christmas. Then they would slaughter the animals to prepare pemmican.

When the captain was ready to leave in the pale light of morning, Paafa Thord said, "Tell Bishop Arne that, with God's guidance, there will be no one in the Northern Settlement next spring."

The colder weather forced the knarr crew to move away from the fast ice clinging to the shore and to be extra wary of the icebergs flowing north. Passage to the Eastern Settlement took twelve long sleeps of little sailing and much rowing.

The captain's experience with the icing process in the southern fjords led him to choose to go up Ericksfjord to the farmhouses opposite the Gardar Kirke. Once again the crew enjoyed home cooking while he walked to visit Bishop Arne.

Bishop Arne was in great spirits. His Nemesis had moved south to Foss in early spring. He had heard word from the southern people that His Nemesis was behaving like a petty king, but the people of the south understood their role in God's world. Even if their hatred of His Eminence was growing, it would not lead to manslaughter if the man would be gone by next spring.

In his own pasture Bishop Arne had personally visited all eight of the kirkes planning to walk to Merica in the years to come. At this time there was little to do except to scheme to prevent His Nemesis from knowing the plan. The *Althing* during the summer had been a small affair. Most of the people from the Northern Settlement chose not to come. His Nemesis also chose not to come "because listing the kirke property in the south was more important."

Captain Gunnbjørn commented wryly, "His Eminence might have come to the *Althing* if he could have walked on water."

Then Captain Gunnbjørn delivered Paafa Thord's and Talerman's messages. When it was time to tell about Talerman's message, Captain Gunnbjørn said, "All Talerman told me to say was 'John 14:3.' Do you know who this man John is?"

Bishop Arne's eyes flashed. He rushed to get his manuscript from the high shelf in his bedroom. He flipped through the pages, found the right spot, and read, "And if I go and prepare a place for you, I will come again, and receive you unto myself; that where I am, there you may be also."

Captain Gunnbjørn guessed, "It means the place is prepared and Talerman will be coming to get you. How did he know all this fancy writing stuff?"

Bishop Arne smiled and replied, "A young man can learn much during a long walk on the ice. What young men learn, they remember a long time. God is truly showing us the way."

As they walked to Merica after Talerman's forty-fifth birthday, the beaver-heads knew the climate had become cold enough to freeze the sea between the Northern Settlement and Merica again. They did not learn that the sea also froze as far south as the southern tip of Greenland.

The chilly autumn before Talerman's forty-sixth birthday reassured him that, at this time, God had very cold hands. Early in the moon of little spirits, he walked on the ice with confidence. He was headed from the fire tower in Ungava Bay to Pamiok Island. He did not know that the coast of Greenland was free of ice halfway between the Eastern and Northern Settlement. Nor did he know the ice and water interface at the edge of the ice was always changing as the Eastern Greenland Current and the Labrador Current floated icebergs toward each other. The pack ice was not freezing enough to stop iceberg movement.

Without that knowledge Talerman hurried to Pamiok Island. There Styrk, Hallgrim, Tjalve, and twelve other beaver-heads were more than ready to go home to the Northern Settlement. Talerman came off the ice after an extended day-long walk. So they stuffed Talerman into a sleeper robe and, without ceremony, pulled the three sleds onto the ice.

In Greenland the same moon was called the Christmas moon. The weather seemed cold in Greenland too. But while Paafa Ketil made his way from house to house to celebrate mass, he noticed that a large ring of the roof area around the fire holes of several houses had melted free of snow. Paafa Ketil thought, "Can the melting on the roofs be a signal that this winter will not be as cold as the past two years?"

By the time of the full Christmas moon, Iqquk had taught forty Norsemen to build icehouses at the mouth of Ranga Fjord. He had taught four Norsemen at a time how to build one icehouse. When the instruction was over, the ten icehouses were functional, but their shapes were nowhere as neat as Iqquk's personal icehouse.

The Norsemen were slightly embarrassed to be taking lessons from a meat-eater. So they reacted to the outcome of their efforts in typical fashion. They made sly and humorous comments about each other's efforts, troubles, and finished icehouses. They agreed that most of the icehouses looked like ice piles. In the Norse language *is* means "ice" and *lo* means, "pile." So the comments went something like, "My islo is a Norse islo; it has a taller peak than anyone's," and "I had to make room for my whole family; that is why my islo is so wide and flat." To the Norse all icehouses became known as "islos."

Then the forty men each built an another islo to train three more Norse men how to build ice houses. The primary purpose of building the islos was to insure that someone on each of sled knew how to make islos if it became necessary.

When the training was finished, there were fifty islos standing in groups of ten. Ten islos were assigned to each kirke and the first ten islos were used as common storage, shelter for the sick, and places to receive the incoming beaver-heads from the west.

Paafa Thord assigned the islos to the kirkes according to the starting sequence. Talerman had asked that the Anavik kirke be last. Paafa Thord would go with Talerman. Paafa Thord decided Paafa Ketil's Amitsau praying house should go first because Paafa Ketil knew the plans and Styrk, the pathfinder, was the man to have up front.

The sakkyndigs of the other two praying houses played three games of chess to determine the placing. The three games turned into seven because of draws, but everybody agreed that the contests took their minds away from just waiting around. The people of the Anda Kirke with Paafa Thorbjørn would go second. The people of the Sandnes Kirke of Paafa Snorre would go third.

Early in winter a written message with a Christmas homily from Bishop Arne had arrived by a sled team. Attached to the message was a request to the priests. Bishop Arne asked the priest of each kirke to carry the mask of the leading patron with him. [See TWELVE MASKS.] When the priests reached Merica, they were to hang the mask in the main shelter. Bishop Arne prayed that he would be able to collect all twelve masks in a few years. Then if the Lord allowed, he would carry all the masks to Eastman Land.

Paafa Ketil and the people of his Amitsau praying house were now ready to go. Forty sleds with six people each would leave from the farmhouses surrounding the Amitsau praying house as soon as they received word that the beaver-heads were here.

Everything among his people looked as good as he could expect. He was getting restless. So Paafa Ketil had arrived at the starting islos two sleeps ago. Then the problems started to come.

First was the man with his dogs. The man desperately wanted to go along to Merica. He would not be denied. Then came the new meat-eater people who made square houses like the Norse. There were three families totaling twenty-one people. They had heard of the walk to Merica. They had walked to Greenland from Merica years ago. They wanted to go back. They built their own islos. They took in the man with the dogs. At the moment, the new meat-eater people and the man were not causing problems, so Paafa Ketil and his sakkyndig decided to wait for Talerman who was expected, with the beaver-heads, from Merica. Paafa Ketil was patiently praying for them to arrive, right now!

Talerman was one of the four pullers. The sun had shone for some time before it disappeared. The southern sky was getting darker again. The stars indicated his time to pull was nearly over. Soon they would stop for food.

Talerman sensed they should be close to Greenland. During the last sunny interval they knew that they were looking at the icecaps on Greenland. Talerman looked down to step over crumpled ice. When he looked up, he saw the firelight.

The firelight was south and east of them. They decided to not make an answering flame because making a fire would take too long. The hunters turned toward the light, and Styrk unwrapped the drum. He began to pound, "Thump, thump, pause, thump," and listen. Soon they heard a responding drum. They stopped the drumming and moved rapidly toward the firelight.

As they approached the light, a figure ran forward. The figure opened his arms wide and said, "Welcome home, father!" Talerman and Bjørn hugged briefly. Iqquk led the group through the darkness to the islo he and Bjørn had been sharing. Iqquk's wife had the seal broth boiling. Eating and conversation started. Ketil came through the entrance tunnel and popped up. The eating and conversation continued. As soon as he determined the plan was going well, Ketil slipped out to send runners to inform the people in their farmhouses.

The four priests and the four sakkyndigs had selected sixteen of the fastest walkers. These men were staying in the islos, four men from each kirke sharing one islo. When Paafa Ketil shouted, "Time to go!" beside the islos, the men crawled out of the entrance tunnels, adjusted their double furs, and strode away into the night. They had slightly less than a two-sleep walk to reach the nearest farmhouses and over three-sleeps walk to reach the most remote farmhouses. The sleds from the near farmhouses would then take more than two sleeps to get back to the islos. When the sixteen men vanished into the night, Paafa Ketil returned to Iqquk's islo to listen to the stories around the boiling pot.

After the sleep Paafa Ketil was waiting near Iqquk's islo when Talerman came out for necessary things. A few minutes later Talerman walked up to Ketil and asked, "You wanted to see me?"

"Yes," Paafa Ketil said. "We have some problems for you to handle." He pointed to a cluster of men wearing meat-eater clothes standing beside their islos in the distance. Just then the sakkyndig for Paafa Ketil's praying house came up to join them. Iqquk and Bjørn came out of the islo while small talk was exchanged among Talerman, Paafa Ketil, and the sakkyndig. Then the group of five walked over to the meat-eaters.

Bjørn interpreted as the meat-eater spokesman said, "About thirteen years ago when the weather was so very cold, we crossed from the west, hoping to find better hunting here. Our grandfathers who were Norse encouraged us to come. They thought the people here might have animals for meat. They said the people here would help us if we asked for help.

"Hunting was good here, but we think it was because the weather was warmer than normal for many years. Now our older men, including me, have observed the weather is growing colder again. Open water was hard to find last winter. We think the temperature this winter will also be cold. Last winter we asked the Norse people for meat, but they drove us away. Only the people that Iqquk knows would trade caribou meat for seal and walrus blubber. Now we want to go with you to Merica because you are going to where the water never freezes. There will be plenty of sea animals for all of us."

Paafa Ketil, Talerman, the sakkyndig, and Bjørn withdrew for consultation. Paafa Ketil expressed his concern, "I do not want to do anything to disturb our plan. We do not have much food to share. Things will be confused enough when we get to the shelters at the low walls without the meat-eaters crowding us."

Talerman was more positive. "They said nothing about sharing our food. They can hunt better on the ice than we can. They might be able to get extra food for us on the Frozen Trail. I do not think they even want to go to our shelters because they will have friends nearby the open waters in Merica."

Talerman and the men discussed the issue for many minutes. Then they all nodded their heads and stepped back to the waiting meat-eater spokesman.

Talerman spoke, with Bjørn translating: "After seven more sleeps, we will not be sending anyone onto the ice for another five more sleeps. During that time you may travel on the ice if you want. We ask that you stay away from our people. We will also stay away from you. At the end of the walk on the ice, we will find shelter near the low walls. We ask that you continue on to find shelter with your friends. You can hunt where the water never freezes if you do not interfere with us. You are good hunters on the ice. We request your assistance in getting extra food. We would be grateful. We have planned our food supply carefully, but if we can move faster than expected we may be able to share pemmican with you later in the travels."

There was no hint of emotion in the stoic face of the meat-eater spokesman. With only a nod, he returned to his people. The meat-eaters discussed the offer for a long time.

Their spokesman returned to Talerman's group and said, "We will move onto the ice after eight sleeps from now. If we have extra meat on the way you will find it stacked inside small houses of ice blocks."

Iqquk commented, "An offer, fair to all men, needs no bickering."

When the agreement was acknowledged, the group of five broke apart. Iqquk and Bjørn walked with the meat-eater spokesman back to his islos. The sakkyndig strode toward the Norse islos. Talerman felt a touch on his sleeve. He turned toward the direction Paafa Ketil was pointing to see Runolf standing between two furry dogs with backs as high as the tips of the mittens on Runolf's hands. The dogs' small ears were standing upright; their mouths were held shut. Talerman thought the dogs looked like Ingjald's Norwegian elkhound. They had the alert foursquare stance, the dark fur coats with the fairy marks behind the shoulders, and the furry tails curved up over the back. Yet there was a difference. Instead of the black facial fur he expected, Runolf's dogs had white fur on the inside of the pointed ears, around the eyes, around the nose, and all the way under the body to their very feet. Their bodies were longer, the necks higher, and they stood about a hand higher than a Norwegian elkhound. Talerman was curious but slightly wary about the dogs as he walked up to Runolf to say, "Runolf, it is a surprise to see you here. There is a lot of land south of here in Greenland."

Runolf responded, "That land would be holding my body, if I had not left."

"You killed a man?"

Runolf looked away to the western horizon. Then he nodded and touched the female dog near his right hand. "The man kicked my dog. When she turned on him, he pulled out his knife. So I pulled mine and stepped in to protect her. I should have been more careful. My knife went into his throat somehow."

Talerman guessed again, "Then you ran away?"

"No, the young pups were in a cage and I could not leave them. Friends of the man caught me at the cage and took me to the sakkyndig. After talking the situation over, the sakkyndig told the family and friends that they were allowed to kill me after the second sunrise. The sakkyndig and the family thought I could not get far away, especially without a boat. So I was allowed to go free to put my affairs in order. Then I took my dogs and ran. The sakkyndig and the family did not know how far a dog team could take a sled in a sleep. With this dog sled, we created a new meaning for fast ice."

Talerman looked at the sled. The sled was similar to the sleds the beaverheads pulled, except it was much shorter. The sled had handles on the rear. The handles were high enough for Runolf to grab comfortably as he trotted along. But a man could not lie down to sleep in the sled. Talerman asked, "How do you get your rest with that sled?"

Runolf answered, "I do not. The dogs must rest too. Then I use the sled for one end of a shelter. I roll up on the ground in a double robe and pull the shelter robe over me. But we can cover about the same distance as four men pulling a sled all the time. I am asking to go with you. I can be a good messenger. I am one man, self-sufficient and traveling fast."

Talerman considered the situation before he answered. "We had not thought we needed a messenger, but someone who can travel from the front of the sleds to tell those behind when we change plans might be useful. Still, you had promised me that you were going to stay far away from Arnora."

"I surely intend to," replied Runolf. "I have been listening. The people tell me you and Arnora will be sledding with the last kirke. I could go with the sleds of the first kirke. If what I have heard is correct, we should be about nine sleeps apart. That is almost the distance from here to the Eastern Settlement."

Talerman said, "Styrk and Paafa Ketil need to be part of this decision. Please tie your dogs and come with me to visit them."

While Runolf was tying his two adult dogs, Talerman chose to ask, "I am curious; where did your dogs get the white markings and the larger bodies?"

Runolf answered, "I do not really know. The Scotsman, Vifill, brought a big mongrel bitch from Scotland. He said her white markings might have come from a breed of dog they call a beagle and, maybe, the larger size from a breed they call a bloodhound, but he was not much of a dog man. All I know is that her pups, which had the pointed ears and white markings, could outfight, outrun, and outlast all of the other pups."

Talerman guessed again, "You bred her to an elkhound?"

Runolf straightened up when his tying task was finished. "Two different elkhound sires. I kept the two best bitches from each litter and bred them to different elkhound sires. The two adults I have now are the best of those litters and my six pups, four she-dogs and two males, are their pups. So, now I have two bloodlines from the original bitch."

Styrk was opposed to the idea of using Runolf as a messenger. Paafa Ketil, who had known Runolf as a young man, was more in favor. So the decision fell back to Talerman, who finally decided in favor of Runolf based on his willingness to talk openly about embarrassing situations. Talerman told Runolf that he and his dogs should move out with the first eleven sleds from the Amitsau praying house. Styrk accepted the decision with reluctance, but told Runolf his place to walk would be slightly behind the utility sled so he would be available to deliver messages.

In the pale light three sleeps later, twelve sleds were aligned in front of the Amitsau islos. The sleds were loaded with pemmican weighing as much as two men. Many of the sleds carried extra pemmican. The men with the sleds had checked their bows, arrows, traps, lances, and harpoons. They had added the hunting tools above the pemmican near the sides of the sleds where they could be reached quickly.

Caribou robes were stacked on top of the pemmican in each sled and arranged so that two people with their feet overlapping could lay on the sled.

In the dawn to the east, several of the arriving seventy sleds were visible as they moved toward the islos. At the departure point, the people on the ice became strangely still with only Paafa Ketil slowly walking from sled to sled checking preparations.

As the sun moved toward the high spot in the sky, Talerman, Styrk, and the other beaver-heads emerged from their islos. They walked along the sled row to talk briefly with the twenty-one men, twenty-two women, nine young boys, eight young girls, and three babies who would be traveling in the first set of ten sleds. Styrk, Paafa Ketil, and Halldis would be pulling the utility sled. Their sons were in the harness of a sled where their grandmother Gudrid was lying between the robes. Gudrid had protested about going because she was too old and because Eyolf had another woman taking care of him in Merica. Styrk finally convinced Gudrid that Eyolf's deep desire to be near her had made the first crossing of the Frozen Trail a reality. Because of that desire, this crossing was possible for her. Styrk knew Eyolf would never forgive him if they left her behind.

Runolf, who was shivering, stood off to the side with his two large dogs in the harness of the sled and the six smaller dogs in collars. He had bartered away his knife, his two cloak clasps, and good fur clothing for pemmican for his dogs.

In the center of the ten sleds Talerman gathered the men around him and checked their preparations. Yes, they had three men, besides Styrk, who could read the Kimal but they had only one Kimal between them. Styrk would wear it. Yes, they knew the position of the stars to tell them when to rotate sleeping and walking. Yes, they had men selected to count paces. Yes, they had men selected to be hunters if pulling was easy. Yes, they knew what

to look for when hunting seal on the ice. Yes, they knew to back up immediately if water began to come onto the ice. Thin ice made of seawater sinks
under too much weight. So backing up was the best way out. Yes, they knew
it was best to stay in place if they became separated. Yes, they knew how to
set ice pointers, if they just had to move. Yes, they knew where the guiding
fires should be seen as they approached Merica. Yes, they knew there were
food reserves on the three islands with the fires. Yes, they knew the food
was to be used only in a desperate situation. Yes, they knew to sit tight during thick fog. Yes, they knew how to keep a line of travel in mist, light fog,
and snow. Yes, they knew what the landfalls would be like.

Finally, Talerman turned to Styrk and asked, "What have I forgotten to
ask or say?"

Styrk said, "I think it is time to step aside and say good luck."

Paafa Ketil stepped in front of Talerman, raised his hand to secure the
silence of all, and then said with a firm strong voice, "The prayer book says,
'Who is this that comes…traveling in the greatness of his strength? I, that
speak in righteousness, mighty to save.'" Then Paafa Ketil raised his right
hand to close with a benediction: "God be with you until we meet again."

The people of the sleds did not say any more. Then the sleepers slid between the robes and tucked themselves in tightly. The forty-three pullers
picked up their harness. When all lines were taut, Styrk leaned into his harness and stepped off. Twelve sleds moved forward with the sun slightly forward of their left shoulder. Nobody looked back.

After the first set of sleds were moving westward, the second set of Amitsau sleds formed up with a lead beaver-head and two men pulling the utility sled. The sun had already slipped below the horizon when the stars indicated the time for the second set of sleds to move out. Although it was
nighttime, the sky was not totally dark. When the eyes became adapted, the
pullers could see well enough to walk with no problem.

When the stars indicated another watch had passed, the third set of
sleds departed. Sigrid and her men set the pace for that group of sleds. Her

nearest neighbors kept their ten sleds closely spaced as if they were afraid of losing their direction in the darkness. When the stars showed the middle of the night, the remainder of the Amitsau praying house went into motion on the ice.

After the sleds were out of sight, Talerman, Paafa Thord, Bjørn, and Iqquk returned to Iqquk's islo for seal meat. Around the boiling pot they agreed the first set of sleds had started well. They talked of the slight improvements in things to say or do tomorrow. Then Talerman, Bjørn, and Paafa Thord slipped into their islos for a long sleep.

There was a twelve-hour intermission in departures as the people of the Anda Kirke began to assemble. Bjørn and Iqquk left for the remote farm. When the sun reached the high point, Paafa Thorbjørn and two other beaver-heads started moving the utility sled for the first ten sleds of the Anda Kirke. A ragged line of ten sleds followed. By midnight of the second sleep, all of the people of the Anda kirke were walking westward. Vifill, the Scot, helped to pull the utility sled in the last group. Talerman had asked Vifill to remain behind at the low walls to supervise the clean-up and to guide the next set of sleds into the shelters.

Then there was a lull at the departing islos. For five sleeps after the word came to them, the people of the farmhouses of the Sandnes and Anavik Kirkes maintained nearly normal routines of eating and sleeping. There were some exceptions. Before this year, eating of healthy dairy cattle was in direct violation of Greenland tradition, which restricted the slaughter of producing cows. But now in most households, the milking dairy cattle were quickly slaughtered. The Merica style of feasting before walking was practiced. The meat not eaten during those feasts was frozen and laid into the sleds to be eaten first on the trail. The people of the Northern Settlement ate themselves out of the dairy business, leaving only the useless hooves of the cattle scattered on the floor.

The in-laws of Tjalve's wife had the largest surviving dairy herd. Within hours of hearing the word from the islos, they butchered the bull. They invited Tjalve, Thorgerd, and the fifteen hungry children to the feast. During the daylight for the four following sleeps, they killed the remaining cows and everyone feasted. Five sets of hoofs were left behind in the butchering room.

For the next five sleeps, Talerman and Paafa Thord were occupied by every little detail that people believe only leaders can solve. Meanwhile the "new" meat-eaters had formed up in a line of widely spaced walkers and they were already out of sight on the ice. During the daylight after the sleep when the meat-eaters left, Talerman and Paafa Thord talked to the first arrivals of the Sandnes and Anavik kirkes. As the sun was going down, Talerman and Paafa Thord were walking back to their islos when Talerman noticed a fast-moving sled coming down the ice on Ranga Fjord. He thought it looked familiar. Then he realized he was looking at the shapes of Bjørn and Iqquk. Beside Bjørn was Arnora. Beside Iqquk was a shape he could not recognize. He saw Bjørn wave, so he turned and walked toward them. He was a little miffed. They did not need to arrive until three more sleeps.

When they reached shouting distance, he shouted, "What are you doing here?"

Arnora shouted back, "Bjørn wants to talk to you."

The distance was closing, so Talerman said loudly, "What for? He was talking to me before he went home. Why didn't you stay until the right time."

Bjørn answered loudly, "Father, I lacked the courage to tell you before. I must tell you now. I want to take Kuptana with me."

Bjarni and the sled came even closer together, he said, "Who is Kuptana? That sounds like a meat-eater name."

Bjørn said, "It is, father. Kuptana is Iqquk's daughter."

Bjarni stopped and stood still as the sled continued to close the distance. He stammered, "You…you…are still so young. How old is Kuptana?"

Arnora said, "She has seen thirteen summers. But her going with us does not mean they are getting married. Iqquk thinks this land will see many more cold years. He wants Kuptana to live in a better place."

Iqquk nodded his head as if he understood.

Bjarni stared at Bjørn in disbelief. He said, "You are encouraging this. You know full well the thing you are talking about is as serious as accepting marriage sometime in the future."

Bjørn answered, "Yes, Father, I know. But while you were away Kuptana has become like a member of our family. Mother likes her. Yngvild likes her. Mother says, by the way I behave, I love her. I think I do, because if you do not let her go, I plan to stay on the remote farm. Mother says I can."

Bjarni turned to glare at Arnora. Even though they now formed a conversation circle, he shouted, "Arnora, what have you done? Those are decisions for men to make."

Arnora smiled. "Yes, Bjarni, they are decisions you must make. But letting Bjørn stay behind is one valid option. The remote farm has kept four generations of your family alive. Bjørn can hunt even better than you could at his age. Another option is letting Kuptana walk to Merica with us and seeing if young love survives. There may be other options."

Bjarni looked around the faces. He saw Arnora with a sly smile, Bjørn with an earnest, almost defiant face, and Iqquk with his wife who had stoic masks for faces. He thought for awhile; then he said, "Since you have come this far, let us walk on to the islos. Arnora, I want to talk with you first. Then, Iqquk, you and I will visit in an empty islo with Bjørn doing the interpreting."

As they separated the harness lines, Bjørn looked at his mother's face. She winked. He swung into the harness with a spring in his stride. Under the covers of the sled, Yngvild felt the sled move forward at a jouncing pace. She had not heard a screaming "No!" from her father. Yngvild had inherited her mother's intuition. She squeezed Kuptana's legs tightly. Kuptana giggled.

On the last evening before leaving, the families in the big farmhouse near the Sandnes kirke had their final, most delicious meal. [See LAST SUP-PER.] As in many farmhouses, a first-born calf was sacrificed along with the sacrificial lamb as mentioned in the praying book. For the first-born calf, Paafa Snorre recited: "Honor the Lord with your substance and with the first fruits of all your increase so shall your barns be filled with plenty." [See PROVERBS 3:9.]

For the sacrificial lamb Paafa Snorre found the proper phrase from the praying book to be: "Worthy is the lamb that was slain to receive power, and riches, and wisdom, and strength, and honor, and glory, and blessing." [See REVELATION 5:12.] He repeated those two phrases in seven different homes that night.

In the pale sky of the approaching dawn, a tired but strangely awake Paafa Snorre tried to sleep. But sleep did not come. Paafa Snorre lay there wondering if anyone else in the world would ever know that a thousand people chose of their own free will to walk across the ice toward the In-drawing Sea. He thought other people might never hear from the people of the Northern Settlement again. He sat up and lit one of the precious altar candles from the flame of the seal-oil lamp. He found his writing quill. He melted the ink and added a little more water. He found a small piece of parchment and smoothed it out on the altar table. Then he carefully printed a short message in Latin.

Tjalve hailed Paafa Snorre from the door of the kirke. Paafa Snorre blew out the seal-oil lamp. He carefully placed the inkstand on one corner of the parchment, the quill across the other corner, and the candle at the top. He blew out the candle.

Paafa Snorre, Thorgerd, Tjalve, the two eldest sons of Tjalve's wife, and the girl who had been tickled pulled one sled. The remaining twelve children were divided into four sled teams where three adults made it possible that two adults would be in the harness all the time.

In the large farmhouse doorway of Thorgerd's in-laws, the old man watched all of the children depart by sled. Only the sled with his wife, his two sons, and their wives had stayed behind. The two sons responded to the old man's wave. They walked back inside the house with their lips pressed firmly together.

When they returned to the sled, the old man laid a bundle of meat at his end of the sled and lay down in the robes with his wife. The young sons joined their wives in the harnesses and pulled the sled away. The old man was relieved for the darkness beneath the robes because he could feel the moisture of the tears around his eyes. Although he had prepared himself for weeks, killing the faithful elkhound was sadder than he thought it would be.

After the acute sadness receded, the old man began to reflect on the deeds of the day. In a way the events had been a blessing. Forever after, he told his grandchildren that those deeds made it possible for him to never desire to go back to his old farmhouse.

At the islos two experienced beaver-heads replaced Tjalve and Paafa Snorre on Thorgerd's sled. Tjalve and Paafa Snorre and Hallgrim pulled the utility sled. When the first ten sleds of the Sandnes kirke moved away from the islos, the five sleds from the orphan house were grouped on the far right end. As they walked, Tjalve and the other pullers of the utility sled checked on the children often.

The second and third sets of sleds from the Sandnes Kirke left the islos at their appointed times with Arnora's father and mother in the second set of sleds. Arnora's father had hidden the lump of coal and the arrowhead beneath the floor of his house. He was still secretly hoping that he might someday return. The last set of sleds from the Sandnes Kirke slid onto the ice in the darkest moments of the night. Gard and two other beaver-heads pulled the utility sled for the last set of sleds. Gard had received from the poor side of life for so long that he accepted his role, which was being with the rear set of sleds going into darkness, as normal.

Ingjald, Thjodhild, and their children had arrived with the second sled from the remote farm while the Sandnes kirke was leaving. Ingolf, his wife, and his in-laws also came with three sleds from their house. Most of the people of the Anavik kirke stayed overnight in the islos for one final sleep.

With Ingolf, Ingjald, and an experienced beaver-head pulling the utility sled, the first ten sleds of the Anavik kirke left at noon as planned.

Talerman's neighbor on the peninsula with the remote farm was one of the pullers of the utility sled for the second group. The second set of sleds left at their appointed time with an eagerness to avoid being left behind.

The pullers of the third set of sleds and their beaver-heads were from Agnafjord, the second most remote fjord in the Northern Settlement. They had their gear together and were in harness, ready to go, long before their time. The beaver-heads on the utility sled shouted to Talerman, "Let us start moving; we will walk slow."

Given their desire to move, Talerman thought the pace would not be slow. Nevertheless, he turned his back on the stars indicating the start time. After a few more conversational exchanges with the sled-pullers, Talerman stretched his arms, yawned, and said, "It must be time to go now." The sleds were on their way, pulled by men setting a brisk pace, before he could reconsider.

All that remained was to assemble the last group of ten sleds from near the Anavik kirke. Talerman, Paafa Thord, and Arnora would pull the utility sled. Iqquk and his wife came up to Talerman. They had been checking the vacated islos for things. They were pulling a sled full of good pemmican, a few bows, several arrows, three sets of mittens, and one boot. In Iqquk's islo they had already stashed five stone boiling pots, too heavy to carry, eight seal oil lamps, unused seal oil and blubber pieces, many pieces of wood, and other items. Talerman distributed a little of the pemmican among the sleds and left the rest for Iqquk. He took the arrows and the mittens, putting them in the utility sled. The rest of the items he gave back to Iqquk. Then he reached under his own parka skirt and pulled out a metal knife that his father Magnus had often carried. He told Iqquk the story of the knife. This was the knife his great-grandfather had used to knock on the remote farm door, long, long ago. He invited Iqquk to stay with his wife on the remote farm for the rest of their lives. He extended the knife to Iqquk, who bowed his head as he took the gift.

Talerman and Paafa Thord gave the same briefing that they had given fifteen times before. The pullers returned to their sleds. Talerman counted and said to Paafa Thord, "There are only nine sleds. I thought you said there would be ten?"

Paafa Thord turned to count the sleds himself. He said, "There are supposed to be ten sleds. Who is missing? Oh, no. I should have known. The Ormsson sled is not here."

The men turned toward the east to look through the darkness of night for anything on the ice in Rangafjord. Iqquk said, "I see movement there." He was pointing near the north shore. No other sleds had used that route. Talerman, Paafa Thord, and Iqquk decided to go look. They took the utility sled. Arnora thought it better to stay in the harness and to go also rather than stand alone in the cold.

The time for the last sleds to leave the Northern Settlement was fast approaching when the utility sled came up to the Ormsson sled.

The reason for the delay was immediately obvious. The runners of the sled were made of bones lashed together. The runners had bowed outward in the center of the sled and then the lashing divided. The sagging load and jagged runners tearing into the ice effectively slowed the sled.

Iqquk surveyed the situation and said in broken Norse, "Can fix. Maybe sunrise. Need fire."

Talerman pulled items from the utility sled, saying, "We have seal oil, fire-starting tinder, and a spark striker, also new lashing strings."

Paafa Thord asked, "Do we hold the other sleds?"

Talerman looked at the Ormsson crew. Valthjof's crew was an old man, who had to slide a foot along; an underdressed boy; Grimhild with Eyvind; and Thurid, obviously heavy with child. Talerman responded, "Valthjof needs four strong pullers. We need time to fix the sled. Take the man and the boy with you. Place them with sleds having five strong pullers. Find more clothes for the boy. Ask four strong pullers, all men, to come back here to help. Then start the rest of the sleds and come back with the men."

The last set of nine sleds left the islos about half a watch later than planned. Four of the sleds were slowed by the loss of their strongest pullers. Two of those sleds were handicapped further because of the boy and the old man. So the entire group of nine sleds moved more slowly than the sleds far ahead of them in the darkness.

The original load in Ormsson's sled was more than twice as much as the sled crew needed. All of the pemmican was stacked on the ice. As he piled on the last parcel of pemmican from the sled, Iqquk said, "No good. Poor fish."

While the Ormsson sled was being fixed, Arnora talked with Thurid and determined that she might be able to walk a little, but she should not pull. Grimhild confided to Arnora that Thurid's child was from their father. Her father could not wait until Grimhild was willing to have sex again. Thurid's resolve had not been as strong as Grimhild's. Arnora insisted that Thurid was so close to birth that she should ride in the utility sled so Arnora would be nearby when the time was ripe.

The sun was above the horizon halfway to the highest point in the sky before the utility sled and Ormsson's sled left the Northern Settlement. They had wisely left the pile of poisonous pemmican on the ice and taken half of the pile given to Iqquk. Valthjof was in the pulling harness with three of the strong pullers. Grimhild, her child Eyvind, and an old married man who had many grown children were paired as sleepers. Throughout the rest of the trip Grimhild would never have to be in the sled with her father. When both were in the pulling harness, they walked in the outside harnesses with two men between.

As they moved past the islos, Talerman and Arnora were pulling the utility sled with Paafa Thord and Thurid under the robes. The sun briefly warmed the cold air. Arnora threw back her hood. Glancing at Bjarni she strode with an exhilarated mood and with a lightness of foot. Even if they were coupled to the most powerful priest in the Northern Settlement and were pulling a sled with a child carrying a child, she realized they were beginning another new life together. During the next moon's time they would be walking on the stone-hard water above the great tidal sea, and then over the humped ice to a new land.

Vignette Twenty
Slippery Water

Gee Hiz had climbed to his highest. The last of the falling leaves lay on the ground. Azon was resting, nearly asleep, against the bank near the waterway when Pitolo came swinging his crutch along the path.

Early in the previous evening, Azon had told the people in the Big House the story about the powvow in the land to the east fooling the bigger, more arrogant powvow. Early this morning, Pitolo had told them about their ancestors leaving home. Both Azon and Pitolo had stayed at the Big House ceremony until nearly dawn. The telling of the quests had been repetitive and boring. Azon was so tired he could feel it in his body, and he expected Pitolo to be tired, too. Pitolo's first words proved that. "Ah, Azon, here we are. Faced with another long day with the living dead and the dead living. I enjoy these Big House ceremonies a lot less than when I was a child."

While Pitolo was hopping across the waterway, Azon said, "I thought you were enjoying the story you told last night. Honestly, I think you behaved just like Talerman must have. I especially enjoyed how you described the Talerman and Bjørn showdown. Many of the older gray-haired people really paid attention."

Pitolo stopped near Azon and retorted, "Well, they should have. All of them have black eyes, which tells me their ancestor mothers might have come from somewhere other than the original blue-eyed Leni Lenape. If I am hearing Maalan Aarum's stories correctly, you and I may even have meat-eater blood in our bodies."

"I have been thinking about that too, but the stories are not over. We call ourselves Leni Lenape, meaning pure men from a decent place. So we must be pure."

145

Pitolo shook his head and said, "I prefer to use the 'decent' meaning for 'Leni.' I looked everyone directly in the eye last night. I saw five sets of blue eyes and two sets of slightly green, but I do not believe those people were any more pure than you or I. I think we are all decent people.

"Speaking of decent, I listened closely as you told about the decent island and fjord in the land to the east. You were careful to say, slowly and distinctly, 'Hrein-aa-byy.'

"But during the breaks many people came up to ask me if there was really a place named 'Lenape' in the land to the east."

Azon smiled. "Many people asked me the same question. I told them that there was still a decent place in the land to the east because the ancient ancestors named it 'decent' seven grandfathers ago. Then I told them that our old ancestors thought this land was better than the decent land, so they all migrated here."

Pitolo studied Azon intensely. "Azon, when we first met I was impressed by your thinking. Now we seem to be thinking alike. If so, that is a good sign for me."

Azon asked, "I wonder if you thought Grandfather was giving us the words at the end of the story again?"

Pitolo started toward the first step. He turned and said, "Sure he was. 'On the stone-hard water above the great tidal sea. Over the humped pack ice.' He wanted to be sure we told about a great tidal sea. We have not seen any tidal seas. He wanted us to know about pressure ridges in packed ice, whatever they are. A frozen sea with pressure ridges rising higher than a man must be gigantic. So, what did you compose?"

Lifting Pitolo at the correct times, Azon said, "Four praying houses went west, sliding on the stone-hard water, on the great tidal sea, over the puckered pack ice."

Pitolo stopped halfway up the steps. Turning to look down on Azon, Pitolo said, "We are beginning to think alike. You are getting better at finding the important stones. My version is, 'On the wonderful slippery water,

On the stone-hard water, all went, on the great tidal sea, over the puckered pack ice.'

"I think Maalan Aarum wants people to be impressed by how hard the pack ice was, how it piled up, and how important the tidal sea was. The sixteen sets of sleds or the four praying houses are minor details, even if he took a long time telling about them."

Azon waved for Pitolo to go onward up the steps. Three maidens were waiting at the top. When Pitolo and Azon reached the top, they stood aside for the maidens to pass, Azon said, "Let me see your engraving for today."

Pitolo held out the bark and said, "I really think Maalan Aarum is losing touch with reality. We know how to draw the ice over the sea, but how do we show the darkness, always darkness, and three moon's passage of time in a simple engraving? Then he wants us to show that three people died and five were born during the crossing. Finally he wants us show the people going into five major shelter areas. I had a tough time. I have drawn the ice and the sea. I show three moons. I stacked up three heads with *x* on them on the 'from' side and five small heads on the 'to' side. Finally, I resorted to five sticks and heads to be the shelter areas. I have a cluttered engraving. Let me see yours."

Azon held out his engraving.

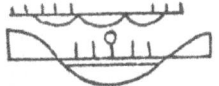

"I have included the sea and ice engraving. Overhead is a solid line to represent 'Always darkness.' The three loops hanging below the line represent the three moons' time for passing over the ice. The five short lines on the left above the line show the births. The three short lines on the right show the deaths. The five lines above the ice with one head indicate the five shelter areas."

Pitolo studied the engraving. "We make it easy for Maalan Aarum's decisions. He will take my verse and your engraving again. Why did you show the births on the left?"

"Because those born came from the land left behind. The marks for the dead on the right show that they went 'to' their final resting place."

"What about the single circle without the hair spike? What does that mean?"

"That represents the head man, Talerman, telling the people to go to five different camps."

Pitolo shook his head in amazement. "It seems so simple when you do it. Those maidens who just passed us reminded me of something I want to talk about. Our villages will soon be going in different directions. We may never see each other again.

Azon asked with a mocking voice, "What? The maidens remind you that we are going to separate? Do you have me confused with my sister? She sat next to you all last night."

Pitolo avoided looking at Azon. "Uh, well, uh, have you thought about how you will find a maiden as pleasant as the quiet maiden when the Big House celebration is over?"

Azon smiled broadly.]"Yes, I have. It is a good thing I am still a growing boy. I did what growing boys do. I asked my mother about it."

Pitolo's face showed his concern. "Your mother! Uh, what did she say?"

"She said my eldest sister has already learned everything that she can teach her. Mother has talked to the mother of the quiet maiden who says the same thing about her. This morning my sister, mother, and father went over to talk with the parents of the quiet maiden. Mother thinks an exchange might benefit both maidens and families."

Pitolo retorted swiftly, "If that happens we will be in the same predicament that Bjørn was."

"I know, but Bjørn did not think it was a predicament."

Pitolo paused to think. He studied the north village where the exchange meeting might have already taken place. Then he thought he caught a glimpse of movement along the path. He waited until the figures escaped the visual obstruction caused by the trees. Then he saw them clearly. They were two maidens running swiftly down the path leading directly to Azon and him. He turned toward Azon, smiled slightly, and said softly, "Nor do I."

After the good news about the impending exchange had been shared, Pitolo glanced at Gee Hiz who had already started to descend. "We can talk more about the plans tonight. We are late again, so let us go hear Maalan Aarum's story for today."

Azon's grandfather was asleep on his side with his knees up toward the tepee wall. Azon touched his shoulder. Slowly Grandfather's legs stretched out and he rolled onto his back. Grandfather tried to rise by pushing down on his elbows and then fell back. He tried again and Azon lifted his shoulders, pulling him to a sitting position with his back against the backrest. Pitolo brought the dipper of water. Grandfather took several sips and put the dipper carefully within reach. Silently he extended a hand, indicating he wanted to see the engravings.

Pitolo was correct. The decisions were easy for Maalan Aarum. Maalan Aarum's voice slowly came back. After a few more sips of water, he was ready to start the story. Azon and Pitolo found places to sit.

"Let me tell you, boys. It was a mob of people, really a mob. Think of taking our two villages and adding eight more. Then shoving all of us out on the ice to walk across Michigamme at the same time. This story stretches even my belief, but it must have happened."

On the wonderful slippery water,
On the stone-hard water, all went
On the great tidal sea,
Over the [puckered pack ice.]

Stories of Maalan Aarum

The Mob

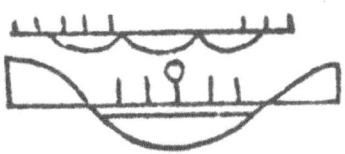

E.S. 3:18

The Migration

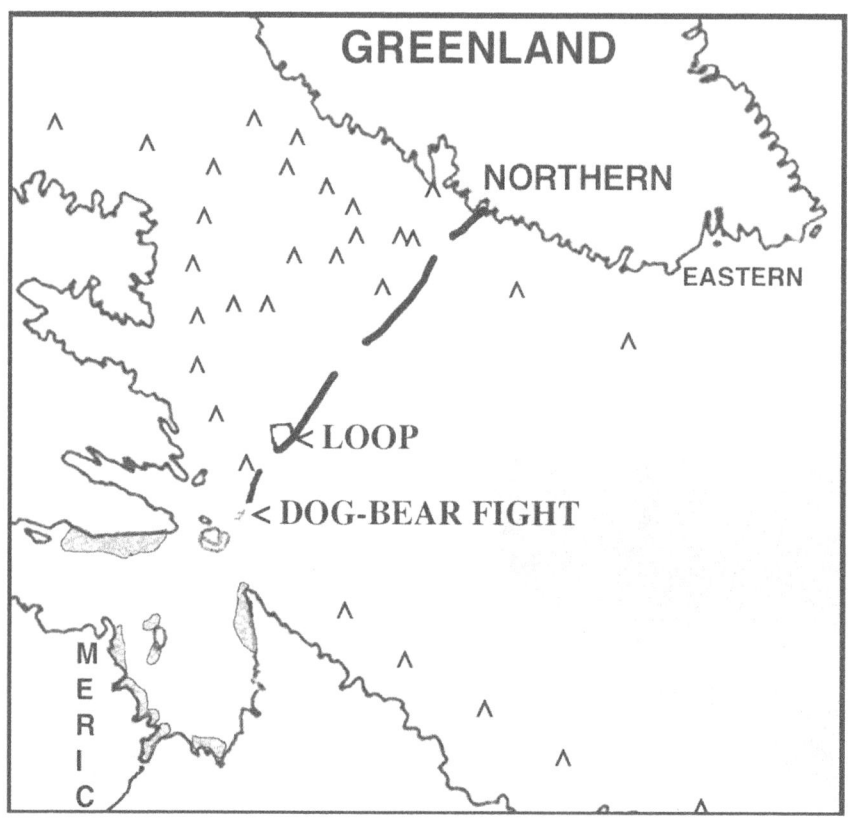

The migration went as planned until Grimhild hacked a horn out of the ice. After that episode a white bear caused a fight.

The Mob

What a mob! What can be said about one thousand people moving across the ice during the dark time of the year? They were each moving inside their own little walking-houses, the double suits of caribou hide. Each sled team was pulling enough pemmican to last two moons' time. They kept moving even as one third of them slept. They knew where they were going by the stars, the wind, and the kimal. The ice was solid, which meant the footing was good.

Each set of sleds moved apart so they could only see the sleds on either side. The wide front enabled them to watch for open water and the possibility of food. They found a few seals, but only enough to enliven a day now and then. When the pullers saw a pressure ridge or a rafting front approaching, the beaver-heads on the utility sled would search for the simplest passage. Then the sleds would move toward that passage to chisel ice steps and help each other, transfer loads, drag sleds over, and reload.

As the pressure-ridge crossings became routine, the working pace hardly slowed. The beaver-heads usually arrived first and hacked out steps up and over the pressure ridge. Next, four of the strongest, most sure-footed men positioned themselves along the top of the pressure ridge. They dropped walrus ropes to the ice below. A sled team pulled up to the ropes. The pullers shouted for the sleepers to wake up and get out of the sled. Meanwhile, the pullers quickly tied the pulling harnesses to the ropes. The sled team emptied the sled by lifting out portions of pemmican and slinging them onto their backs. They placed a bundle strap around their forehead, leaned forward, and tied the bottom of the bundle onto the waist. They leaned into the load as they climbed single-file up the icy steps. At the top of the pressure ridge, they turned around and descended, backwards, to the ice on the other side.

Meanwhile the four men on the pressure ridge pulled the sled to the top of the ridges. Two people of the sled team guided the sled, if necessary, by using following ropes. When the sled reached the top of the pressure ridge, two guide ropes handled by men on the far side were attached. The men at the top of the pressure ridge and the men with the guide ropes lowered the sled to flat ice on the far side. Then the men untied the guide ropes from the sled and tied them to lift ropes. The men at the top reeled in the lift ropes, untied the guide ropes, and wrapped them around a lance stuck into the ice. Then they dropped the lift ropes down for the next sled.

On good pressure-ridge crossings, there was a steady line of climbers on the icy staircase. The sled lifters would be lowering a sled to the far ice in time for the sled team to reload and get out of the way. The first sleds over the pressure ridge moved to the right or left to clear the passage. Usually the first full set of eleven sleds was over the pressure ridge and moving again when the second set arrived. Successive uses of the steps and sled paths made the task easier for the last set of sleds.

The activity and the routine enhanced the co-operation of the people in the groups. Members of isolated farmhouses who had rarely talked to the neighbors before were calling out often to those same neighbors on their left and right. There was a festive feeling in the air. The people had decided. The people had acted. The people were leaving the freezing cold of the gates of Hel behind them. The weather felt warmer already.

Styrk in front, Hallgrim and Tjalve in the middle, and Talerman at the rear were aware that the weather was warmer than usual. The ice was slippery. The icing on the sled runners was melting faster than it should. Many people were throwing their hoods back.

When the sun peeked briefly above the horizon about four sleeps after Talerman moved onto the ice, the towering icebergs from the breast of Hel could be seen to the northwest. Styrk would be the first to know if the icebergs were moving south. Hallgrim figured that the icebergs must surely be moving, but because he was seven sleeps behind Styrk, he had to trust

Styrk's judgment. Then, in the moonlight, Hallgrim saw a man and dogs approaching.

Runolf called for the dogs to halt and was catching his wind when Hallgrim came up to ask, "Did Styrk send you?" Runolf still could not speak clearly, but he panted out, "Yes."

After several moments Runolf caught his breath enough to talk clearly. "Styrk says the icebergs are moving south fast. He says he shows he is two notches above the line to Merica, whatever that means. Should he angle more south than west until he gets on line?"

Hallgrim responded, "I see two and a half notches above the line. Yes, Styrk should go much more south until he has gone south two full notches. We must hurry. Tell him to move faster but beware. This is not a cold year. Tell the other sleds on your way back to Styrk. We will pass the word back.

Runolf said, "My dogs and I slept only a watch ago. I will start back."

Hallgrim nodded and added, "A regular run back and forth would be helpful."

Runolf's whip cracked through the stillness of the moonlight. The dogs leaped forward as he shouted back, "I think so, too."

The sleds angled more south than west as Styrk eyed the large iceberg looming in the northwest. When the Amitsau sleds passed west of the iceberg, Styrk asked another utility sled to move up to become leader. Styrk decided to stay behind to keep an eye on the iceberg slowly coming south.

The Anda sleds moved west of the iceberg but snaps and cracking of the ice were heard. Styrk sent Runolf back at a fast pace to encourage the Sandnes sleds to hurry. When Runolf arrived, he found that Hallgrim had already figured that speed was crucial. The Sandnes sleds were moving as fast as they could without the people sweating. Hallgrim urged Runolf to go further back to the Anavik sleds. Runolf hesitated. He said, "It is not wise for me to do that. I have an agreement with Talerman that I will stay away from him."

Hallgrim said, "Talerman will be with the last sleds. At least tell the first sleds; they can relay the word back to Talerman." Runolf nodded and guided his dog sled toward the east.

The large iceberg slowly moved south. The Sandnes sled teams walked west of the iceberg. Then the last of the Anavik sleds moved west of the looming iceberg as the sun was rising one morning. That morning men were taking off their mittens for several moments at a time. The cracking of the ice was so loud that sometimes conversation had to be halted. The skilled hunters went north to the edge of the open waters behind the iceberg. They killed many seals.

When the time for necessary things came, Talerman told the sled teams to take a little longer rest to recover the energy used up by the fast pace. The people on the sleds broke out the best food they had. A fire was started and passed throughout the sled teams. The first seals from around the iceberg were pulled up and divided. The children enjoyed the taste of fresh blubber.

Grimhild had taken Eyvind north, away from the sleds, to avoid having to talk to her father. She put the toddling Eyvind down on the ice and helped him walk. When she was satisfied that he would stand by himself, she stepped off to do her necessary things. Eyvind looked around. He noticed a slender horn somehow trapped in the ice. The horn was sticking up, out of a small pressure ridge. Most people, who talked it over later, were sure the horn was still attached to a narwhal. Eyvind toddled over to the horn and took hold of it. He wiggled the horn back and forth. Then Eyvind cried for Grimhild to help him. Grimhild returned to the sled to get the large cooking knife. She began to chop a larger hole around the horn. When she thought the horn was nearly free of the ice, the big narwhal moved. The pressure ridge suddenly broke apart.

"Thwack!" With a sharp thunder crack, the iceberg moved. [See **HORN**.] The ice floe split. The split, opening wider and wider, angled off to the south-west.

Grimhild grabbed Eyvind and ran east, away from the open water of the split. Talerman and the other beaver-heads jumped to their feet. With the instincts of a lifetime of unexpected events, they turned the last set of sleds around and encouraged everyone to run eastward.

A few hours later the iceberg lurched again. Even larger cracks radiated outward. In two sleeps the iceberg smashed through the spot were the sleds had been. In the days to follow the iceberg crashed south, appearing smaller with each passing day. Another iceberg, spun off the cold breast of Hel in the north, followed in its wake. The churned-up ice in the wake behind the iceberg was not freezing fast. The weather grew warmer, and the ice began to melt during the brief hours of sunlight.

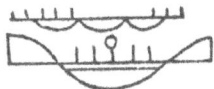

Soon after the retreat eastward, Talerman and Paafa Thord were relieved they could account for all the people and the eleven sleds of the last group from Anavik Kirke.

Paafa Thord asked, "What do we do now? If we return to the Northern Settlement, His Eminence Ivar Bardarsson will find us. Yet we cannot stay here."

Talerman replied, "We can stay here for a while. We have food reserves for an extra moon's time. The hunters are having good luck hunting seals and birds. Perhaps we or Styrk can find a way across the scrambled pack ice."

"Then we should build icehouses and settle in?"

"No, we should keep moving with the routine we had before. If we stop, too many useless disagreements may start. We do not have to walk as fast and we do not have to climb every pressure ridge, but if we keep moving we will have a moon's time to think of what to do.

"I suggest we walk east for two watches to get away from the fractured ice. Then we can walk north a sleep, east a sleep, south a sleep, and west a sleep. When we get back to the southeast point on the seventh time around, we will have to do something else.

"You go with Arnora and the sled. We will get another man to help. I want to scout the path of the icebergs."

The next day in the brief sunlight, Talerman saw Hallgrim and Runolf waving at him to go to a narrow place in the open water. He used signs to tell them everyone was alive. He learned from their signs that all the other sleds on Hallgrim's side were safe. He signaled for Hallgrim to move the sleds on. He signaled for Runolf to bring Styrk back to look for a path across the churning pack ice.

In the four sleeps that followed Talerman searched the churning pack ice for a safe passage. Then it was time to meet the sleds as they returned to the starting point. He was relieved to find that the mood remained positive even after the four-sleep circuit.

Talerman did not hear from Styrk for four more sleeps and he grew concerned. In the daylight the sleds were due back for the second time. He slept in his small islo and arose before the dawn to wait for the sleds to come from the east.

Talerman heard a single bark from the north. Then there were more barks like elkhounds chasing a fox. He turned to look north. A man, a sled, and two dogs were kicking up a plume of snow crystals as they came.

When Runolf recovered his breath, he explained, "Styrk went three sleeps along the iceberg path and looked even farther from the top of a high iceberg. The pack ice in the open water is not freezing like it should. On his way back Styrk took another look at a big old iceberg that has tipped over. The bottom that was melted by the sea is now on top. The former bottom has rounded edges almost like a big islo except it is about twice as long as it is wide.

"The iceberg is jammed crosswise in the iceberg path. There is smooth ice almost to each end of the iceberg. Styrk and two other beaver-heads carved steps to the top. They crossed over to this side of the iceberg to see if a passage was possible. They came back to our side to pull up the dogs, the sled, and me. Then they lowered me by rope to the ice on this side.

"Styrk told me to find you. They will have the steps and a passageway across the iceberg in better shape when your sleds get there."

Talerman listened closely to Runolf. He appreciated the resourceful man even more.

"The pot was simmering when I came out of the islo," Talerman said. "Please come in to rest and eat. The utility sled with Arnora on it will not get here before the sun's high time. You can be out of sight when it arrives."

The sled-pullers were excited when Talerman told them to pull north toward the fourth iceberg. They would make the passage to the west there. When Thord and Arnora arrived, Talerman slipped back into the harness of the utility sled. He enjoyed the pleasure of walking beside Arnora for the first watch. She brought him up to date on the minor events that happened while the sled teams walked around a square. She said most people understood and accepted the reason to keep walking. There had been a few complaints, a little bickering, and two minor fights, but she thought the incidents were caused by anxiety of the unknown future. Most also knew the food supply was getting closer to the point of no return. The majority of the sixty-two people behaved with heroic resolve to survive as long as possible. She told of the constant attention that Thurid needed. It was difficult to fend off Valthjof, even now with his daughter as big as a small whale. On one occasion Arnora took up her lance to make Valthjof back off.

After the next rest for necessary things, Paafa Thord joined Talerman in the harnesses. They strode along for nearly half a watch before Paafa

Thord commented, "Talerman, I have rarely seen you so quiet. We are planning to cross over an iceberg. There must be things we should talk about."

Talerman looked Paafa Thord in the eyes and said, "I am worried about Valthjof Ormsson. I do not know if he does things deliberately. But wherever he is, things go wrong. I cannot think how he can mess up crossing an iceberg, but my gut tells me he surely will."

After several more strides, Paafa Thord replied, "Perhaps, if I walked next to him, I could defend against his evil doing. The praying book says, 'Put on the armor of God.' I could encircle him with God's armor."

Talerman retorted, "You could put God's armor only on one of four sides. Besides Bishop Arne told me once that we 'should not tempt the Lord your God.'"

"To take action is not tempting God," responded Paafa Thord. "Doing nothing is tempting God. While my body can be only on one side, my prayers can encircle him. I will join his sled at the next rest."

"I do not know how you can." Paafa Thord chose not to reply and, once again, they settled into the steady strides without talking.

After the next rest stop, Talerman was adjusting his feet under the sleeping robe to avoid undue pressure on Thurid's stomach when he saw Grimhild step up to Arnora. He heard Grimhild say, "Paafa Thord says I am big enough to help you pull the utility sled and that I should be here because Thurid's baby may come any moment."

Talerman heard Arnora start to respond, "I do not think…"

He shouted out, "We planned it that way."

Arnora continued, "… we will not have any trouble pulling this sled, the runners are still well iced."

Talerman lay back to ponder the ways of God, briefly, before God granted him blissful sleep.

Crossing the iceberg was a relatively easy task, relative to crossing a dangerous jumble of ice and open water. Talerman and Styrk chose to move half of the people over first, then the sleds, and finally the last half of the people. The first thirty-one people, mostly women and children, scaled the iceberg five man-heights high with the assistance of a knotted walrus rope tied to a spear imbedded into the ice at the top of the iceberg. The spear was jammed into the ice at a forty-five-degree angle. Styrk's men had heated the spearhead and sunk it into the ice. The spear handle had frozen solidly in place as Styrk's group waited for Talerman's sleds to arrive.

The slippery trail across the iceberg was too difficult for two people to walk side by side, so each person moved slowly across the iceberg in single file. A walrus guide rope gave flimsy help because the rope was tied to a few spears jammed into the ice but not sunk and frozen solidly. At the far side four large men with their feet planted in holes chiseled into the ice tied on harnesses and lowered the people, one by one, to the ground.

After the first people had crossed over the iceberg, five sleds were lifted up and moved across. A man in front and a man in back guided each sled during the crossing. Then the sleds were lowered to the solid ice on the west side. The ten pullers and pushers came from the dwindling group on the east side of the iceberg. When a man stood at the edge of the iceberg to lift an unloaded sled and then its separated loads, he lashed himself into a harness secured to the spear in the ice.

When the load on Valthjof's sled, sixth in line, was lifted from the ice, the lifting man was surprised by the weight. His foot slipped as he dropped to a knee. He lunged forward. Then, knowing how much he had to lift, the lifter braced himself, leaned into the harness, and slowly lifted the pemmican again. A man watching the spear shouted, "Drop it! Drop it!" The load of pemmican crashed back to the ice below. Upon the iceberg the spear was nearly vertical. The tension on the rope had caused the spear to rotate upward. A crack had formed in the ice above the spear.

After much discussion, the men on top of the iceberg decided that the spear would still work if someone held the upper end down to the correct angle when a tension load was put on the spear. Ten more men lifted, pulled, and pushed the last five sleds across the icy path on top of the iceberg. As they moved across each puller and pusher took their turn holding the spear in place. Then the last puller and Arnora, who had been tending Thurid, used the knotted rope to climb up the slippery steps.

At Talerman's direction Grimhild and her son had waited behind with Thurid. Their father, Valthjof, had insisted it was his role to stay with his daughters. Talerman had wished for a better arrangement, but he could not think of one. A strong beaver-head who was best able to lift Thurid had stayed behind at Talerman's request. Paafa Thord, always standing close to Valthjof, stayed with the group on the Greenland side of the iceberg.

When she reached the top of the iceberg, Arnora moved over the ice to relieve the last puller holding the spear. The strong beaver-head made his ascent. He put on the harness connected to the spear and dropped the sling for Thurid. Talerman and Paafa Thord followed the lift of Thurid with intense anxiety. Paafa Thord gave a silent prayer of thanks as the sturdy beaver-head on top of the iceberg carefully picked up Thurid. The beaver-head moved carefully over the path to the spot near the spear. There he set Thurid on her feet. Arnora took hold of Thurid from the back. They used all four legs for balance as they slowly walked over the iceberg while the beaver-head held the spear handle for the next climber.

At a nod from Talerman, Valthjof began his climb. Talerman and Paafa Thord watched with even more anxiety. But Valthjof reached the top of the climb without incident. Valthjof moved across the ice to hold the spear end. Then Paafa Thord made the climb. Paafa Thord put on the harness and lowered the sling. Grimhild tied her child, Eyvind, into the sling and signaled Paafa Thord to start the lift.

When Eyvind was standing on the top spot next to Paafa Thord, Grimhild started the climb. Meanwhile Paafa Thord slipped out of the harness and guided Eyvind toward Valthjof. When they were within reach of each other, Valthjof grabbed Eyvind, lifted him onto his shoulders, turned, and began to stride across the ice. On the first step his feet flew up waist high. Eyvind fell backwards. The spear began to move. Grimhild felt the rope go slack. Her feet slipped from their toehold. She clung to the rope.

In that same instant, Paafa Thord planted his left foot in the hole in the path near the spear. His right hand caught the spear handle and pushed forward. He dropped his right knee to the ice with his leg aligned with the slippery slope. His left hand swung forward and caught falling Eyvind at the chest. Valthjof's left shoulder hit Paafa Thord's left knee and Valthjof was knocked up slope. He rolled stomach down and grabbed the spear just above the rope knot.

For a few breaths Paafa Thord took time to think a prayer of thankfulness. Then he stood Eyvind against his left leg. He advised Valthjof where to put his feet and how to move carefully. He told Valthjof that Grimhild, who was just reaching the top spot, would take the child. Valthjof moved slowly across the iceberg on his knees, keeping two hands on the guide rope.

Grimhild, standing at the top spot, watched Talerman climb. When he reached the top he asked, "Is everything good?"

Grimhild responded, "Yes, thank God, no trouble at all."

Runolf and his dogs stood at a distance as Arnora was lowered from the iceberg. When he saw Talerman and the four strong beaver-heads descend, he swung his dog team to the west and cracked the whip. He thought, *Ten sleeps to make up. The front sleds should be seeing Merica by now. Even if I cover the distance of two of their sleeps for every sleep I take, I cannot catch them for nearly five sleeps. Still, Styrk told me to get the word to them as soon as possible. The people of the Sandnes Kirke can take a few extra sleeps in the shelters by the low walls.*

He cracked his whip over his dogs, whose flying feet were throwing ice crystals in his face.

Talerman's sleds quickened the pace so people were almost sweating. They sustained the pace from rest period to rest period. The rest periods were uncomfortably short, but Talerman wanted to get his sleds closer to the sleds ahead if he possibly could.

Talerman, Styrk, and Paafa Thord were aware that their lateness would affect the departures from the low-wall shelters. The plans called for only a five-sleep rest by the people of the first kirkes and then they would move on. Styrk wanted desperately to be back in the lead. He, Paafa Ketil, and Halldis forged on ahead. The two sleds from Styrk's group that had stayed behind at the iceberg with him tried to keep up.

Clear skies, pleasant breezes, and long stretches of smooth ice made the progress, as one old man said, "almost as boring as walking in squares." But it was fast.

Talerman saw the light ahead and slightly to the right. The light on Bjarni Island was visible where it should have been. During the following day the pullers could see the high ground on their right shoulder. The people who had not walked the Frozen Trail before were awed to learn they were walking over the Indrawing Sea. As the daylight paled, Talerman looked ahead hoping to see the light on Akpatok Island. He saw nothing. He turned back to look for the light from Bjarni Island. It should be to the rear right. The light was not there. He felt the mist on his face. He looked up to see no stars. He shouted for a halt.

For the next three sleeps, they sat still on the ice. When the daylight briefly returned all they could see was a white mist. When nighttime descended it was incredibly dark.

Because he believed doing something was better than doing nothing, Talerman used the first daylight to align the sleds in single file in the direction they were facing. Then he had the front pullers move the sleds until the pullers behind told them to stop because they were almost out of sight. Then the rear sleds would move up one by one, checking their alignment after each move.

Talerman insisted the sled-pullers keep moving during their watch assignments. They did that by slowly walking around the column of sleds while waiting for their turn to move their sled.

In the darkest time of night the sleds were touching. The people on walking watch moved down one side of the sled column and then up the other side as they held on to the sleds. The same old man commented, "This is much more boring than walking in squares."

But not even his humor lightened the darkness.

The mist was becoming lighter on the fourth morning. That morning was when Thurid gave birth. Arnora and Grimhild attended the very difficult birth. The delivery on the utility sled went well under the circumstances. Meanwhile the rest of the column of sleds had advanced away from the utility sled, which was used for the birth. The last sled was barely visible in the mist to the west. Arnora wrapped the child. She checked Thurid once more and decided Thurid was still alive and only sleeping. She lay the child inside Thurid's hood. She had sent Grimhild to the other sleds to look after Eyvind.

Bjørn and Kuptana came out of the mist. They were carrying pemmican and soup to Arnora. They also had instructions from Talerman to ask Arnora to move the sled forward as soon as it was possible.

A dog barked loudly from somewhere to the rear of the utility sled where Thurid lay with her child. Then two dogs began barking a loud chorus of alarm. Bjørn looked beyond Arnora and immediately recognized the white bear coming out of the mist. The bear had reached the sled on the side away from Arnora and was raising its left paw toward Thurid and the newborn child.

Bjørn's automatic reaction was rapid. The harpoon was in his hand before the pemmican hit the ice. A flick of his left hand freed the harpoon rope from his waist. He rocked back and then hurled the harpoon with all his weight swung into the throw. The harpoon caught the bear in the right shoulder. Bracing against a small pile of snow frozen to the ice, Bjørn pulled the rope and bear toward him. The bear turned, swiping at the rope with his left paw. The two barking dogs came out of the mist on bear's right rear. The bear stopped turning, but still tried to slice the rope.

Arnora reached down into the sled. She found her lance. Suddenly the bear severed the rope and was on all four paws moving toward Bjørn. She chose the broad expanse of the neck just in front of the shoulders as the target. Like Bjørn, she rocked back and swung forward to transfer all her weight into the lance. She saw the lance hit the white fur. Blood painted the bear's right paw. A spot of blood appeared on the left side of its neck.

The snarling and barking dogs came closer. The bloody bear turned toward them. The bear swiped at the dogs with his left paw. The claw caught the skin of the nearest dog just below the jaw, drawing blood. The dogs jumped back and moved to their left, pulling their sled behind them. They stopped to face the bear again and barked even louder. The bear turned right to follow them and took a step toward them.

Bjørn drew his knife and came running forward. The dogs jumped to their left again to a spot beside the utility sled where Thurid was struggling to rise with the child. Arnora, on the side of the sled away from the bear, reached for the baby. The bear turned toward the barking dogs again and raised his left paw to swipe at them. They backed up against the utility sled and were caught in the harness as the two sleds tangled.

Bjørn saw his chance. He put the cold knife in his teeth. He grabbed the harpoon, which was still stuck in the bear's right shoulder, and pulled hard. Bjørn slipped and went down on his seat. He swiftly spun to his knees and hands. The bear tipped to the right. The bear put its left paw down to the ice to recover its balance. Balance was difficult to get in the slippery pool of blood under the bear's feet. Again the bear, ignoring the snarling dogs, swung right toward Bjørn. Bjørn took the knife from his teeth and scrambled backward. The bear lunged.

Bjørn rose with arms outstretched. He wanted the bear to rise too, so he could duck in to plant the knife below the rib cage. But the bloody bear slid to the ice in front of Bjørn. Bjørn, the bear, Arnora, and Thurid froze in place. The new baby did not cry. Only the agitated barking of the dogs signaled that a life-and-death confrontation was happening.

Runolf came running out of the mist. He saw that the bear was lying in the red circle of blood. He commanded his dogs to be quiet and lay down. They did not obey. He grabbed their harnesses and pressured them to lie down on the ice. Dropping to a knee he stayed between them to hold them down.

Bjørn studied the bear in the circle of blood. He grabbed the harpoon still stuck in the right shoulder and rolled the bear onto its left side. Talerman came swiftly out of the mist, shouting, "What is happening here?"

Bjørn smiled as he unhooked his harpoon. "Oh nothing much. Mother's lance just cut a bear's bloody vein."

As the first men came to the rescue, Runolf and his dogs moved back into the mist. Much later a message passed along the line of sleds that Talerman should come to the front sled. When he saw the dogs near the front sled, Talerman realized Runolf was still nearby. Runolf stepped out of the darkness. "Styrk sent me to tell you. The word about the iceberg splitting the ice was passed all the way to the front group of sleds. Actually, your rear group of sleds had been moving too fast so that you were only three sleeps from the first group of sleds.

"Anyway, all the sleds slowed down to about half pace. The ice looked good. There was enough food. So they took longer rests and did not hurry. Then an ice breakup at the Indrawing Seas caught them. The front sleds had to wait five sleeps to be sure the ice was solid. After that came a clinging, miserable fog.

"The result is that you are not far behind. Styrk, Hallgrim, and Tjalve say that the Big House celebration you were talking about can still happen. They will go slower. You should keep moving fast."

Talerman replied, "When the fog lets us, we will be moving. Runolf, you have good and faithful dogs. Does Arnora remain a compulsion to you?"

Runolf studied Talerman. Then he said, "No, I guess not. Arnora is not a compulsion to me anymore. My dogs and Arnora were both in the bear fight. I worried about my dogs. I did not think about Arnora.

"I am proud of my dogs. I am relieved they survived. The wound upset me, terribly, but they have caused worse when they fought between themselves.

"When I think about the bear fight afterwards, I felt absolved of past difficulties between Arnora and me. If my dogs had not been there, Arnora, Bjørn, and that lady with her baby may have all died. But I am grateful to Arnora too. If she and the lance had not been there, my dogs would surely have died. When I remember the effect of the lance in that fight, I am thankful that I have only a little scar on my side."

Talerman smiled and said, "Then please join us for soup. I would like to know more about your dogs."

The following morning the white mist was lighter. A few of the pullers thought they saw a flicker of light ahead. Talerman agreed the light must be on Akpatok Island. He formed them in a broad front and they advanced toward the light. As the daylight faded, they walked through the darkness with the firelight showing ahead of them. They took a path to the right of the fire to avoid the pressure ridges and the open tidal sea around Akpatok Island.

Slowly the fire moved to their left. As sunlight came through the mist in mid-morning. the bulk of Akpatok Island could be seen below the fire.

Darkness came back. The night was dark black with no moon and low clouds covering the sky. As the Akpatok fire settled toward the southeast horizon, the pullers began to worry again about how to maintain direction. Then straight ahead a dim fire rose out of the ice. There were shouts of exclamation as the walking pace increased. The light was on the fire tower. The fire tower sat on an island near Merica. The people in the last sleds from the Northern Settlement of Greenland were now Mericans.

Vignette Twenty-one
In the Darkness

A day like that day happened only once every year. The trees had begun to turn color weeks ago. The day before they had leaves of light brown, red, and deep purple. Then the cold air of the night before had settled softly among the trees. On that day the wind hardly stirred the leaves. Yet throughout the forest the leaves began to fall in earnest. The leaves fell as if some invisible force was pulling all the trees' dresses down.

Azon and Pitolo stood at the top of the steps watching the falling leaves. Pitolo said, "If only all dying could be so pretty. How many days do you think Maalan Aarum can last?"

"The Big House celebration is over in two days. I am sad to think about it, but I would prefer to see him die before we have to set him out in the cold.

"Come. Let's get on with it. Show me your engraving."

Pitolo said, "Here. What a mess! I want to see how you showed all kinds of clans and all kinds of men coming from everywhere and then showing that all, absolutely all, came."

Azon looked at Pitolo's engraving. He had to agree it looked like a mess. Instead he said, "Yours does look confusing. Here is mine."

"Grandfather said to show all, but he only mentioned three directions, three clans, three types of important men, and three variations of ordinary

171

men. So I made four little engravings; one for directions, one for clans, one for important men, and one for the ordinary men."

Pitolo said, "Once again your engraving is better than mine. Except I cannot quite understand the lower right engraving. What are you trying to show?"

Azon replied, "The cross line on top of the three vertical lines is for all the ordinary men. Every ordinary man believes in the *T* symbol. Some believe it to be a hammer. Some believe it to be a cross. The circle on the right shows the wives that most men have. Most wives help their families believe in the Great Spirit. The *T* is for those men who make wives of their daughters. They are the men who still believe the *T* is a hammer, because men who truly believe in the Great Spirit do not use their daughters as wives. The three vertical lines are for the dogs that men who cannot live with women keep for company.

"Grandfather wants this engraving to show that everybody came along. The men with wives are the normal men, the men with daughters are the few who are shunned by everybody, and the men with dogs are the totally isolated loners. Yet they all, everyone, made the walk on the Frozen Trail."

Pitolo sighed and said, "Well, I have a difficult time seeing the concept. What did you say for the verse?"

Azon turned to start toward the palisade.

"Row on row the sleds went west.
They climbed ice.
They felt through the fog.
They fought bears and came out best."

Pitolo, who was skipping to keep up, said, "Oh Azon, did you forget your own engraving? Maalan Aarum added the iceberg, the fog, and the bear fight to show how difficult the Frozen Trail was. But for our grandsons' grandsons the important thing to remember is that all of them, a big group, walked and walked in the darkness of winter."

"What are you going to say?"

Pitolo pulled Azon to a halt just before the palisade entrance.

"I tell you it was a big mob, in the darkness.
All in one darkness, to Akomen,
To the west, in the darkness, they walk and walk, all of them."

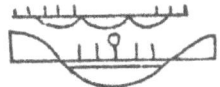

Grandfather was lying on his back with his eyes closed. His left arm was lying on the ground at an angle to his body. His breathing was so shallow Azon could not tell if Grandfather was still alive. Azon reached down to pick up the left arm. As he placed it on Grandfather's chest, Grandfather's eyes opened. He stared at the roof of the tepee for a long time. Then he spoke in a very soft voice. Azon leaned closer to listen.

Then Azon said, "He wants to hear our verses. Here, Grandfather, is mine." Azon said his verse.

Then Pitolo said his verse. Grandfather lay still for a few moments then he pointed to Pitolo.

Grandfather held his left hand up as a signal to see the engravings. He looked at Pitolo's and laid it on his chest. He looked at Azon's and, with his right hand, took it and laid it on the engraving pile. With his left hand he returned Pitolo's engraving.

Then Grandfather tried to raise his head. Azon caught him under the shoulders and pulled him into a seated position. Pitolo brought the dipper of water. The two boys sat down and waited as Grandfather sipped the water.

Grandfather finally spoke. "Boys, it will not be long now. Our ancestors have reached Merica in our story. But they are only halfway to Akomen.

The fog in the east is tame compared to a blizzard sweeping off the great ice in the west."

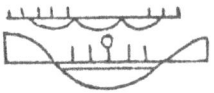

[I tell you it was a big mob]
In the darkness, all in one darkness
To Akomen, to the [west], In the darkness
They walk and walk, all of them.

Stories of
Maalan Aarum

The Men

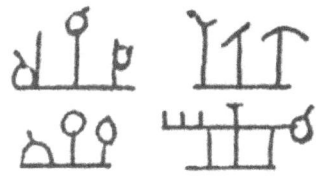

E.S. 3:19

The Migration Continued

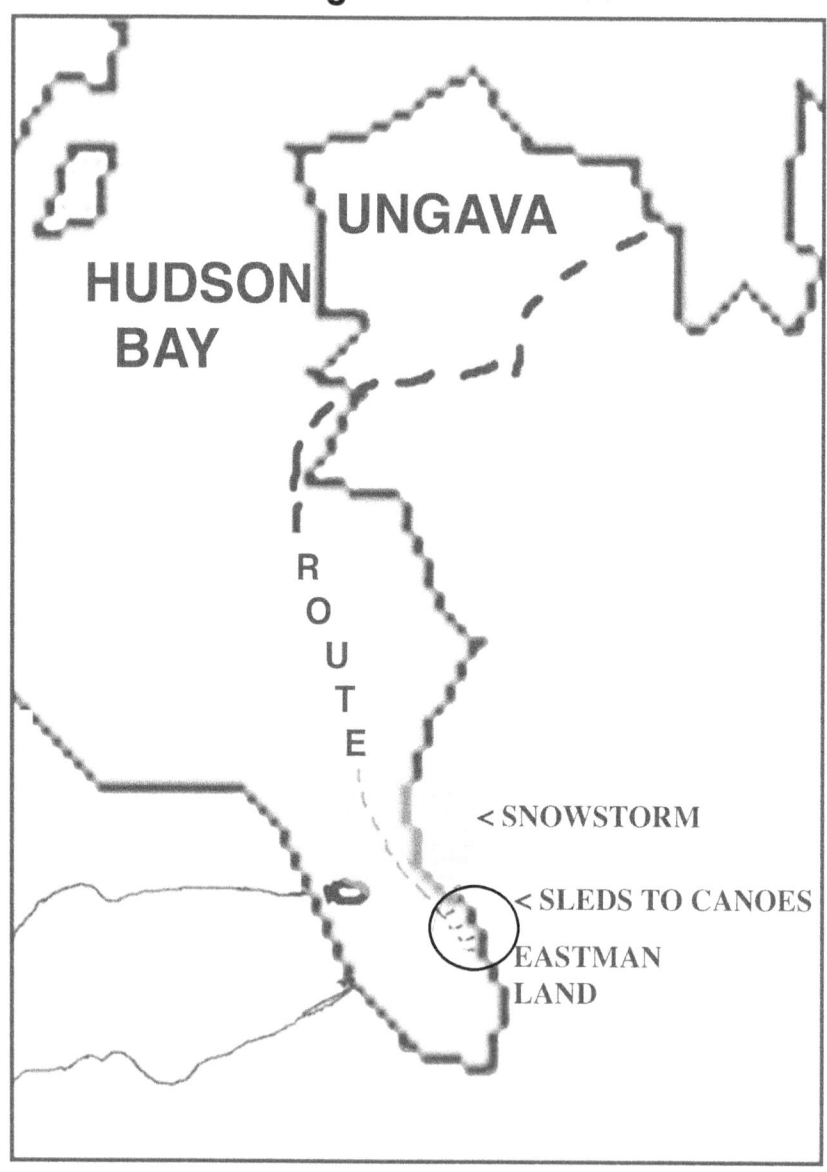

The migration continued without serious mishaps until the snowstorm hit. Days later the people went to land.

The Men

One sleep later the snow-covered rocks became visible through the mist rising from the open-water marvel. The ice was cracking and rumbling. The tide was going out, so the ice floes were settling. Although it was his turn to sleep, Talerman was walking beside Arnora and Paafa Thord.

He pointed to a path of smooth ice, saying, "There is a safe path through the ice. Can you handle it? I see Hallgrim and Gard on shore and I want hurry to talk to them."

Paafa Thord said they could certainly walk a patch of smooth ice to a visible shore. Talerman left them with the utility sled and walked swiftly ahead. A little while later as they approached the smooth ice, dense fog rolled in from the open-water marvel to the south. Paafa Thord shouted to stop all sleds. They stopped in place and waited for the fog to clear.

As the sun rose higher in the sky the dim outlines of men standing on the rocky embankment began to appear through the fog. Arnora tried to see who they were. From their relative size, she thought that Hallgrim, Gard, and Talerman were straight ahead of her, but a fourth person was there also. After a long interval the fog began to clear. The sleds started moving slowly forward. As she pulled on her harness, Arnora saw that the other person was standing very close to Talerman. Arnora felt a tinge of resentment. She rarely stood that close to Talerman in public.

Then the sun stabbed through the mist and shone on Talerman's group. The other person was carrying a bundle with both arms tucked under it as if the person was holding a baby. Then, the person turned and quickly walked away. Long black hair flowed over the hood that was thrown back. Arnora felt her resentment grow. She thought, *Men do have long hair. But men do not carry a bundle that could be a baby. Men do not stand that close to Taler-man.*

When the mist cleared Talerman walked out over the smooth ice to help guide the sleds to the Big House. Paafa Thord and Arnora pulled the sled with Thurid to the south entrance of the Big House. Thurid was placed to the right just inside of a low stone partition. Talerman waved a family with two grown sisters into the area beside Thurid. He told Valthjof and his two male companions to move into an area at the other end of the Big House. Robes of four other single men were already hanging in that area.

Talerman told Arnora that their family would take the area to the left of the center firepit near Thurid. Grimhild and Eyvind would be with them. Bjørn, Yngvild, and Kuptana came through the doorway with their robes and were directed to Arnora's area.

During the remainder of the daylight and through the first sleep, Arnora had no chance to ask Bjarni about the fourth person she had seen through the mist because other people were always around. When the dawning sky began to grow pale again, Bjarni rose from the robes and said he wanted to talk to Gard, who would be outside at the other end of the house. After waiting a brief time, Arnora, too, stepped outside to follow Bjarni. She could see Bjarni and Gard discussing things as they stood on the rock embankment near the other door of the Big House. She walked half the length of the house and then waited out of hearing range.

When Bjarni turned and walked toward her, Arnora stepped away from the stone wall and, before he could say anything, she asked, "Who was she?"

The startled look on Bjarni's face was not reassuring to Arnora. Bjarni said, "Huh? Oh, you must mean Nokla. She is the daughter of my friend Naigu. I have told you about how helpful Naigu has been to us. She just wanted to show me her baby. It was born a few moons' time ago. In fall, I think."

Arnora did a quick mental calculation. *Born in fall. So go back to summer, to spring, and to winter. Probably conceived in winter. Last winter Bjarni was at home with me or on the ice to Merica. Why am I suspicious after twenty-seven years with Bjarni? Maybe the stress of Thurid's baby, the bear, and the long time on the ice is upsetting me. Be calm.*

Arnora fell in beside Bjarni as they walked toward their end of the Big House. Then she suddenly asked, "Why is Gard here?"

Bjarni retorted with an irritated tone of voice, "You sure ask a lot of questions. He came down from the northern shelter to tell me everything is under control up there. He is one of my better helpers. He is reliable and resourceful. I depend on him as much as Styrk, Hallgrim, or Tjalve, especially because they are now ahead of us on the trail.

"Gard is going to stay here while I make a personal survey of the situation in the shelters just north of here. We want the people there to close the shelters so they can be used next winter without many repairs. Does his presence bother you?"

Arnora paused before she calmly answered. "No, you forgot that he is respectful, too. I almost regret the…Maybe you should be the one who is bothered by his presence."

Bjarni stopped, grabbed Arnora's arm, and swung her to face him. He studied her face. Then he said, "Ah, Arnora, it is good to see you smile again."

During the second sleep in the Big House, Arnora was so blessed with her first good slumber in three moons' time that she gladly curled up in the comfort of Bjarni's arms. In the morning Bjarni was already gone when Arnora awoke, but she remembered he had told her that he was going to walk to the shelters just north of the Big House. So for the first time in three moons, Arnora had time to just lie in her robe and think dreamy thoughts.

After a few fleeting visions of earlier enjoyable times, her dreamlike thoughts returned to the four people standing in the sunlit spot in the swirling mist. She begin to think: *Bjarni said the other one was Nokla, a woman with a baby. Why was she showing the baby to him and not the other*

men? Gard probably had not seen the baby before. Then Nokla walked away
carrying the baby on one arm. One arm! And not on her hip. A baby born in
fall, five to eight moons' time ago, would have been riding a hip. Bjarni
said…Oh, what do men know about babies? The baby was younger than Bjarni
said. That means it was started last spring when Bjarni was—here!

Arnora bolted up to a seated position, slipped on her inner caribou
suit, and rolled from her robes with a determined face. She told Grimhild
to prepare food for her family and to tend Thurid with her baby. Arnora
found Yngvild and Kuptana already making snowshoes and encouraged
them to continue. She asked Bjørn to go through the Big House and help
others make their snowshoes. Then Arnora pulled on her caribou suit with
the fur outside. She told Grimhild that she might be out until late. She had
a task to do that might take her well into the night. She told Grimhild not
to alert the beaver-heads unless she was not back by tomorrow's daylight.
Then she picked up her lance and walked out of the Big House.

Once outside of the Big House, she looked for a beaver-head. There was
one to the left and none to the right. At eye level on the embankment next
to the Big House she saw legs. She looked up. There was Gard standing with
a group of Tunit men. She struggled to climb the path up the embankment
through the powdery snow. She finally reached the top of the embankment,
where she stood on a rocky spot and waited until the men parted to go separate ways.

Gard and another beaver-head turned to walk further north, away from
her. Arnora hollered, "Gard!" The two men stopped and turned to look.

Gard recognized the lance and realized the voice came from Arnora.
He told the other man to go ahead without him. Then he turned and walked
toward Arnora. At a distance beyond the range of a held lance, Gard stopped
and shouted, "Arnora, walking around without snowshoes will rapidly wear
you out. Do you need something?"

Arnora blurted out, "Can you take me to Nokla, the daughter of Naigu?"

Gard instantly recognized the situation. He considered his options. Finally, he said, "I can remember the way better if I am carrying your lance."

Arnora retorted, "I do not intend to use it. I only want to tell Nokla to stay away from Bjarni."

Gard replied, "If you are not going to use the lance, then I can, at least, carry it to improve my memory."

Arnora and Gard locked eyes and silently waited for the other to give in. Finally Arnora realized she was the one who was being the more foolish. If she found Nokla's place, she could always go back to it. If Gard did not get the lance, she would not find Nokla. Arnora laid the lance on the ground and stepped back. Gard came forward to pick up the lance.

Then Gard asked, "Are you carrying a knife or an axe?"

Arnora scowled at him, but she did raise the outer jacket hem to reveal nothing tucked into waistband of the inner suit.

Gard said, "Stand where you are. You will need snowshoes. I will go tell another beaver-head where we are going and get good snowshoes for you. You stay here because we are going west from here across that rocky ridge."

When Gard returned, the tide was starting to rise, so he hurried Arnora over the ridge of rocks from Pamiok to the mainland. "The water rises higher than these rocks. We cannot return until the tide goes out again."

As the sun passed its height and began to descend, Gard led Arnora through soft snow for a thousand paces facing directly into the sun. They followed the path taken by the people of the first two kirkes who were already walking west across Ungava Peninsula. Then they walked out onto a ridgeline looking over a small bay where water was surging upward. Gard pointed down and to the right of the ridgeline to a tepee. "Nokla is there with her father. The tent is away from the others because Naigu is sick. He may die soon. Do you want to go down?"

"Yes, but please let me go far enough ahead so you cannot hear what I may say. I do not want you telling my words around the campfire. It is time. A festering boil is best lanced soon."

Nokla was sitting on the sunny side of the tepee with her back to them. Arnora on snowshoes walked through the soft snow for fifty paces before Gard started to follow. Gard continued to watch Arnora closely. He held the lance ready. At a hundred paces more, Arnora stopped just up slope from Nokla. At that very moment, Nokla removed Awasos from her breast and held him up to admire. Arnora could see him too. The baby looked just like Bjørn when he was a baby. Nokla leaned forward to lay Awasos on a fur. She readjusted her own furs.

Arnora asked in a loud voice, "Is Bjarni the father of that baby?"

Nokla quickly scooped up Awasos again and turned to face the intruder. Arnora continued, "What a healthy baby. What is his name? Is Bjarni the father?"

Nokla smiled. Looking down at Awasos, she said, "Awasos means bear. His father is Talerman."

"Awasos looks just like my son Bjørn when he was a baby. Bjørn means bear. Awasos's father is really named Bjarni. That means bear also."

Nokla's eyes snapped back to look directly into Arnora's. Nokla said softly, "Arnora. Oh, I am so glad to meet you. Talerman told me so much about you."

Nokla lay Awasos down again, and started to move toward Arnora. Arnora faltered. She signaled for Nokla to stop.

Things were not happening as she thought they would. Arnora thought, *Nokla knew Talerman, but not Bjarni. That means that she does not know*

Bjarni well. Nokla said that she was glad to meet me. That means? Well, what does it mean?

It must mean that she wants to plead to live with Bjarni in our house. I hate her for bearing Bjarni's baby. But really, even if it is Bjarni's baby, we cannot possibly feed another mouth.

What have I been thinking all day? Yes, a festering boil needs lancing fast. Do it now!

Arnora said emphatically, "Nokla, you and Awasos cannot live with Talerman in our household, because we cannot feed any mo…"

In that instant, Nokla realized the real reason for Arnora's visit. She cut Arnora short with one peal of laughter. "Ha, I never, never want to move into your household! But if you need food, I will give you caribou meat."

Arnora became flustered. "Wha…why do you not want to move in with us?"

"My father taught me. He said, 'The best blessing a man can have is a woman who loves him. But a man creates his own blessings by desiring the woman above all others.' So it is wisest for me to live with a man who desires to be with only me. Talerman is already living with you and your children. He talked about you every day. Besides, now, he has a thousand people to guide. He thinks of them all day long. Can Talerman possibly desire to be with only Awasos and me? I do not think so. Besides he is…a little, old man. I want a younger, bigger one."

Arnora was taken aback by Nokla's unexpected perspective. She was also affronted by the reference to the "little, old man." She retorted, "You already have a baby from that 'little, old man.' How will you find a young, bigger man who desires to be with only you?"

Nokla turned and reached down to pick up Awasos because he had begun to whimper. As she brought Awasos up to her chest, Nokla faced Gard. Nokla appeared to be paying attention to Awasos. She rocked him gently, but she was looking at Gard as she replied to Arnora, "Two young Tunit men have already asked for me. They are now at the northern shelter showing people how to make snowshoes. I told them I would decide who I would live with after two moons' time passes."

"A wise mother lives with a hunter before the baby is born. Why are you waiting two months more?"

Nokla continued to rock Awasos and to occasionally brush the fur around his face. She remained with her body turned toward Gard. She answered Arnora, "Because I have seen many beaver-heads, including Talerman, come and go through this land. But I have seen enough of a certain beaver-head to know that he would think of only me and I would like to live with only him.

"He does not now have a woman. Yet he keeps his distance from me. I cannot make him understand that I am interested to be his woman. Maybe he thinks I am only interested in Talerman. The big man only came to our shelter when Talerman was there. He is loyal to Talerman, and Talerman was in my robes during all of the sleeps the man stayed in our shelter.

"I wanted to wait until your people passed out of our area. I have been hoping for a chance to be with him without Talerman around. If I fail to make him interested in me by then, I will chose a Tunit man to raise Talerman's son."

"Do I know this beaver-head?"

Nokla nuzzled Awasos with her nose, brought her gaze up to Gard, then turned to answer Arnora, "I think so. He is reliable and resourceful."

Speechless, Arnora watched another cycle of nuzzle, glance at Gard, and look at Arnora. Then she guessed, "He must be respectful, also."

Nokla made one more nuzzle, glance, and look cycle before she said, "And quiet, gentle, and kind. He would be a good father to Talerman's baby. He has blood similar to Talerman's."

At a loss for words, Arnora reached out, indicating she wanted to hold Awasos. Gard stiffened and took several steps closer. Nokla hesitated and then passed the baby to Arnora. Arnora held him close to her breasts, looking at the wide black eyes. She lifted him to her face and kissed him on the forehead. Awasos' eyes drifted closed. Arnora held him a little longer then gently handed him back to Nokla. Nokla lay the baby back on his robe. Then both women looked each other in the eyes. One at a time, with Arnora first, they both stole a glance at Gard. They smiled. Then they hugged.

After much talking, Arnora asked to see Nokla's father. Nokla explained that before he got sick, her father had gone north looking for the caribou. But the weather was so cold, the herd had already moved west to the ice and then back south. Naigu had returned with swollen legs and stomach aches. He said many of the other caribou men had the same problems.

Arnora asked, "Were the men forced to survive on caribou meat only?"

"There were two moons' time when the men had to live only on caribou meat. But Müsqá Naigusson and some others did not get sick. My father could not understand why, because Müsqá ate everything. He ate complete birds except for the feathers and the beak. He ate arctic hare. Müsqá even ate the droppings of arctic hare. He should have been sick for all the bad food he ate, but he was not. Müsqá is leading the caribou men now. They are going south to meet the spring caribou migration."

"Are you still eating caribou meat?"

"Yes, all of the seals and fish were saved for your people coming off the ice. We have enough caribou meat to survive until Müsqá and the other caribou men return with fresh meat."

"Nokla, you cannot survive on caribou meat alone. The caribou have very little fat now. You must have other food. You must have seal blubber to make the caribou meat work correctly."

"What can I do? The men bring the food. Even if I know what to do, they will not listen to me."

Arnora looked first at Nokla, and then she signaled Gard to come closer. "Let us go to make your father comfortable. I will ask Gard to give you the lance. He can get the boiling pot hot to heat our pemmican. It has fat in it. We will leave it for your father. Then we will go back to the Big House tonight. We are going to talk with a bear."

The sun had gone below the horizon, but the wood fires in the Big House gave a warm glow. Talerman had returned to find both Arnora and Gard gone, "until later." Arnora was right; their absence together did bother him. He reflected on the situation and decided the wisest action was to continue to trust the two people he trusted most. So without saying a word, he joined the men at the central campfire just in time for the hanging of the masks.

Tjalve had collected the masks from the Amitsau praying house and his own Sandnes Kirke. Those masks were already hanging on the sidewalls of the big house. Gard had brought the mask from the Anda Kirke people who were still resting in the northern shelters. Paafa Thord hung the Anda and the Anavik masks as the people in the Big House quieted in solemn reverence. Paafa Thord gave a special blessing for the masks and then he repeated vespers for the evening.

Then the lighter part of the evening began. Talerman, Tjalve, and other beaver-heads began planning for the next day. Included around the main fire were Vifill, Runolf, Paafa Thord, and several other beaver-heads.

Styrk, the pathfinder, was somewhere in front, walking fast to get to the front of the people from the lead two kirkes. Hallgrim, still up north, could be trusted to shut down the shelters no longer needed this year. In three sleeps the people in the Big House would walk the trail again.

Talerman had a few changes he wanted to make. He wanted Vifill to stay behind to help close the shelters. Also he wanted Tjalve to remain behind because he wanted Tjalve's talents during the last meetings with the local meat-eaters and the Tunits. Leaving as good friends would make the local people more helpful next year when the next migration came again. Talerman suggested Tjalve and Vifill join Valthjof's sled team. He wanted Paafa Thord to lead the last group of people onto the trail. That way Paafa Thord would make early contact with the Eastman Land people. His black robe would earn respect.

Paafa Thord questioned the wisdom of leaving Valthjof without the armor of God nearby. A beaver-head gave the opinion that Tjalve would have been a priest himself if the cold climate had not altered his life. Another beaver-head suggested that Valthjof really needed understanding compassion. Tjalve was even better with people than Paafa Thord. The discussion went on until Paafa Thord decided that the Great Spirit was calling him to lead the Anavik people to the land they would possess.

Then there was little pressure to get more planning done. Everybody relaxed. Talerman was enjoying the laughter of a joke made by another beaver-head when he saw the startled look on Tjalve's face. Tjalve was looking toward the south end of the Big House. Talerman turned to see what was going on. He saw Nokla carrying Awasos and Arnora carrying her lance. She was not just carrying it, but was striking her left hand with the shaft in cadence to her steps. Talerman said, "Uh, uh. Trouble. Double trouble."

Then Talerman quickly rose to his feet saying, "Do you ladies want something?"

"Yes," said Arnora, "we want you to do something. We want you to take seal blubber and fish to the grandfather of this baby, right now, in the darkness of night before the tide washes over the path. This baby is yours, Talerman. Are you willing to let his grandfather die?"

Talerman responded, "If I knew what to do, it would be done. But the man is sick and the Great Spirit..."

Arnora said emphatically, "The man is not sick; he feels bad because he has not eaten the right food. He and his people have saved the seals and fish for us. I tell you, he needs seal blubber. Now!"

The point of the lance moved as she talked. The point stopped, aimed for Talerman's nose.

Tjalve sprang to his feet. "Talerman, that will be no problem if someone can lead the way."

Nokla said, "Gard knows the way." She turned and walked swiftly to join Gard, who was standing at the exit at the end of the house. Tjalve tapped two other beaver-heads. They scrambled to pick up a lamp, seal blubber, and fish, and then they followed Gard and Nokla.

Arnora's lance returned to rest in her crossed arms. With a nod she said, "Good. Now, Talerman, I request that you allow Nokla and Awasos, your son, to travel with me in another utility sled. Nokla needs more time for her future plans to develop. I request you have an extra sled take Naigu to his home at the Walled Hut. Also arrange to take many, many seal and fish for the caribou people there."

Talerman smiled and bowed, saying, "I was just going to make those suggestions myself. Will I be facing one hellion or two in the future?"

The direct personal question flustered Arnora. She hesitated, then recovered. "She has the baby. I have the lance."

Arnora, holding the point of the lance over her right shoulder, spun around and walked to her sleeping area.

For a few moments, Talerman was fearful he had been disgraced in front of everyone. Worse yet, would Arnora still live with him? Would either woman live with him? His thoughts raced, trying to find the right thing to say, as he turned back toward the fire. Then he heard Vifill say to Runolf with a voice loud enough to carry to both ends of the Big House, "I always said that a man who can live with the hellion is a man to follow to the ends of the ice."

There was a swelling of laughter mixed with comments throughout the Big House. A smiling serving woman gave Talerman a large dipper of bva. He relaxed and settled down to listen to the stories going around the fire. In the following days Talerman's position with the people grew with each repetition of stories ending with "I always said that a man who can live with the hellion…"

Hallgrim and Tjalve stood on the hill overlooking the solid härbret base at the mouth of the Arnaud River. Hallgrim thought the solid härbret base could be the Hammer of Thor. Tjalve kept insisting that it looked like a poorly made cross. In a friendly way they had argued about the solid härbret base every time they had passed it. The only thing they agreed upon was that the pointer on top of the solid härbret base was definitely pointing upriver.

Hallgrim was keeping tally of the people passing by. The people of the Anda Kirke had already passed. According to Hallgrim's count, two hundred of the Anavik people had gone by. The people in snowshoes were leaning forward into the forehead straps of their backpacks because they had restocked with pemmican. They were walking single file, uphill through deep, fluffy snow. Unlike when they were on ice, if they made a new path through the snow over unknown ground, they often uncovered unwanted problems.

There was a small interval between groups before the last group would pass the solid härbret base. Tjalve commented to Hallgrim, "We are watching all types of Greenland people pass by. Most of the people of the north have gone by. But we had two families that returned to Sandnes from the Eastern Settlement so they could migrate with us. A family from the very south of Greenland walked with the Amitsau praying house. So we have had people from the north, from the east, and from the south. There will be more people from the east and the south in the years to come."

"Where they came from is not as important as the family connection," responded Hallgrim. "Remember the people of Akomen called Styrk 'the white wolf.' Well, his sons have led the wolf clan to the west. The wolf clan may be turning toward Akomen now. Then your clan, all those young kids, will be called the beaver clan in Akomen, because they called you 'the blond beaver.'"

Tjalve smiled. "You may be right. I may have to find another beaver tail. But you are still wearing your feathers. You wife's relatives know they are part of the eagle clan and you are bringing home more people of the clan. So now we have changed from being Norse to being the eagle clan, the beaver clan, and the wolf clan."

Hallgrim nodded. He made a tally as five strong beaver-heads and their wives, wearing well-built snowshoes, walked past the solid härbret base. He said, "There goes the best group of men in the whole migration. They are people we could always count on."

Tjalve pointed to the group behind the best men. Three large men and one man who was short and heavy were walking up. The heavy man, who carried no backpack, was struggling to lift his snowshoes. Tjalve said, "Here comes the richest man in the Northern Settlement. Now that he has abandoned his ships, he will have to find another way to accumulate wealth. Perhaps he is already thinking about the way."

Hallgrim said, "Best men and rich men are good. We need them to make a good life for all. But here comes the most important man, Talerman and his family. The headman, the most important man, is coming last as usual."

"He has always done it that way. He feels responsible for all the people. He comes last to be sure all the people have made the journey."

Hallgrim swung his head to the west to look at the people going over the ridgeline. He swept his arm along the line of people as he turned back to Tjalve. "All of the people have made the journey. See all the men with wives."

Hallgrim pointed to Valthjof's sled. "Even those men who must sleep with daughters have made the journey. Everybody has come."

Tjalve smiled. He pointed to Runolf's sled and dogs just going to the top of the ridge. "Men who must sleep with daughters are near the bottom of the pot. But the real proof that everybody came is when men who can only live with dogs are also on the trail."

A moon and a half later, two utility sleds, one pulled by Arnora and Nokla, and the other pulled by Talerman and Gard, were sliding easily on smooth ice. They were heading south into a warm wind. They had passed the long island off to the east. They were past the point where the shore angled south by slightly east.

Gazing at the shore through the haze, Talerman and Gard felt like they were coming back to a familiar old neighborhood. Talerman asked, "I wonder how many paces it is from here to the shore?"

Gard on the outside of the four pullers quickly replied, "Five hundred."

Nokla on the shore side said, "I think it is seven hundred."

Gard said, "Well, we are not going to stop to walk it, so we will never know, will we?"

Talerman said, "Hallgrim would not be satisfied with that answer. We started the sleds three hundred paces apart. Now they are starting to slant to the east to follow the shoreline. But only four sleds are clearly visible."

Talerman went through his clumsy mental arithmetic of adding 300 to 300 and doubling that sum. Finally he asked, "Nokla, how far ahead is the furthest sled we can see?"

Nokla looked, hesitated, then said, "It is less than twelve hundred paces. I would say eleven hundred paces."

Talerman smiled and nodded to Gard, who preferred to walk on with his usual quiet demeanor.

Midday passed with very little conversation. Then Gard commented, "Now I can see only two sleds ahead. There is light snow in the air. The wind is much softer now. Maybe we should think of preparing for a blizzard."

Talerman concurred. "Maybe you are right. Those black clouds to the west look menacing, and those in the north have been moving closer against a south wind. Someone is coming toward us from up ahead. That must be Runolf and his dogs. Look how fast they are traveling."

"Someone is running with Runolf, and the sleds ahead are turning toward the shore to find protection in the snow."

Runolf and Ørn Aslakson came up to Tjalve's sled on the run. The pullers of Tjalve's sled stopped when Runolf held up his hand. Ørn had barely shouted the words, "Stop and prepare for a blizzard! Go to the snow on the shore," when Valthjof took his knife and slashed his harness loose from the sled.

Without saying a word Valthjof walked to the side of the sled, reached under the robes, and yanked Eyvind onto the ice. Valthjof grabbed him by the collar and dragged him to the front of the sled, saying, "I say we keep moving. Start pulling or I will hurt this boy."

Runolf saw something bad was going to happen. "I have to tell Talerman about the storm." His whip snapped. The dogs raced toward Talerman.

Grimhild rolled out of the sled as Tjalve tried to calm Valthjof. "Valthjof, Eyvind is your own child. Why would you want to hurt your own child? Can we do something for you?"

"It is better that he dies quickly than to freeze to death slowly just because a black-haired brown piece of…Where are you going!" Valthjof shouted to Ørn who was walking away from the sled, toward the shore.

Ørn answered calmly. "I have to go into the woods. I cannot wait."

"Oh, you dumb, blacked-eyed goat. There are no woods here," replied Valthjof.

"You know what I mean," said Ørn, putting his hands on the seat of his leggings.

"Get out of my sight, you black-eyed rabbit, and be sure you stay up-wind, too." Valthjof turned back to Tjalve to renew his command. "Let's move now!"

Tjalve tried to change the mood. "Valthjof, look, the snow is falling faster. Already we can barely see the sled ahead of us. They are moving to-ward shore. We must, too. The wind will rise soon. Do you think we can walk in a blizzard?"

Eyvind screamed. Grimhild shouted, "No!" She ran to Eyvind, who was holding his right cheek. Blood was flowing down from under his mitten. She turned to Tjalve at the sled and begged, "Please move. When he is like this he hurts us if we do not follow his orders. Please, there is not a blizzard yet. Do what he says. In time he will be nice to us. Just do not disturb him now."

A man who would hurt his own son puzzled Tjalve. He could not see the sled in front. He turned and saw that Talerman's sled was coming from behind. Gaining time for the sled behind to catch up would be good. So Tjalve leaned into the harness and said, "We are moving." Very softly into the ear of the pullers on each side of him he said, "Slowly."

Moments earlier Runolf and his dogs came to a sliding stop beside Taler-man and Gard. Runolf puffed loudly. "Talerman, hurry, Valthjof is doing crazy things up ahead."

Talerman could barely make out the sled ahead because of the snow-fall. Talerman turned and shouted at the sled, "Vifill!" but Vifill's legs had already popped out from under the robes.

Snatching the third harness from the front sled peg, Vifill said, "I heard the dogs coming. Let's go." The three men lunged forward with the utility sled.

Runolf took several breaths to catch his wind. Then he turned to catch up to the utility sled. When he came alongside, Talerman said, "I can barely see Tjalve's sled. Stop and stand still just before you lose sight of Arnora."

Runolf slowed the dogs and looked back. Arnora and Nokla were dim shadows in a field of swirling snow. Runolf had trouble stopping the dogs that were still eager to run with the sled in front of them. When they finally lay at his feet, he turned and looked again for Arnora and Nokla. All he saw was swirling white. He raised both arms high and held the whip with both hands. He wanted to be as visible as possible for Arnora and also signal Talerman's sled to stop.

Gard glanced back every other stride. Through the snow, he saw Runolf's raised arms. Gard said, "He has stopped already and he is getting hard to see. I will stay with the sled. You two go ahead." Talerman and Vifill slipped from the harness and raced on.

Vifill said between gasps, "The sled ahead does—not seem to be—closer."

Talerman, also huffing, answered "It is—but it—is moving."

Finally Talerman thought he was close enough that the pullers could hear him. He shouted, "Tjalve, stop!"

Valthjof heard the shout. He stopped and turned left as he pulled Eyvind in front of him. Tjalve and the pullers gladly stopped. Valthjof asked, "Who is that?" Talerman and Vifill came out of the swirling snow.

Talerman said, "I am Talerman. We must stop and prepare for a blizzard."

"We never stopped for a blizzard all the way from Greenland. Your words were always, 'Keep moving, do not freeze.' I am not going to stop when we are so close to a safe camp," answered Valthjof.

Talerman responded, "Valthjof, we were lucky on the Frozen Trail. Since we left the Big House we never had a snowfall where we could not see the people or sleds ahead, but this blizzard will be worse, much worse. Stop now!"

"My child will never freeze to death," shouted Valthjof as he raised the knife above his shoulder. He was ready to plunge it into Eyvind.

Grimhild grabbed her father's arm crying, "Please, father! These men are going to move." Turning toward Tjalve and Talerman, she pleaded, "Please, move."

Talerman nodded to Tjalve and the other pullers. They began to walk at a slow pace. When he was satisfied the sled was in motion; Valthjof turned around and began to walk. His left hand held Eyvind's right hand. Grimhild took Eyvind's left hand in her left hand and walked slightly behind him, holding her right mitten over the cut on Eyvind's right cheek. Valthjof led his family into the swirling snow, shouting loud enough for the other men to hear, "No filthy black-eyed goat will freeze my family to death."

Talerman followed the sled. Vifill dropped to the ice and quietly began to prepare to make an ice pointer. The other pullers heard Tjalve ask very quietly, "Ørn, what happened to Ørn?"

Ørn had faded into the snow. He counted his paces from leaving the sled. As he kept count, he also was thinking, *This will be like catching a moose that is backtracking to settle down. Go toward shore until out of sight, maybe two hundred paces. Turn. Two hundred fast paces to the right. Turn. Two hundred fast paces to the right. Turn. Be ready. This is a man, not a bear. Go left.*

When he had counted two hundred paces, he was alone in a swirling white world. The men and the sled could not be seen or heard. He stopped and carefully aligned his feet. Then he turned his right foot until its toes were at a right angle to the left foot. He bought his left foot around and stood still, feeling the wind. He thought, The wind is on the left cheek. It has started to turn. Then he ran forward, fast, for two hundred paces.

He stopped once again in a swirl of snow. He made his deliberate turn to the right. Then he ran forward two hundred paces. He crossed sled tracks. They were just-packed ridges of snow on the ice. The rest of the snow had blown away. He thought they were tracks from the sled ahead. He turned right again. He pulled out his knife and held it in his left hand, blade up. Then he started forward at a fast walk, counting the paces.

On the forty-third pace Ørn saw shadows to his right front. He crouched and angled toward a spot in front of the ghost-like figures. When he was aligned head-on with the three figures, he began to run toward them.

A small adult was on his right. A child was in the middle, and a large adult on the left. *The big one is the one I want,* thought Ørn. He aimed for the center of the looming hide jacket.

Grimhild saw him first. Her mitten snapped up to stifle a warning scream. Valthjof was startled by the hurtling shadow. Then he raised his knife.

Ørn increased his speed and placed the right hand under the left. When he felt the point touch the jacket, he raised up, putting all his strength into both arms, shoving them upward. He felt a tug on his left legging. He plunged over the child. The child fell backward, pulling Grimhild to the ground on her right side.

Ørn spun rapidly to his hands and knees, ready for a counterattack. But he saw that Valthjof had fallen forward as most dying men do. A pool of blood was already spreading on the ice. Ørn then saw Grimhild struggling to rise. He took her left hand and helped her up. He pulled her into him and held her facing away from the scene behind them. Eyvind took her right hand. Grimhild asked, "Is he…?"

"Dead," answered Ørn. He felt her quiet sobs.

Tjalve, the other pullers, and Talerman had been far enough back in the swirling snow that it looked as if the action happened in a shadowbox. They quickly came upon the final tableau. Talerman glanced at the scene and began to direct the action. He said, "Pull the sled up here by the body. Put the sled upwind. Ørn, where will the wind come from?"

With his left hand, Ørn pointed back along the trail and slightly to the right. The men quickly placed the sled crosswise to that direction. Then they pulled the body into position along the runner that would be away from the wind. They pounded bone stakes into the ice to hold the upwind runner. The sled had two robes secured to the frame. They were left in place to block the wind. The men pulled the six sleeping robes out of the sled. Three of the robes were placed on the ice next to the body. Three were lashed to the sled for an extended covering downwind.

The snow was falling heavily and the wind was beginning to blow when the other pullers, Grimhild, and Eyvind, slid under the robes. Tjalve and Ørn went with Talerman to find Arnora and Nokla.

At first they could not even see Vifill while they had the sled in sight, but then the snowfall eased slightly. Talerman was able to pick him out. Leaving Tjalve to make an ice pointer, Talerman and Ørn walked to Vifill. Vifill was shivering from the cold, congealing the sweat on his body. Gard was not in sight, but Vifill pointed in the direction where he was last seen. Ørn suggested that Vifill should be moving, so he volunteered to stay in the spot. Talerman and Vifill, walking in tandem with twenty paces between them, found Gard and their sled before Ørn was lost to sight. Then, by the same method, Talerman and Vifill reached Runolf standing in a drift of snow covering his dogs.

Runolf was shivering with cold also. "I thought you were going to leave me. What happened up there?"

Talerman said, "Valthjof is dead. They are making blizzard camp. Where is Arnora?"

Runolf said, "She was right there." He was pointing away from his left side. "I saw them, but dimly, just before I stopped, but when I looked up after getting my dogs down, there was only snow."

Talerman had Vifill take Runolf's spot and make an ice pointer. He and Runolf took the dogs in the direction where Arnora was last seen. When Vifill became a gray ghost in the swirling snow, Talerman stopped and asked Runolf and the dogs to go as far as they dared to look for Arnora.

The wind began to pick up, the snow was driving horizontally, and darkness reduced visibility by the time Runolf returned to Talerman. Runolf said, "They are not in sight. When I last saw her, we could not have been more than eighty paces apart. I have looked back along the path for a hundred paces. My dogs have not smelled anything. She has vanished."

Talerman was distraught, but he said calmly, "She has not vanished. When the first heavy snowfall hit they were not more than three hundred paces away from Valthjof's sled. They must have tried to come ahead and missed us. It is getting dark. To try to find them at this time when we do not know where they are would risk too many lives. She is with Nokla. If anyone can think of a way to stay alive in a blizzard, Nokla can."

So the men returned to the blizzard shelter by Valthjof's sled. On the way they cut more ice pointers to mark the spots where each man had stood. In the darkness they added Talerman's sled and robes to the shelter. Then they all lay side by side with their clothes on, feet against Valthjof's body, and their heads toward the flap serving as a doorway. Ørn lay behind Grimhild with his arm around her waist. He could feel her sob silently. He quietly asked, "You loved him?"

A murmured "Mmm-Mmm" and faster sobbing was the reply.

Ørn said, "I am truly sorry."

Grimhild said through sobs, "It had to be." Then Grimhild took a deep breath and let it out slowly. She fell asleep before Ørn did.

Everyone in the blizzard shelter slept soundly through the first night. The next day was fretful. Everybody, of course, had to go out for the necessary things, but they did not go far. They squatted next to the robes on the side having the least wind. They tried to pass around pemmican and eat. Mostly they just lay there listening to the strong wind roar and whip the loose ends of the robes. When more than one became uncomfortable on one side, they all turned to the other side. They all were chilled, but none felt that their hands or toes were freezing. They were thankful when darkness and sleep time returned, but they could not sleep. Nighttime was worse than the day. Only Ørn's prediction kept their spirits up. At the end of the first sleep he had said, "This is a fast-moving storm. It may be clear by tomorrow's dawn."

Slightly after dawn Talerman stuck his head from under the flap and said, "Let us go; it is clear. I can see the ice pointers behind us." All of the men scrambled to get out of the blizzard shelter and join the search for Arnora and Nokla.

Soon they all stood around the ice pointer marking the spot where Runolf had been when Arnora disappeared. To the southeast they could see seven, some said eight, groups of men strung out along the shoreline. The sled teams ahead were digging out of their snow shelters. To the north they saw nothing but low snow streaks on the ice. The west was the same. To their east the shoreline was hard to define because it was covered in white.

Runolf commented, "They did vanish."

Ørn asked, "How many paces did they have to make to catch Valthjof's sled when you went ahead, Talerman?"

Talerman answered, "They had about three hundred paces. We could see that Valthjof's sled was stopped. But it moved again."

Ørn said, "So Nokla would have gone forward only six hundred paces and stopped. We can see at least five sleds along the shore beyond our blizzard shelter. We cannot see Arnora and Nokla's sled on either side of the trail. That is a good sign."

Talerman asked, "Why is that a good sign?"

Ørn replied, "Because we can see they did not freeze to death out here on the ice. Did Nokla, by any chance, know how many paces it took to get to shore?"

Gard spoke up. "Yes, she thought it was seven hundred paces."

Ørn said, "They were pulling into a light wind when the heavy snow started. They thought they could pull into the wind and walk the correct line through the snow. But the wind was changing rapidly. So they missed Runolf and his dogs. They may have been close, but the snow was too thick. They also missed Gard and Valthjof's sleds.

"Nokla would have stopped and stayed right there, but they did not have enough robes to survive a blizzard in the open, especially one with the wind that strong. If Nokla knew the shore was seven hundred paces away, she would have turned to the left and walked for not more than eleven hundred paces before stopping. They are somewhere on the shore, right there."

Ørn was pointing east to a spot just south of the point of the land.

Gard asked, "How do you know what Nokla would do?"

Ørn smiled. "She is Naigu's daughter. Naigu and my father always talked about weather. Müsqá and I also learned about weather from them. Nokla was always nearby."

Talerman assigned the men sectors to search in the area pointed out by Ørn. Gard had seen Ørn point directly at a clump of small trees. He offered to go there. Talerman agreed. The men spread out and walked toward shore. Gard counted the paces. After seven hundred and eleven paces, Gard was standing on the shore at an intersection with the bank of a small stream. Ahead of him was a clump of willows. His eyes searched the white snow-banks to the north. At first he did not recognize the handles of the sled. But sensing that something about the snow and trees was not correct, he looked again. This time he picked out the carved wood of the sled handles.

With a few quick bounds, he was at the sled. He quickly scooped away the snow with his snowshoes. He found the sled stripped bare.

Gard thought to himself, "Ørn would say this is a good sign. They did not freeze in the sled. They must be close by."

He shouted, "Nokla, Nokla." He listened and he looked. He saw only snow and nothing else. Nothing except the wind twitching the bare willows. Then he realized that the wind was calm and only one willow branch was moving. He hurried along the ice on the stream until he was standing opposite the twitching willow. Then he noticed the lance also moving in small circles from the side of the snow bank.

Gard removed the snow with his snowshoe. At the same time he shouted, "Nokla." The back of Arnora's jacket was uncovered first. She rolled halfway out and said, "It is me, Arnora."

Gard hardly stopped digging as he said, "Good. Where is Nokla?"

"She is at my feet and Thurid is at my head."

By now Gard was puffing very rapidly, but he shoveled the snow away in front of Nokla. Nokla reached out with both arms. Gard started to pull when Nokla said, "Wait, get Awasos first." As Arnora rolled completely out of the snow bank, Gard found Awasos and lifted him out. Then Gard returned to Nokla. He pulled her out and to her feet. Then he hugged her.

Right then Arnora knew her scheme with Nokla was going to work. Nokla hugged Gard for a brief while; then she said, "We must get Thurid out. Please help Arnora do it." Gard and his snowshoe flew back into action. Arnora and Nokla stood back. Nokla had Awasos cradled in her right arm. Arnora took Thurid's baby when Gard handed it out of the snow. Finally Thurid was lifted out of the snow cave. Soon three women carrying robes and two babies walked on the ice of the small stream back to the sled. Gard followed with the rest of the robes.

When they reached the sled they quickly cleared it of snow. They replaced the robes and pulled the sled over the low pressure ridges between shore and the firm ice. Gard went ahead onto the ice, and by waving his arm in an overhead circle he signaled the other searchers to come to him.

Ørn, Talerman, and Tjalve converged on the sled almost at the same time. Gard was pulling the sled with Arnora on one side and Nokla on the other. Thurid, her baby, and Awasos rode toward the blizzard shelter. Gard waited until the right time, when the other searchers could hear, but before the questions started. Then he said loudly, "It is a good sign, they did not freeze in the snowbank either."

About midday the sleds were reloaded and ready to move. Valthjof's body was covered with snow, making a dignified mound. The men and women gathered around the mound. Tjalve said all of a prayer he could remember, "Our Father, who is in heaven. Hallowed be your name. Your Kingdom come."

The men backed away and moved to the sleds. The women touched the kneeling Grimhild's shoulder and then also came to the sleds. Grimhild knelt for a few moments longer before she rose. The other sled-pullers were tying themselves into the harnesses. They thought she would want a solitary place to cry, and they left a sleeping spot for her. But she walked directly to Tjalve, took the harness he was holding, and said, "It is my turn to be in the harness."

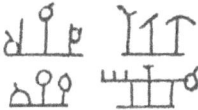

That afternoon 177 sleds moved south in a line on the ice of James Bay. Then the first sleds moved past a spot on the shoreline at dawn. The next dawn the last sleds of the line moved past the same spot. Alas, there were only two sleeps of cold weather. The morning after the blizzard, the ice began to melt, slowing the progress. On the third dawn, Styrk, who had made it back to the first sleds of the column, saw water on the ice near the shore. Styrk said, "I wish Ørn were here. I think it is time to leave the ice."

Styrk's eldest son looked back up the column and said, "Here he comes, and he is waving toward shore." Styrk turned all the sleds toward shore. Following their example, the entire column did a left flank movement.

When the sled-pullers reached the shore they walked onto melting snow. Muddy earth poked through here and there. Most of the pullers thought they were in a brand-new country. But, really, it was near the spot where the first Christian blue-eyes had met K'nistenaux black-eyes three centuries ago. During those centuries, at least six thousand young men from Greenland had already passed the spot on their way to find black-haired wives.

Even though they had been told that friends would meet them, the people on the ice did not know what to expect in the forest. Knives were positioned in waistbands. Bows and arrows where placed handy in the sleds. Lances were moved to the top of the pemmican. Arnora started to move her lance to a handier spot, but Talerman, with a smile on his face, told her to leave it alone.

The sixteen utility sleds each moved to a position in the center-rear of their own group of ten sleds. As the sixteen groups of eleven sleds came close to shore, the pullers in each group saw hunters standing on the shore waiting for them. Some hunters were beaver-heads, some had black hair, and a few were blond. All carried only knives in their waistband and all were smiling broadly.

When the sleds came off the ice, there were many greetings of joy and much news was exchanged. Then the hunters on shore guided them to a pre-selected camp spot. From sixteen winter camps, the local people emerged to welcome the people of the nearest eleven sleds. The winter hunting camps of five to eight wigwams each were located about three thousand paces apart along the shore. Each hunting camp had prepared a special kill: a moose, a bear, caribou, or several deer, for the sled people.

The feasting and the conversation that night were forever in the memories of both the sled-pullers and the awaiting villagers. In the dawn after the sleds reached shore, a beaming Ørn led Talerman and Arnora to a white-haired, blue-eyed man sitting in a wigwam with his black-haired wife. Aslak's first words were, "I have waited a long time for you to come home, young wise one."

With the dawn after the second sleep on land, settling in began. The villages had collected poles for ten or more wigwams in each village. The women of the villages showed the sled women how to set up and cover wigwams. The men were shown local hunting and, more importantly, fishing practices. The fish were starting to come upstream. By the end of the third sleep after coming ashore, 177 empty sleds were leaning against warm wigwams

The people from each kirke began to blend into the hunting camps that had absorbed them. Four small tribes of four villages each were formed. After the flower moon came to the sixteen villages, the canoe building began. Usually building a canoe took the local people about half a moon's time. But the sled people were learning a new skill. Because the new canoe builders were learning, one or more restarts were made. The flower moon passed rapidly. Slowly, as summer came, the sled people became floating people.

When the full strawberry moon shone, Talerman, Arnora, Yngvild, and Bjørn were special guests at two wedding feasts. Paafa Ketil performed the marriage ceremony for Gard and Nokla. Gard carried Awasos during the visiting after the ceremony. Awasos, who laughed often and occasionally tugged on Gard's ear, was obviously pleased to be held by Gard. Arnora felt joy, without reservation, for both Gard and Nokla.

Then seven sleeps later Paafa Thord and the powvow from Aslak's village blessed the union of Ørn and Grimhild. Little Eyvind was also happy. He looked stylish. Like the other young boys in the village, he had black painted stripes on both cheeks. The paint covered his scar.

In the time of the moon of wild rice, Talerman and Arnora traveled through the sixteen villages. They stayed two nights in each village. During the talks around the firepits, Talerman told the village leaders that his role and the role of the other beaver-heads on the trail were ended.

Talerman reminded the people that he and the other beaver-heads had promised the people of the Eastman Land that everyone would move south and west toward Michigamme. He explained that the best way to move would be to go as tribes of people from the former kirkes. Each tribe would row south in forty canoes divided into smaller traveling bands of ten canoes each. Many of the men in the original hunting camps that took in the travelers were from Eastman Land. They would serve as guides to the new locations along the rivers flowing south and west of Eastman Land.

At the start of the moon of falling leaves, four fleets of forty canoes each moved south along James Bay's eastern shore. In the lead canoes Styrk's sons, performing as pathfinders, talked with Haki and his men, serving as guides to Michigamme. Shortly after the last fleet pushed away, a canoe carrying Styrk, Halldis, Gard, Nokla, Vifill, and Runolf with his dogs shoved off and headed north.

Arnora watched the canoe pull away with interest. The canoe carried two of her lifelong friends, one new friend, and three men who still gave her terrifying memories of being trapped alone in a cold, isolated room. But the three men worked well with Bjarni. Bjarni would be in the last canoe. So that must be why he put the men in the first canoe.

Following the first canoe, Talerman and Arnora joined twelve beaver-heads with their families paddling north. They were going to Merica to pre-pare the low-wall shelters for the migration of the people who "Hrein-aa-byy."

Vignette Twenty-two
Those with Dogs

Azon and Pitolo entered the Big House in their expected positions in the parade. They both moved along the people standing along the side walls. They both visited with the people, but both were also sorting, in their minds, the details of the story they were going to tell later that night. They moved to their usual places to the side of the big house. Each was pleased to find their favorite maiden, the quiet one for Azon and Azon's sister for Pitolo, sitting beside them. Then they mentally withdrew from the surrounding activity, and they began to visualize their stories, with gestures, in their heads.

The leader of the Big House ceremony gave a few brief remarks. The powvows called forth the blessings of the Great Spirit with a minimum of words. The drums began the low, slow ruffle. The leader of the Big House called out, "Pitolo and Azon, please go to your speaking spots."

The quiet maiden nudged Azon and told him to go to his speaking spot. He was surprised. Azon looked across at Pitolo. Pitolo was bent over to recover his walking stick from the ground. He must have been surprised, too. They met at their speaking spots and turned to face the leader of the Big House. He signaled them to turn around.

Then the leader of the Big House said, "We all know that even if the outside air is cold enough to freeze water, the air inside this Big House just gets warmer and warmer as the night goes on. Later when our aarum-tids talk to us, they will want to be cool. They will not want to wear the heavy jackets they will be wearing in the villages this winter. But we think you should see them in their jackets. So we want the aarum-tids to try on their jackets now."

The drums had slowly increased the loudness of the ruffle. The lead drum made a quick "thump, thump" after the word "now." Both drums settled into a walking rhythm. Azon's sister and the quiet maiden held up the jackets for all to see. Then they carried the jackets to the aarum-tids and slipped them onto Azon and Pitolo

The murmur of approval came from the people. Azon turned to look at Pitolo. He saw a competent, very well-dressed man. He found it hard to believe the young man was the anxious boy who had entered their tepee about a half-moon's time ago. Then Azon realized, "I must look similar to Pitolo."

The leader of the Big House called for the parents of Azon and Pitolo. The parents knew what was going to happen. They were sitting near the front end of the Big House. They went forward with swiftness.

The leader said, "During ten nights in the Big House we have given feathers to the many young men who have finished their quests. We have before us two young men who have taken on a task more difficult than a quest.

"We have seen them grow before our eyes from boys who could hardly speak to competent aarum-tids. We can hear the voice of Maalan Aarum behind their stories, but their growth into aarum-tids is because of the families who taught them about living through difficult situations. So, I present these feathers to the families and request that they present them with pride to their sons."

The two fathers took the feathers and raised them high for all to see. Then they carefully laid the feathers into the hands of their wives. The two wives turned around and placed the feathers into the hands of two maidens. Pitolo's mother passed the feather to Azon's sister. Azon's mother gave the feather to the quiet maiden.

In time with a light cadence, the two maidens walked side by side to Pitolo and Azon. Then they put the feathers into the hair of the young men. The quiet maiden placed her left hand on the lower back of Azon's neck while she reached to secure the feather. Azon's back shivered and his skin made pimples as if he were cold. Azon wondered, "Does she know the sensations her hand is causing?" The quiet maiden gave the hair at the base of the feather a pat with her right hand. The feather was in place. She gave a squeeze with her left hand before she took it away. She knew.

The next morning Azon sat on the ground near the top of the stairs. He was leaning back against a tree. Azon's sister and the quiet maiden approached him with warm meat in two bowls. They studied him. Then they set the food softly on the ground beside him. They smiled and darted down the earthen steps toward the waterway. Azon, bathed in the afternoon sun, was asleep.

Pitolo saw the maidens walking to the Big House as he crossed the stepping stones. He made his way slowly up the earthen steps. The "swoosh, swoosh" of the leaves did not waken Azon. Pitolo found the meat in the bowls. He picked up one and settled onto a leaf-covered mound near Azon. He reached out with his walking stick and nudged Azon in the ribs.

Pitolo asked, "Should I eat your meat, too?"

Azon woke up looking into the branches of the trees above him. He said, "Uh, it looks like a fish net will catch us all." Pitolo nudged him again.

Azon said, "Oh, hello, Pitolo. I was finally catching some needed rest."

Pitolo tapped the second bowl with his stick, saying, "You should catch some food also. It will be a long time until the feast tomorrow morning. I hope the Great Spirit lets the women talk all the time, every day, so they will have few words left to say during their time to speak in the Big House."

Azon was fully awake now. He smiled. "We now know why the women have been given the honor of speaking the night before the last dawn. There is no doubt they will find enough words to fill the night until dawn."

Azon picked up his bowl and began to eat. They ate in silence.

Pitolo set down his bowl and said, "There are a few things I am beginning to like about being an aarum-tid. Eating is one of them. But we better pay attention to our roles. If we do not, Maalan Aarum may not reach the end of his story. What is the verse?"

Azon replied, "I am confused. The drums last night made it difficult to think. I guess the verse is something like:

'They all came off the ice.
They walked over the land.
They waited through a storm.
They found friendly people in a new land.'"

Pitolo smiled. "You are a good listener but a poor observer. Your verse does not match the engraving."

"I was not able to make the story match the engraving. The words at the end were worthless."

"Old Maalan Aarum is still alert. Maybe he thought he could not make it to the end. He put the words up front, when Hallgrim and Tjalve were talking near the big, solid härbret base. The verse he wants us to remember is:

'The men from the north, the east, the south,
The eagle clan, the beaver clan, the wolf clan,
The best men, the rich men, the head men,
Those with wives, those with daughters, those with dogs.'"

"Oh, I remember those words, but they made sense only in the story."

"They do not seem to make sense for history, but they do. The people from the three directions mean the Frozen Trail went across the sea to the last direction, west.

"The three clans are those who followed the bear clan. People of those four clans are found in most villages today. The clans help us determine who can marry whom."

"The three types of important men remind us to respect the important men in our villages: the powvow, the powerful trader, and the sachem. The three types of lesser men tell us that everyone came."

Azon shook his head. "I had most of that figured out, except the three phrases at the end, 'Those with wives, those with daughters, those with dogs.' I could not make sense of them."

Pitolo tilted his head and remained silent for a moment. Then he said, "I had trouble with those phrases, too. I think the meaning is that the 'men with wives' tells us that all of the families came. The 'men with daughters' means that even the men having to use their daughters for wives brought their families, too. There was probably a stigma around those families, but because they came too, we know that the whole village came."

Azon waited, but Pitolo seemed to be finished, so Azon asked, "What about the men with the dogs?"

Pitolo responded, "How many men do you know who prefer to live with only dogs?"

Azon thought about it. Then he said, "Only two men. When our people were sure they wanted to live with only dogs, the village made them stay behind when we moved. Oh? Do you think that phrase means that everyone, really everybody, came?"

Pitolo pulled Azon to his feet. "That is what I thought it meant."

Pitolo reached into his medicine bag. He pulled out an engraving.

The engraving showed two rounded mounds on a flat horizon. A vertical stick held a cross stick on the mound on the left, the "from" mound.

A bare head was mounted on the side away from the "to" mound. A single symbol of an evergreen tree stood on the right mound, the "to" mound.

Azon looked at the engraving for a long time. Then he said, "Interesting. Let me guess how much you tried to say with these simple symbols. The sticks on the 'from' mound represent the cross without a top, similar to the crosses the women sew into their designs?"

Pitolo nodded "yes," with a hint of a smile.

Azon replied, "And you put the head away from the 'to' side to show the reluctance to come to Evergreen Land?"

Pitolo nodded confirmation.

"And the single Evergreen means you think the people in the 'to' land are coming to the tree of lights or life that we have in our old myths?"

Pitolo's smile showed teeth, but he said, "Azon you pushed it a little too far. An evergreen tree is an evergreen tree. Two trees would have been more difficult to draw simply. Besides, I just got tired."

Azon studied the engraving again. Then he looked Pitolo in the eyes and said, "Pitolo, I cannot improve on what you have. I will show Grandfather my engraving because he wants to see it, but let us not waste time looking at mine now. He will choose yours."

Pitolo nodded and led the way, up the path with the slight grade, through the palisade entrance, along the worn path between the tepees to Maalan Aarum's tepee. Azon's mother, standing in the tepee doorway, saw them as they entered the palisade. She reached down to pick up the rectangular water basket. She turned away from them. When they came near enough to turn into the tepee, she walked away to get water. Neither Azon nor Pitolo saw her tear-stained face with the darkened eye sockets.

Once again, Grandfather was lying on his back. The left knee was raised, giving the illusion of more life than before. Azon shook the knee several times before Grandfather's eyes opened. Slowly the right knee rose to match the left knee. Grandfather turned his head left and slowly right. When the head stopped on the right side, Grandfather indicated by the fingers of the right hand for Pitolo to say his verse. Then Azon said his verse. The finger pointed to Pitolo.

The right hand rolled palm-up. Grandfather's eyes looked at Pitolo. Pitolo placed his engraving in Maalan Aarum's hand. Maalan Aarum's head rolled face-up and the hand moved the engraving close to his eyes. Then the right hand placed the engraving on the pile beside Maalan Aarum's right side. Azon was relieved that he was not asked to show his engraving to Grandfather.

Grandfather raised both arms. Azon put his head between those arms. He slid his hands under both of Grandfather's shoulders and slowly raised him to a sitting position, then slid him back to the backrest. Pitolo brought the water dipper. Grandfather took it and sipped slowly. Gradually his eyes began to move more. He wiped his lips with his tongue several times. Then he nodded and began to speak:

"So, the people of the north had walked the Frozen Trail. But only four masks, of the four northern kirkes, hung on the walls. Eight masks were still hanging in the cold kirkes of the land across the sea. During that cold, cold winter, the people in those kirkes were praying for the beaver-heads to return to show the way to the land prepared for them."

The men from the north, the east, the south,
The eagle clan, the beaver clan, the wolf clan,
The best men, the rich men, the head men,
Those with wives, those with daughters, those with dogs

Stories of
Maalan Aarum

Evergreen

E.S. 3:20

Genealogy

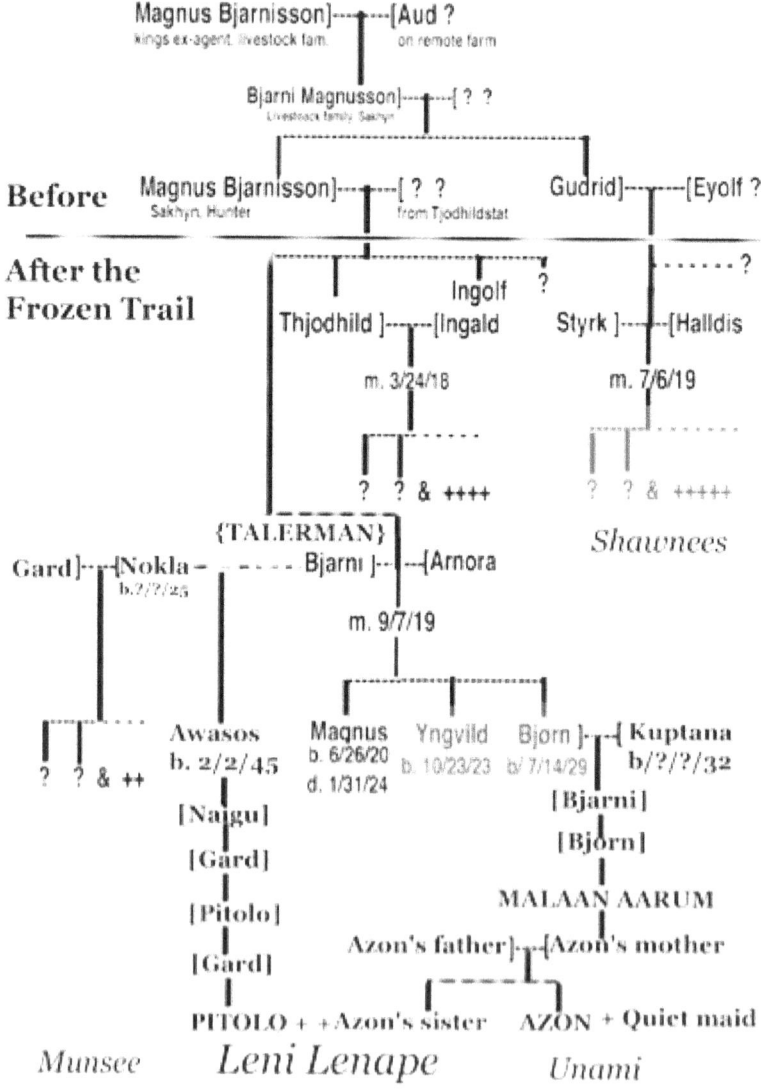

Before

Magnus Bjarnisson] ---+--- [Aud ?
kings ex-agent. livestock fam.   on remote farm

Bjarni Magnusson] ---+--- [? ?
Livestock family. Sakhyn

Magnus Bjarnisson] ---+--- [? ?   Gudrid] ---+--- [Eyolf ?
Sakhyn. Hunter   from Tjodhildstat

After the Frozen Trail

Ingolf   ?   . . . . . . ?

Thjodhild] ---+--- [Ingald   Styrk] ---+--- [Halldis

m. 3/24/18   m. 7/6/19

? ? & ++++   ? ? & +++++

{TALERMAN}   *Shawnees*

Gard] ---+--- [Nokla –   Bjarni] ---+--- [Arnora
b.?/?/25

m. 9/7/19

? ? & ++   Awasos   Magnus   Yngvild   Bjorn] ---+--- [Kuptana
b. 2/2/45   b. 6/26/20   b. 10/23/23   b/ 7/14/29   b/?/?/32
          d. 1/31/24

[Naigu]   [Bjarni]

[Gard]   [Bjorn]

[Pitolo]   MALAAN AARUM

[Gard]   Azon's father] ---+--- [Azon's mother

PITOLO + +Azon's sister   AZON + Quiet maid

Munsee   *Leni Lenape*   *Unami*

Pitolo followed his people to the east where they were called the Mun-
sees. Azon followed the Unami Lenape to the Chesapeake Bay.

Evergreen

I n the summer when Talerman was forty-five years old, Ivar Bardarsson was again residing in Gardar at Einarsfjord of the Eastern Settlement. He became more and more excited as the summer passed. The ice had begun to thaw a whole moon's time before summer. The pack ice began to move away from the shores at the beginning of summer. In the middle of summer, the icebergs from the south flowed northward to smash the last of the pack ice, which swiftly melted. Finally, Ivar Bardarsson thought, he could get to the Western Settlement.

Ivar Bardarsson asked Bishop Arne to get him ships. Bishop Arne suggested one boat would do. "No, two ships," said Ivar Bardarsson, who was afraid of armed resistance in the Western Settlement. He wanted two ships. One ship to land men, who would scout the area, while the other ship, with him aboard, would stand by at sea. Bishop Arne's repeated arguments about the absolute necessity of using all the ships during the brief opportunity to hunt whales went past Ivar Bardarsson's closed ears. Finally Bishop Arne did what he had resolved never to do—he went begging.

He went begging to the shipping agent, the king's agent, the ivory trader, and the fur trader. They operated out of a big common room, which was their office in the daylight and their living area at night. After hearing Bishop Arne's request, the shipping agent and the king's agent considered the benefits of their relationship to the king in Norway against the damage the king's ombudsman could do to them.

The shipping agent was aghast to think anyone with sense would even think of using precious knarrs just to travel to the Northern Settlement. The king's agent, who knew the Northern Settlement was probably empty, also saw the folly of sending forty good men instead of six men in an oared boat. The ivory and fur traders were noncommittal, but they did have small coastal boats that they used for hauling trading supplies. Because trading was slow in the Eastern Settlement, they were willing to send their boats in case a chance to trade with the Northern Settlement was still possible. Bishop Arne, who had a knack for knowing the moods of people, sensed a great deal of hostility during the discussions, but the four of them finally agreed to two coastal boats with crews of ten each.

When Bishop Arne reported the arrangement, Ivar Bardarsson sensed that, finally, he was on his way to the Western Settlement. It was about time!

Eight sleeps later eight men with weapons disembarked from the lead boat. They landed near the first farmhouse on the north side of the short fjord leading to the Sandnes Kirke. Two men stayed with the boat. The eight men walked to the farmhouse and pushed the door. It opened. They looked in, walked down to the shore, and shouted to Ivar Bardarsson, "There is nobody here."

Ivar Bardarsson pointed to the other three farmhouses visible up the fjord and hollered back, "Check those out. I see sheep and a cow." There was nobody there, either.

Finally Ivar Bardarsson chose to go ashore himself. He landed near the Sandnes Kirke. First he looked into two nearby earthen houses himself. He emerged from the first with a frightened look on his face. He did not stay in the second house very long. Then he walked to the Sandnes Kirke. He looked into the dim interior. The sun's rays stabbed through the smoke hole. The sunlight fell on the simple chancel. A piece of parchment lay on the chancel. Ivar Bardarsson went forward to read what was on the parchment. The letters, made with bold hand strokes, said in Latin, "AD AMERICAE POPULOS SE CONVERTERUNT." [See **TO AMERICA.**]

In four locations south of Eastman Land, that same fall, more than forty canoes arrived and unloaded people who where strangers to Eastman Land and Akomen. In each of the four locations, the local people lined the pathways as their friends led the wide-eyed strangers into a towering forest along a flowing stream to a large clearing surrounded by twenty-five tepees. The celebration feasts were held in an open circle around a roaring fire. Dancing was a part of the celebration.

The strangers tarried in a place that seemed like the land ready for them to possess. The lingering warm weather was another blessing, making the land truly a paradise.

But all too soon the tepees were taken apart, and the people who had walked the Frozen Trail to Akomen started their hunting walk away from the Eastman Land. The people who had walked the ice knew that other kirkes would be coming to the Eastman Land during the next summer.

Everyone, except the very sick or lame and the young women who had been successfully courted by Eastman men that summer, moved toward the winter hunting territories. They hunted south by southwest. It was a big land and the paths were many. In the spring they would gather together in a summer camp by a flowing stream many moons' time away from Eastman Land.

Further north in Merica that fall, Talerman and his team of beaver-heads engaged in preparing the shelters for the next migration. On Talerman's forty-sixth birthday, the ice was firm enough for the beaver-heads to walk straight to Hrein Island in Einarsfjord in the Eastern Settlement. Arnora, Halldis, Nokla, and other competent women who knew the migration experience stayed in Merica. While they waited for their men to return, they prepared the final details for the next migration of people coming off the ice.

Under Bishop Arne's guidance the people of the Eastern Settlement had agreed that the kirkes furthest north should migrate first. The people thought it only fair that those who would to be trapped by ice first should go first.

Bishop Arne had a different reason to encourage the kirkes furthest north to migrate first. His Nemesis, Ivar Bardarsson, was at Foss in the south again. He would not notice the absence of the small Middle Settlement or the kirkes furthest north in the Eastern Settlement.

Each kirke of the Eastern Settlement had more people than the former kirkes of the Northern Settlement. So the 176 sleds could only accommodate the people of three kirkes. But when Talerman and the other beaver-heads arrived in the Eastern Settlement, they were convinced the climate was colder than usual. The cold climate meant that the solid ice from Hrein Island to Merica would last up to nine months. So just before the first wave of the migration from the Eastern Settlement left Hrein Island in the moon of rising spirits, Talerman sent messengers to the next three kirkes who were to migrate. The messengers told the kirke people to assemble at Hrein Island at the same time during the moon of the snow crust. Talerman had promised that he and the beaver-heads would be back to lead a second migration in the spring.

Then Talerman and the beaver-heads guided the first set of 176 sleds from the Eastern Settlement to Merica. At the shelters in Merica, they left the migrating people in care of Ørn, Müsqá, and other competent guides from Eastman Land.

Then Talerman and his crew turned around and walked back to Hrein Island. Late in the spring the second set of sleds from Hrein Island filtered through the fog into the arched houses on the shore of Merica.

Hallgrim and Gard had guided their people into the longest shelter at the north end of the northern open-water marvel. They had coordinated the change from sleds to snowshoes. The weather remained cold, even for the late season. Things appeared to be going well.

Hallgrim sensed that things were going too well. He suggested to Gard that they make plans to leave early the next day. They spread the word among the people in the shelters to prepare to walk when the sky became pale. That evening before going to sleep, a few women began to cut the roof panels loose from the shelter. They chose to start on the side away from the light wind. A concerned Hallgrim asked the women to stop taking down roof panels until everyone rose in the pale light. Because it was already time to sleep and because the wind was very still, Hallgrim allowed the removed panels to be left off.

During the night Gard heard the wind increase. He scrambled up to check on the roof. He looked out of a space where a panel had been removed. The snow, driven into his face, blinded him. He knew instantly that it was unthinkable to lead people into such a snowstorm. He hurriedly woke Hallgrim. Shouting above the wind, they moved through the house and quickly spread the word for the people to stay in place under their robes. Some people, who were already up getting ready to go, shrugged and returned to their robes to catch more sleep.

The wind increased even more. The snowstorm became a howling blizzard. The wind funneled through the open panel slots and rammed into the opposite side wall. A few of the sidewall panels fluttered open, but most of the panels had been frozen into place. The wind pressure on the downwind wall caused the poles to bend and the whole arch to lift. On the windward side the arches lifted high enough to allow the wind to sweep into the gap between the walls and the roof panels. The downwind poles, which were bent against the rock walls, snapped. In moments, the whole shelter was blown off the walls.

Most of the pemmican was packed and the packs stayed in place. Some of the people in the shelter were still in their full walking suits under their robes. But many more people had taken the outer walking suit off and stored it either in their sleeping robes or within reach nearby. By swift action most people were able to save their outer walking suits and to squirm into them while still holding onto the flapping sleeping robes. Once they slipped on their outer walking suits, they moved their sleeping robes to the lee sides of the two low walls. There they burrowed into the snow sifting back, and they survived the snowstorm. Many even slept in comfort.

In the daylight after the storm had abated, Hallgrim and Gard could see that most of the roof poles were a scattered tangle downwind. Half of them had the end broken off at wall height. Considering the weather conditions they faced, the best course of action was to get everyone walking on the trail.

As Gard led the column of people away from the flattened shelter, Hallgrim stood beside the path asking each survivor if they had lost anything of value. He was pleased to hear only a few comments: "A needle, a handle for a metal tool, about twenty glass beads, a small wooden doll's head, a copper knife about two centuries old, another handle for a metal tool, an arrow with a metal arrowhead, and thirty beads scattered all over." [**See Artifacts from Greenand.**] As the last family passed him to get on the trail, Hallgrim took a look back at the scattered remains of the shelter and thought to himself, "Things are still going good, but not too good."

When the priest for the people of the kirke, which had been at the northern low walls, added their mask, nine other wooden masks were already hung in the Big House at Pamiok. All the people from the ten kirkes had walked across the wonderful slippery ice and were on the trail to the land they could possess.

Finally that fall, when the last wave of people reached the forests of Eastman Land, everyone in the region, including the beaver-heads, had themselves one tremendous feast. The eating, the dancing, the courting, and the storytelling went on into many dawns.

Back in the Eastern Settlement, throughout the three fjords from Hrein Island north, the people who remained in the earthen houses spread out. After every sleep, small groups of people moved their personal items to an empty house left to them. The new people in the formerly abandoned houses tended the livestock left behind and consumed the frozen seals. Within a moon's time, every abandoned farmhouse was occupied. The Eastern Settlement looked, from the outside, as it did before two migrations had left. From the inside three-fourths of the people, nearly two thousand souls, were gone.

During the early spring when Talerman was approaching his forty-seventh birthday, he asked Tjalve to send out messengers with an invitation. Talerman invited the people who were important to the Frozen Trail crossings to remain behind in Merica and plan to meet in the Big House on Pamiok Island when the strawberry moon became full.

So they assembled. They were Styrk, Hallgrim, Tjalve, Müsqá, Ørn, Gard, Runolf, Vifill, and Gunnbjørn.

The meeting was not closed. Other people were welcomed, but the nine people named were the only ones to receive a gift of a full suit of deerskin clothes. Talerman had told Tjalve, "We should not use Hrein gifts anymore. That will end by next spring." So Tjalve had asked Hallgrim's wife to have the village women make the deerskin clothes. Each of those receiving gifts knew, by tradition, they would be expected to give a gift or service of even greater value sometime in the future. In fact, most were more than willing to accept the gift because they felt proud to be included in the assembly of the most powerful men in Akomen and Merica.

After the evening feast but before the big stories started, Talerman signaled the drummer to call for attention. Then Talerman began speaking:

"Men, as you are well aware, we have led three large groups of people over the Frozen Trail. In the coming winter we will lead the last large group out of the Eastern Settlement. Hallgrim tells me this last group will be all of the people who want to walk the Frozen Trail at this time.

"After the last group arrives from Hrein Island, we will proceed as usual, with each house carrying their roof panels. We will take down the arches as we leave each house. We can take some of the timber for firewood and store the rest for the Tunit, the meat-eaters, or in case others from Hrein Island come over the Frozen Trail on their own.

"We have been very, very fortunate. Hallgrim please tell us the numbers."

Hallgrim stood up and said, "So far we have guided two thousand, seven hundred, and eighty three people to Akomen. More than eighteen hundred people are now south of the Sludd River in Eastman Land. They have set up summer camps in their new territories. They are on their way to Michigamme.

"This year we lost eleven people. Three elderly people died. One old man died peacefully in his wigwam. An old man and his wife chose to go outside together on a very cold night. Two mothers died in childbirth. One of the babies lived. A bear killed a boy. Some families fought. Before the priests were able to stop the string of violence, three men and one woman were killed. The eleven for this year means thirty-eight people have died since the first group of sleds started over the Frozen Trail. The important thing to remember is that, while we have had nearly three thousand people in the migration to a new country, we have not had any deaths that can be blamed solely on the hazards encountered during migration. Nobody fell into the sea. Nobody froze to death. Many people went hungry many days, but none of them died. We have not had to fight other people to find a place to live."

Talerman said, "Thank you, Hallgrim. Your last statement about not fighting others for a place to live reminds all of us how fortunate we are to have our friends, the Tunit, the people from Eastman Land, and the people from west of the big bay."

Talerman allowed time for comments and suggestions about the final migrations. The meat in the boiling pots was replenished more than once. The beaver-heads talked late into the night until Talerman thought most plans had been settled and most people knew their roles for the last migration from Hrein-aa-byy. Then he asked, "Hallgrim, you have been keeping track as usual. Can you tell us what supplies will we need, and when do we need to have them?"

Hallgrim stood again, holding his chin in his hand and gazing at the end of the room as though sorting things out in his mind. Then he stepped forward and said to the assembly, "Actually I think the numbers and the timing we used last time will be good. We could use more poles and wood to burn at all the sites, but the greatest need is for new poles at the longest house, which is also furthest north, just south of the Indrawing Seas. Last spring when the people were leaving, they had taken panels off of one side of the roof. Then the wind shifted and came very strongly from the northwest. Most of the poles broke off where the stone walls held them."

Captain Gunnbjørn said, "I sense the climate will give us only one month of sailing water this year. If the weather allows, I will have my other boat bring a load of poles to the southern houses. They will be the smaller poles to build the snowshoes, trade for meat, and provide fire. I think I can make one trip to the northern houses. I will carry longer poles to be used to rebuild the roof that was blown away."

Two moons' time later Hallgrim, with his crew of Tunit and beaver-heads, had carried new roofing panels to the northern house. They had collected the poles that were left and sorted them for possible use. Hallgrim was thinking of the possible ways to make a shorter arch when a beaver-head shouted, "Sail in sight!" Hallgrim and most of the crew went to the shore to await Gunnbjørn's landing.

To Hallgrim it looked like Gunnbjørn had the landing area in sight with a following wind filling the sails and the tide flowing toward shore. But then the wind died. The boat crew reefed the sail and began to row. The boat was heavy and Gunnbjørn had only eight oars on his knarr.

Later in the day, chunks of ice began moving away from shore. The Indrawing Sea was flowing out. Then Hallgrim heard a long resounding "cr-rraaack." He looked north and saw a large ice floe coming straight at him. The icebergs in the Indrawing Sea were shoving the northwest end of the ice floe, rotating the southeast end of the ice toward Hallgrim standing on shore.

Gunnbjørn's boat was blocked by the rotating ice floe. The crew turned the boat. They began to row with the outgoing tide. The pack ice surrounded them and carried them along.

For three sleeps the boat floated, back and forth, encased in the ice in the Indrawing Sea. The icebergs coming down the Indrawing Sea from the northwest blocked movement up the strait.

When he looked in the dawn's light after the forth sleep, Hallgrim could not see the boat. Hallgrim had not slept much because he was distressed about Gunnbjørn and the crew of seventeen in the boat. Hallgrim knew the Indrawing Sea would deliver them to the cold current filled with pack ice and icebergs, which was moving south. Assuming they could escape being smashed between icebergs, there was little chance of escape unless the boat could sail a long way south into the warmer sea or east into the warmer waters near Hrein Island. The ice flowing south moved at one notch per moon's time. It would take at least ten moons' time to reach the warmer water free of ice. That would be much too long for the crew to survive in the cold, even considering normal fishing luck.

Even if the boat could get into the water near Hrein Island, it probably could not get to shore because the fast ice on the Hrein shore was not melting and was not being broken up by the tides. The only remote hope for escaping the ice was to get into the open warm water with the icebergs flowing north and then go south against the warm flow to the warm water flowing east. This course would take all of Captain Gunnbjørn's sailing skills, and an unreasonable amount of luck, too.

Hallgrim stood on shore consumed with his distress. He knew, in his heart, the Frozen Trail had just swallowed its first eighteen victims. It was even more distressing to know that he had baited the trap. Hallgrim stood alone on the shore for several minutes. Then he turned toward the group of beaver-heads and Tunit behind him and said, "Let us start building the house using what we have. We will make lower arches. The boat will never make it here."

A larger-than-normal house sat on an island on the north side of Hrein Island, near the shipping wharf. The shipping wharf was across the channel from Hrein Island. The people in the house were first generation to Hrein-aa-byy. They had come from Norway for the king's or merchant's business. The leading men in the house were the ivory trader, the fur trader, the shipping agent, and the king's agent. With the exception of Ivar Bardarsson and Bishop Arne, these men were the most powerful men in the settlement. Two of the men had wives from Norway. Two had Hrein wives from powerful families in Hrein-aa-byy.

The wives worked together and visited among themselves every day. Lately they agreed that maintaining a home in the mound of frozen earth was becoming almost impossible. They were now routinely talking about how they could possibly survive if the cold lasted. The nineteen children in the house were bad enough. But the four men who stayed underfoot in cold weather were nearly as bad as the children. Food reserves were running low. Their men depended on others to do the hunting and expected the wives to trade for the food. But the other hunters had disappeared, which made it difficult to find people willing to trade. Everyone was saving their butter and pemmican for some precious reason.

The living arrangements in the mound of earth allowed each family a set of rooms connected to the larger common room. Most of the people went to the common room for the evening activities because the fall chill was already being felt in the house. The more people in the common room, the less seal-oil that they had to use. One night, after the evening food was eaten, two of the men had set out the chessmen. The shipping agent had just moved the first pawn when there was a knock on the door.

"Oh, no," said the shipping agent. "It must be His Eminence again. You would think he could just look at the ice in the fjord to know the ship did not come."

The king's agent went to the door to ask who was there. "Bishop Arne," was the reply. They opened the door for him and exchanged greetings. Another bundle of caribou ribs was cut open and offered. Bishop Arne chose to drink just water rather than bva.

After a period of talk about small things, the king's agent decided to open the serious discussions of the evening on his own terms. He asked, "Bishop, do you know anything about people vanishing?"

Bishop Arne replied, "What do you mean by 'vanishing'?"

"Oh, do not be coy, Bishop. You have been preaching for years that the people of Hrein-aa-byy should migrate to Merica. Then two summers ago Ivar was able to go to the Northern Settlement. The fool thinks it was the Western Settlement. But the point is that he found nobody there. A thousand people vanished.

"Then just this winter, I could find none of the Sakkyndigs in the middle settlement or in Breida and Isa fjords. There were people in the houses, but they looked like people I have seen before in Eiriksfjord."

The fur trader chimed in: "Then this summer we checked closer. We know there used to be up to nineteen people on each farm in the Eastern Settlement. I know. I was with Ivar when he counted them. Last summer there were less than five people on every farm in the northern fjords. There are about a hundred and forty farms in those fjords. That means that nearly another two thousand people have vanished. Do you know anything about it?"

Bishop Arne held up his right palm. "Yes, I do know where the people went. They did not vanish. They still walk the earth. In fact, I came tonight to discuss a unique opportunity for you to join them. I can arrange to get three sleds for you."

The ivory trader responded, "Why would we want to trade for sleds? I am hesitant to talk about opportunities with you, you crafty old…"

A ladle slapped against a doorframe. The ivory trader looked up into the glaring eyes of his Hrein wife who stood in a doorway with her crossed arms. He looked around the room. He saw three other women glaring sternly at him. The crafty ivory trader hardly missed a beat as he continued to say, "On the other hand, we have nothing else for entertainment this evening, Bishop Arne. Let us examine this opportunity."

In the middle of winter at Hrein-aa-byy, the sky was growing pale in the east. The last ten sleds to leave Hrein Island were lined up side by side off the west shore of Hrein Island. There was no one to see them off because the sixty people at the sleds were the last people in the last kirke that chose to leave Hrein-aa-byy.

Suddenly they heard a sound behind them, from up the fjord in the direction of Gardar. Bishop Arne looked back. He saw three men on small ponies. The ponies were trotting. The men were bouncing and waving. When a pony hit a snow bank, the flying snow created a burst of whiteness. The men and ponies looked like ghosts.

Then words could be heard: "Wait! Stop! Wait! Stop!"

Bishop Arne said to Talerman, "It is His Nemesis. I wonder what took him so long?"

Talerman shouted over to Gard, "Move them out, but keep us in sight." Gard started the other nine sleds down the fjord. The three Shetland ponies came up to Talerman and Bishop Arne's sled. His Eminence turned his pony in a circle trying to stop it. Finally he jumped off close to Bishop Arne and came up half falling and half running.

"Where did they go? Where did they go?" shouted His Eminence.

"Where did who go?" asked Bishop Arne.

"The people in the Eastern Settlement! Nobody is in any of the houses from Hrein-aa-byy north," huffed His Eminence.

Bishop Arne smiled and said, "They have all chosen to walk to Merica."

His Eminence's face showed his disbelief. "They have all walked into the Indrawing Sea? Are you saying that FOUR THOUSAND people from Greenland have walked into the Indrawing Sea?"

"Yes," said Talerman, "and fewer died than if they had stayed here."

"Oh! Oh!" exclaimed His Eminence, who could not control his rage. "Where are the ivory and fur traders, the king's agent, and the shipping agent?"

"They are a sleep ahead of us, Your Eminence," said Bishop Arne. "They hesitated until the very last to come with us. They had roles with high esteem in this land of frozen mounds. They really did not want to leave their frozen mound."

"But, but, you, you deceived them, you old, old devil," sputtered His Eminence. Leveling his finger at Bishop Arne, His Eminence shouted, "You are excommunicated!"

"You want to cut me off from this land of frozen mounds where people die a little bit every sleep? I accept that," replied Bishop Arne. "But you cannot excommunicate me. I am the bishop here. You are only the Pope's ombudsman."

"But you are Bishop—here!" screamed His Eminence, pointing at the ice.

Bishop Arne reached down for the harness and began to tie it on. He said, "People or place. The Popa always has a problem with people or place. Four out of five of my people are in front of me in Merica. I choose to go with them. The Popa can have this place."

"But, but, what will I tell the Popa?" screamed His Eminence.

"Tell the Popa I died and went to the land prepared for me," answered Bishop Arne.

Big Raven Arne leaned into the harness and said to Talerman, "I cannot wait to get there. Let us go."

A moon's time later, at the Big House on Pamiok Island, Talerman came in from the outside. He lifted the flap of the Big House and held it open. Styrk, Hallgrim, Tjalve, and Gard filed into the warmth of the Big House. Halldis recognized Styrk. She stepped over legs, dodged the fire pits, moved children aside, and danced around a man to get to Styrk. She remembered they were in a room full of people, so she just touched both of Styrk's shoulders while saying, "Welcome home."

Styrk smiled and said, "All the other shelters are already on the trail to Akomen. This house will be the last of the last."

Halldis turned to Talerman and said, "Arnora is at the far end of the house with a sick child."

Tjalve, not wanting to disturb the other people, asked, "Is everyone awake?"

Halldis replied, "I do not think so, but we have eaten the morning food a while ago. Those asleep are only napping. We can wake them."

"Good," said Hallgrim. "We will pass along each side of the fires to tell them about the last feast in this Big House. Tomorrow the people in this Big House, the final shelter of the people of the last kirkes to come over the Frozen Trail, will walk on to the land of the spruce and pine."

That day they made preparations. Tjalve retrieved the eleven wooden faces from safe storage and carefully hung them on the arches of the Big House. He also asked a woodsman to make two larger faces, one painted red to represent the sunrise and the other painted black to represent the night. He located the red mask at the south end of the Big House. The red face was set at an angle to the axis of the Big House. Tjalve opened a hole in the roof so the morning sun fell on the red face. At the north end of the house he placed the big black face at an angle so that it looked out the passageway to the western horizon.

As the sun touched the western horizon, the drum rang out inside the Big House, starting slowly, then increasing in rhythm and intensity. The people in the Big House had removed most of their furs and had tried to improve the looks of the clothes they wore. The drum stopped. Big Raven Arne rose to spread his black wings. There was silence. Without a word Big Raven Arne took the wooden face from the priest of the last kirke. He held the wooden face in his hands while he said a short prayer:

"Thank you, Great Spirit, for bringing us here to the land prepared for us. Thank you, Great Spirit, for watching over us on the Frozen Trail. Bless all of those people from the eleven kirkes that have passed this way before us. Thank you for watching over the people of this kirke. Guide their steps on the path to come. These people are the last of those who chose to come to a new land that we can possess. We thank you for guiding so many of us from the land of freezing Hel. Be merciful, Great Spirit, with those remaining in the land to the east. Provide them with strength for their ordeal. Great Spirit, guide us in this land onto the paths of humility. Amen."

Then Big Raven Arne returned the wooden face to the priest, who hung it onto an arch pole of the Big House. When that was accomplished, twelve wooden masks, representing the Greenland ancestors that built the original twelve kirkes, were hanging in the Big House in Merica.

Then Talerman assumed the role of the lead man for the feast that followed. His assistants did the many odd things needed to make a big gathering go smoothly. Styrk, Hallgrim, and Tjalve served the food to the people gathered around the firepits. Talerman told the people that whatever could not be carried away tomorrow should be consumed during the following night.

Tjalve found and led the next speakers to the center of the house. During the feast the headman of each household came forward to give praise for their safe passage or told of an event that would interest the others. There was much mirth, good-natured ribbing, and even ribald comments, mostly about who slept together in the sleds.

There was a period of time when the necessary things were done. After the period was over, but before Talerman took full control again, people began to exchange items to show their appreciation of other families. Neighbors in Hrein-aa-byy, who had always carefully guarded their personal items, now exchanged those same personal items. An ivory cross went to a young woman who helped take care of the children of sick and weak mothers. New mittens were given to an old man without a woman to sew mittens for him. Beads went to the woman who was always patching the splitting furs for everyone. Those with nothing to give said a simple, "I am glad to know you. Thanks for all you have done." Many responded, "Thanks, me too."

When the drum called the people to Talerman, he asked his helpers to say anything they wanted about the past and about the walk yet to come.

Styrk spoke of the details of the path. Hallgrim spoke of food and housing details. Tjalve spoke of what to do if sickness came and how to behave with the local people. He closed with a plea for everyone to encourage each other.

Then it was time for another relaxing break. The drummer played interesting rhythms while people circulated and talked. Talerman noticed with a slight concern that Arnora, Halldis, and Nokla were talking earnestly in the far end of the house.

Talerman gave the drummer a sign to call the group back to order. When the drumroll ended, Talerman said, "In my youth, we young men often ventured to test our skills. Big Raven Arne, Styrk, Hallgrim, Tjalve, and myself ventured together to Akomen during the second long cold spell. The things we learned on that venture have helped all of us. You young men here have had the venture forced upon you by the cold. Most of you did not plan to walk the Frozen Trail. Yet you too tested your skills and found they were adequate. Few people in the future will believe the ordeal you have survived. Please rise and tell us about your experiences so that the storytellers can tell of your actions for the future generations."

Tjalve had already picked a young man to lead off the stories. Tjalve reached down, took his hand, and pulled the young man to his feet. He told of his house preparing to survive the cold in Hrein-aa-byy. He told of storing food, blubber, and fur. He told of his family's callowness toward his neighbors. His family was planning to fight the neighbors when the food ran out. Then he told how Bishop Arne visited their farmhouse and personally argued with the headman in the house until the man agreed to walk the Frozen Trail with the family. The young man saw how the actions of people on the Frozen Trail changed everyone for the better. He saw men working together. Everyone was pulling a sled. He saw people sharing food. On this night, he knew the people in the Big House were much better people than they were in the earthen houses they left behind. Yet they were the same people. He himself wanted to be like Tjalve, who cared for people like a priest.

The first young man set the tone for the stories to follow. As Talerman listened he was thankful that the people in the house would be mutually supportive during the rest of the walk on the Frozen Trail to Akomen and during the confrontations with the wolf packs in the future.

When the last young man finished, Talerman signaled the drummer to announce a necessary break. Then Talerman turned to steal a glance at the far end of the house. He said, "Uh-oh!"

Tjalve said, "What is the matter, Talerman? You look as if we are under attack."

Talerman said quickly, "The last time I saw that lance carried like that, life became twice as difficult."

Tjalve turned to see where Talerman was looking. Arnora with the lance in her hands and Nokla were almost upon them. Behind the approaching women, the other women and girls were on their feet. Tjalve heard a rustling behind him and swung further around to see Halldis pulling women to their feet. Soon all the women in the Big House were standing.

Arnora and Nokla stopped in front of Talerman. The Big House was silent. He rose and asked, "Do you women want something?"

Arnora said, "We want to be heard also. We have pounded the pemmican, nursed all these young men, pulled the sleds, woven the roof mats, sewed the clothes, carried the water, and much more. We women are part of the people in this Big House, too. We want to tell our names, what we are good at doing, and what we are thankful for."

Tjalve chimed in, "If it were not for the women, what could men be thankful for?"

Styrk offered his opinion. "Living with them will be better if we listen to them."

Hallgrim said quickly, "We have enough time before sunrise."

Talerman turned to signal for the drum to give a summons roll and then realized it would sound silly. The Big House was already very silent. Smiling at Arnora, Talerman turned and said to all in the Big House, "We have saved the best for the end. We all know we would not be in this land and could not possess it without the efforts of our women. Would you please, one by one, tell us your name, what you are good at doing, and what you are thankful for."

Arnora folded her arms around the lance, stepped forward and said, "I am Arnora. I am a good cook. I am thankful that Big Raven Arne listened carefully to the Great Spirit."

Then Arnora pointed to the woman to her right. She said, "I am Hallveig. I am a good sewer. I am thankful for Styrk's ability to find the right path." The next women said, "I am Thorbjørg, I am good with sheep, I am thankful to be away from the frozen mound of earth."

Each woman to the north end of the Big House, south along the other side, and back to the leaders, spoke in turn. When her turn came Halldis said, "I am Halldis. I am good at caring for men, including my husband." The laughter made her hesitate before she continued, "I am thankful Talerman was our friend." Then she pointed to Nokla, the last woman to speak.

Nokla looked straight at Talerman and said, "I am Nokla. I am a good comforter of people in distress. I am thankful I comforted Talerman." A subdued murmur of laughter came from the crowd. The parentage of Awasos was known to many in the Big House. Talerman swung to look at Arnora, who just smiled back. Nokla continued, "By comforting Talerman, I met Arnora."

The drummer signaled the ending with a double thump. Talerman looked toward the south end of the house. The pale sky was visible through the hole above the red mask on the post. The red face was standing out from the darker sidewalls. Talerman pointed to Big Raven Arne.

Big Raven Arne stood up and said, "My children, now is the time to leave this Big House of restoration. We still have many sleeps to walk to reach the land we can possess. At that land there are many paths into the future. May the Great Spirit place your feet firmly on the path you desire. May he bless the animals that will give you food. May you remember the spirits of those animals that give their life for you. May the Great Spirit give you the strength, intelligence, and endurance you need to live. There are many paths in Akomen, so my body will be separated from yours, but I will always go with you in spirit. Amen."

There was silence. Then the drummer started slowly with a soft beat. As the drum grew louder, a "thwack, thwack" matched the rhythm. After the sixth "thwack" from a woman's axe, a panel of caribou hide on the east side of the Big House fell away. The sun stabbed brilliant rays into the house. Bishop Arne took the masks from the sidewalls and gave three each to four young men who had volunteered to carry them. The two big posts with the faces carved into them were left standing. Maybe someday the site would be used for another Big House. People scurried to collect their things for the start of the last walk on the Frozen Trail.

The drummer tried to match the "thwacks," but they were coming from all sides. So he rolled to a crescendo and went silent. The "thwack, thwack" continued while Styrk led the people from Hrein-aa-byy toward the land they would possess.

Vignette Twenty-three
They All Came

"Thwack, thwack," the knives resounded. The women were cutting the sinews holding the Big House roof panels. A roof panel fell away. Daylight flooded into the Big House, illuminating the women methodically taking the house apart.

In the morning light Azon and Pitolo skipped slowly, in tandem, on the path from the Big House toward Grandfather's palisade. Four women each carrying three masks followed behind. Other women were carrying the other twelve masks to Pitolo's tepee.

Pitolo sighed. "Oh, what a long, long night. What do you think about it?"

"I agree about the long night," said Azon, "but I think it is good that the men listen to what the women say. Everyone is better because they hear the women."

"You are wise."

Pitolo stepped off the path. Azon came to stand beside him. The women with the masks continued toward the palisade. The young men looked through the trees toward the east where Gee Hiz, clothed in red, was rising. They stood silently, appreciating the beauty of the morning.

Azon broke the silence. "The women have good thoughts and we need to be reminded how valuable they are. I just wish they could whittle words away as you do."

Pitolo started toward the palisade entrance. "The words of last night will be easy for me to whittle away. I fell asleep when the big fat woman started to talk. I hope you have a good verse for Maalan Aarum. I would be ashamed if we used mine for history."

Azon was not at all sure of his verse, so he just said, "We will see what Grandfather thinks. If he still breathes."

When they reached the tepee, Azon's mother was seated on the large rock a few paces away from the tepee. She saw them coming. Then she quickly looked away as if she was watching a bug in the grass. They entered the tepee.

Grandfather was lying flat on his back. His eyes were open, but he did not raise his head to look at Azon. With a slight turn of the head, he refused the water Azon offered.

Grandfather whispered, "We'd better hurry. Can I hear the verses? Pitolo first."

Pitolo said, "Every one came.

"They wintered at the forest by the sea.

"The men from the east also came, though they were reluctant

"to leave their homes behind."

Grandfather's eyes blinked. The tip of his tongue parted his lips. He whispered, "Azon, what do you have?"

Azon knelt down to speak quietly into Grandfather's ear. He said:

"They all came.

"They tarry at the land of the spruce-pine.

"Those from the east came with hesitation,

"esteeming highly their old homes at mound land."

Grandfather's eyes went shut. Slowly his head rolled away from them. Then he took a shuddering breath. The head rolled upright with eyes open and a slight smile on his face.

He was whispering as he said, "I am thankful to know. Now both of you are good engravers and both can make good verses. Today, I choose Azon's verse."

Pitolo said, "Maalan Aarum, your judgment is still excellent."

Grandfather said, "My young men, I have no story today. I think there is not enough time for one."

Azon said, "Grandfather, Pitolo and I have been wondering. Have all those people, who you told stories about, just vanished? Will anyone but us even know they were on earth?"

Grandfather lay with his eyes open, blinking only once in a long while. Then he said, "I will not be able to tell about all of them. Please, Pitolo come close on my left side to hear my words."

Pitolo moved alongside Maalan Aarum's chest and knelt. As Pitolo adjusted his position, Azon moved up closer on the right side of his grandfather. Grandfather spoke with long pauses between words: "Big Raven Arne will be well known by many people who will still deny that he ever was in this land. The older people of this land will know that he lived near the cave on the Nemiskou until the Great Spirit came for him.

"Thurid, Valthjof's second daughter, who gave birth on the ice, joined a young rebellious man who would not listen to the elders. He took her and the child to join a band of wild young men and a few foolish women who went to Hochalaga to fish. All of them were food for the wolf packs.

"Runolf is already forgotten. He stayed north with the dogs he loved. Everyone in the cold country knows the descendants of his dogs.

"To find a new start in life, Grimhild and Ørn Aslakson took Grimhild's firstborn, Eyvind, west. They had other children. Their descendants, called 'Blackfeet,' still hunt where the earth is black.

"But, unfortunately, warriors from a small group of people called 'Sarcy' captured Eyvind's daughter. They carried her away to replace a wife who died in childbirth. Somewhere, in the far west, there are storytellers who still tell the story about Eyvind trying to pull the horn from the ice.

"Gunnbjørn and the boat escaped the sea ice and made it to the island of ice in the east. Nineteen other boats sailed to the island of ice that fall. All of them stayed through the winter because the sea ice surrounded the island of ice. In the summer, Captain Gunnbjørn and the boat sailed to Norumvege. The crew of Gunnbjørn's ship joined a band of red-haired, white-skinned people called the 'BEOTHUK.'

"Captain Gunnbjørn's Kimal will be found in the future and will be seen by a large host of people. For four grandfathers' time no one will understand the Kimal, but eventually a few men will be able to explain it.

"Vifill traveled to Hallgrim's village with him. At a summer camp of many villages, Vifill fell in love with one of Aslak's black-eyed daughters. Their wise, fearless descendants have always followed the descendants of Talerman. In the future they will choose to place themselves between the wolf packs and our people. They will settle on a river shaped like a giant fish hook, You will call them the 'Mahigans.'"

Grandfather's eyes closed. His breathing was hardly visible. Azon reached his right hand up to hold Grandfather's right hand. The hand was cold to Azon's touch, but he felt a twitch of the fingers. Grandfather opened his eyes and continued with a dry rasping whisper, "Tjalve's son from Thorgerd married an Eastman Land woman who wore black clothes and a hat like a cone. We call their descendants the 'Conoy.'

"Hallgrim always went back to his first robe-warmer who had waited for him. They had three children, and all of them could think with numbers. When the children were grown, she left her village to follow Hallgrim. They were always wise to cook their seafood. Their descendants lived through many cycles of the yellow death. We call their descendants the 'Nanticoke.'

"The descendants of Styrk and Halldis are still finding paths for our people. Right now their descendants are far to the south, so we call them the 'Shawnee.'

"Pitolo, Talerman was your ancestor via Nokla and through Awasos. Awasos's half-siblings who came from Gard and Nokla have been important sachems of our people. They continue to guard our people. They look out on a big bay at the mouth of a river. Their descendants will continue to call themselves the 'Munsee' group of the Leni Lenape.

"Azon, our ancestors were from Talerman and Arnora through Bjorn and Kuptana. Our people have become the main group of the Lenape. We call ourselves the 'Unami.' All Leni Lenape are in the grandfather group of the Algän kin. Your descendants will always call themselves the 'Leni Lenape,' real people from the decent place. The decent place, called Hrein, will still exist, but only a very, very few here will believe your ancestors could have walked from there.

"Pitolo, because of your way with words, you will be known by many in the future as the 'Author.'

"Azon, you will be known for your creations. Many will call you 'Historian.'

"There will be many who will not believe you even existed, but what you and your descendants create will exist for ten grandfathers' time. Someday wise men will make studies of your engravings and verses. They will be confounded many times, but finally someone will understand."

Grandfather paused. The eyes closed. After a long moment Pitolo said quietly, "People will remember you, Maalan Aarum, forever."

Grandfather's eyes flickered and opened. A brief smile formed on his lips. He whispered, "Something like that. Pitolo please hold my left hand."

Pitolo reached up with his left hand to take Maalan Aarum's left hand. It felt cold and lifeless.

Grandfather's eyes closed. He said, "I am seeing green grass on soft earth, under spruce and pine trees. Gee Hiz is going down to his boat over a pretty lake. Is this where they will put my body?"

Azon was filled with choking emotions, so he was surprised to hear his own voice say calmly, "Yes, Grandfather."

Grandfather's eyes remained closed, as he whispered, "It is a very good spot to put a body."

Pitolo and Azon each felt a slight tightening by the cold, feeble fingers. They leaned close to hear the words Maalan Aarum formed with his last three shallow breaths: "My spirit—goes with—you."

They all come.
They tarry at the land
Of the spruce pines,
Those from the east
Some with hesitation.
Esteeming highly their
Old home at the mound land.

Factual Fiction

ALTERGANG—Today, in Norway, *Altergang* means "communion." The story assumes that, in earlier times in primitive locations, "Altergang" meant what it says: "going to the altar (to pray)."

The Algonquins had: (1) a Great Spirit, (2) a name that sounds like "Jesus" for the light of the world, (3) priests called *pavow*, similar to *paafa*, (4) cross tokens, both regular and tau, (5) a word *quash* for "cross," 6) altars in their tepees, and (7) a word *attaboan*, to mean prayer, that could have derived from *altergang*.

The cluster of evidence implies that the Algonquins were originally Christians. The *attaboan* word implies that the Norse Christians also became part of the Algonquin culture sometime after A.D. 1000 when the Norse converted to the Christian religion.

ARTIFACTS FROM GREENLAND—The artifacts listed in the story were found during an excavation of the longest and northernmost set of low walls. Plumet (1985) wrote the report in French. He omitted any mention of these artifacts in the abstract, which was written in both French and English. Even though he had dates for the occupation of the low walls, Plumet said (in the French text) that, except for the copper knife, the artifacts could not be dated. The copper knife was of European manufacture in the twelfth century. Plumet proposed that an Eskimo walked to Greenland to trade for the knife.

Plumet's primary research motivation appears to be that he wanted to show that Thomas Lee's hypothesis of a Norse origin for the low walls was not valid. Plumet's repeated rebukes of Thomas Lee appear in the abstracts of many of his research reports. Summaries of the real physical evidence did not appear in the abstracts (Plumet 1982, 1984, 1995). The irony is that Plumet had valid carbon-14 data showing that the walls were built before the Viking era and only re-used during the Little Ice age.

BELL'S PALSY—Bell's Palsy is a nonprogressive facial nerve disorder characterized by the sudden onset of facial paralysis. The paralysis results from decreased blood supply and from compression of the seventh cranial nerve.

The early symptoms of Bell's Palsy may include a slight fever, pain behind the ear, a stiff neck, and weakness and/or stiffness on one side of the face. The symptoms may begin suddenly and progress rapidly over several hours, and sometimes follow exposure to cold or a draft. Part or all of the face may be affected.

In most cases of Bell's Palsy, only facial muscle weakness occurs and the facial paralysis is temporary (*The Family Doctor*, 3rd edition).

BEOTHUK—The words, drawings, and descriptions in the HNAI vol. 15 Beothuk chapter point toward a hypothesis that the Beothuk were early fifteenth-century Norse, perhaps from the remaining people of the Eastern Settlement of Greenland.

The Beothuk had a story of a man being burned at the stake because of committing adultery. The last Norse people who left Greenland after 1410 had a tale of a man burned at the stake because of committing adultery. Burning a man for committing adultery is rarely mentioned in the history of many cultures, especially those of America.

FIRE TOWER—Lee (1970/71) took a photo of the ring of large stones described as a base for the fire tower in the story. The ring of stones is located at the north end of a small, flat island off the northeast coast of Ungava peninsula. The island is near the center of the eastern edge of the northern open-water marvel. The largest twelve or more stones in the ring weigh more than a man. They are placed tightly together in a ring, except for two gaps where there are no stones. Other stones are visible in the distant background, but the effort to select and move the big stones to the ring obviously required several men working for several days (Lee 1970/1971, fig. 22A).

FOUR THOUSAND—The *Inventio Fortunatae* author wrote of "…nearly 4,000 people who 'entered the Indrawing Seas [beyond Greenland] who never returned'" Seaver 1996).

The *Inventio Fortunatae* author is thought to have returned on the same ship(s) that returned Ivar Bardarsson to Norway.

HORN—Sarsi Migration Myth: "…when ice was on the water, the people went traveling across it. There was no snow on the ice. Half the people got across. Some were still on the ice and some had not started across. Among those on the ice, a small boy saw a horn imbedded in the ice. He asked his mother to get it for him. He cried. She took a large knife and began to chop it out. When she had nearly released it from the ice, the animal (a water monster) moved, and the ice was suddenly broken up" (Curtis 1928).

KOKSOAK—Koksoak is the first major river south of the River of Leaves. The location, 150 miles south of Pamiok, is south of the tree line. The site has one of the few härbret bases not located on a hilltop (Lee 1968).

LAST SUPPER—"The hooves of these five beasts (cows) were scattered among food remains on the lower layer of one room. The larder contained the bones of a lamb, a new born calf, and the skull of a large, elkhound like hunting dog" (Brian Fagan 2000).

MAMMOTH ROOF—A sketch of a *mamateek* (Mammoth Roof) is shown in the HNAI, vol. 15, p. 102, fig 2.

POSTHOLES—Although the sites are all well north of the Arctic tree line, researchers have found evidence of wooden posts in all the low-wall sites investigated. The postholes in Longhouse 2 at Pamiok Island are adjacent to the interior sides of the rock walls (Lee 1971; Plumet 1982).

The holes have a position and spacing similar to the spacing of posts erected for arched Big Houses.

SECOND USE—The carbon-14 data indicate that the longhouses on Ungava Peninsula were used for the second time during the Little Ice Age, 1300 to 1360. The data also indicate the sites were not used between the Dark Ages and the Little Ice Age, or since then to modern times (Plumet,1982).

STONE TOWER—Verrazzano (1524) reported that the people near the lavabo said they lived in "Agonsy" (Stromsted 1973), The "other places" included, in colonial times, "Akomac," an early name for Plymouth; "Akomenack," meaning "Haakon's people's country" but recorded as "of which Massassoit was sachem"; the rivers Akhushnut, Akoont, Akoakest, and Akqussent. There were also tracts of land, hills, and necks of land with names like Akawmack, Akashewah, Akomonticus, Akoakset, Akockus, Akoughcouss, Akquiatt, Akushnet, and Akushena.

The stone tower, a lavabo, and keep of a medieval church still stands in Newark, Rhode Island (Holand 1958).

TO AMERICA—The phrase "AD AMERICAE POPULOS SE CONVERTERUNT" means, "To the people of America we have turned" (Mowat 1965).

Bishop Oddson, of Iceland, wrote the information in his journal c. 1360. At that time Ivar Bardarsson may have stopped over in Iceland on his way back to Norway.

TWELVE MASKS—The decision of twelve praying houses in Greenland to migrate conforms to the Lenape tradition of twelve tribes represented by the twelve masks in the Big House (Bleaker 1953).

WHITE FALCONS—White falcons were a rare gift often exchanged between powerful people in Europe. Many Europeans thought the white falcons came from Greenland (Ingstad 1966).

The most productive source of white falcons was Ungava Bay, especially Gyrfalcon Island near the River of Leaves.

YELLOW DEATH—Warren Rasmussen discussed the yellow death in a public forum in 2001. The yellow plague episodes are believed to have been recurring events. A very bad episode occurred just before the Pilgrims landed in 1620. Rasmussen believed tainted shellfish during a very warm climate caused the yellow plague. The story has the Greenland priest dying in 1335, the warmest year in the previous twelve years.

Word Meaning

Many words used in the story are related to Old Norse. A pattern is followed in the word derivations below.

If the modern spelling of an Algonquin word has a very similar spelling and sound as an Old Norse word, then the Old Norse meaning will be given directly. For example, *tepee (teppa)* means, "enclosure."

If the modern spelling of an Algonquin word has major changes from an Old Norse word, then the Algonquin word is shown as derived from the Old Norse word before the English meaning is given. For example, "caribou" is derived from *kare* meaning "raking" combined with *bu*, meaning "cattle."

Aa-byy means "abide" or "to live at."

Asvaldson is the son of a very powerful man. *Ás* means "god," and *vald* means "ruler."

Beothuk may have derived from *beo(rdre)*, meaning "direct," and *tokt*, meaning "cruise."

Eyvind: *Ey* is "a gift" or "happiness, good luck," and *vind* means "the one who wins."

Grimhild: *Grim* means "mask" or "face shield," and *hild* means "clean" or "pure."

Hallveig means "stone" plus *veig*. *Veig* was used in Iceland long before 1335, but no one, today, has managed to translate the meaning of *veig*.

Hrein-aa-byy means 'to abide in Hrein." There was an island and perhaps a fjord named Hrein in Greenland. *Hrein* means "decent," as in "a decent place."

Koksoak may mean "Beaver house land," where *kobi*, for "beaver," has been shortened to *ko* and *kso* was derived from *kasse*, meaning "box (house)."

The *ak* is a Norse ending meaning "plenty of." The *ak* also indicates that the word is Norse.

Kuptana is the name of an Eskimo woman.

Mahigan was derived from *moki*, meaning "fish," and *gagn*, meaning "instrument." The people may have been named after the river they lived upon. *Maghigan* means "fishhook." The Hudson River is shaped like a fishhook, with a long shank north from the mouth and a definite hook to the source in the west.

Mamateek is a "mammoth roof," where *mama* was derived from *mammut*, meaning "mammoth," and *teek* was derived from *tekke*, meaning "roof."

Manalthing—*Manalting* is a word used in the *Walam Olum* 4:4. The word, in Lenape, means "meeting in council."

Müsqá means "bear" in the K'nistenaux language.

Nanticoke may mean "people that cook." *Nan* was probably derived from *man*, which means "people." *Ti* was derived from *det*, which means "that." *Coke* was derived from *kokke*, which means "cook."

Narragansett—*Narra* means "narrow," *gan* was derived from *gang*, meaning "passageway," and *sett* is a place designator

Ormsson means "son of worm."

Runolf—*Run* means "hidden knowledge, secret," and *olf* means "wolf."

Sigrid: *Sig* is from *siger*, meaning "victory," and *rid* means "beautiful."

Thorbjørg means "Thor" (the Thunder god) and *bjørg*, "protection."

Unami may have been derived from *uni*, which was used for the definitive, "the," and *mye*, which means "plenty (of)." The name may mean "the main (most numerous) group of the Lenape."

Valthjof means "someone who steals from graves."

Vifill means "we will." Usually the name of a priest.

Selected Bibliography

Adams, Arthur T. 1951. *The Explorations of Radisson*. Minneapolis: Ross & Haines.

Allen, Paula Gunn. 2003. *Pocahontas*. Harper San Francisco.

Arms, Myron. 1998. *Riddle of the Ice*. New York: Anchor Books, Doubleday.

Bial, Raymond. 2000. *Ojibwe*. New York: Benchmark Books, Marshall Cavendish.

Bleeker, Sonia. 1953. *The Delaware Indians*. William Morrow & Company, Inc.

Boland, Charles Michael. 1963. *They All Discovered America*. New York: Pocket Books, Inc.

Brinton, Danial G. 1885. *The Lenapé and their Legends*. Philadelphia: D. G. Brinton.

Burland, Cottie. 1985. *North American Indian Mythology*. New York: Peter Bedrick Books.

Carlson, Susan D. 1998. The Decipherment of American Runestones. In *Across Before Columbus*, ed. Donald Y. Gilmore and Linda S. McElroy, Edgecomb, Maine: NEARA Pub.

Cookman, Scot. 2000. *Iceblink*. New York: John Wiley & Sons.

Coulter, Tony. 1993. *Jacques Cartier, Samuel de Champlain, and the Explorers of Canada*. New York: Chelsea House Publications.

Courtauld, Augustine. 1958. *From the Ends of the Earth*. London: Oxford University Press.

Cox, Ian. 1960. Eskimo Remains on Akpatok Island, North-East Canada. *Scientific Results of the Oxford University Hudson Strait Exploration, 1931*. Oxford: Oxford University Press.

Curtis, Edward S. 1928. The *North American Indian*. Vol. 18. New York: Johnson Reprint Corp.

De Bremen, Adam. 1070. *Descriptio Insularum Aquilonis* (quoted in Olsen and Bourne. 1906. *The Northmen, Columbus, and Cabot*).

Douglas-Lithgow, R. A. 1909/2000. *Native American Place Names of Massachusetts*. Bedford, Mass.: Applewood Books.

Drake, Benjamin. 1852. *A History of Tecumseh and of His Brother the Prophet*. S. & J. Applegate & Co.

Edinger, Ray. 2003. *Fury Beach*. Berkley Publishing Co.

Enterline, James Robert. 1972. *Viking America*. New York: Doubleday and Company, Inc.

Fell, Barry. 1976. *America BC*. New York: Demeter Press.

——————. 1982. *Bronze Age America*. Boston: Little, Brown & Co.

Fitzhugh, Ward. 2000. *Vikings: The North Atlantic Saga*. Washington: Smithsonian Institution.

Freuchen, Peter. 1953. Vagrant *Viking*. New York: Julian Messner, Inc.

——————. 1955. *Arctic Adventure*. New York: Farrar & Rinehart.

Gabrielsen, Egill Dave. *English-Norwegian, Norwegian-English, Concise Dictionary*. New York: Hippocrene Books.

Galbraith, John S. 1957. *The Hudson's Bay Company as an Imperial Factor, 1824-1869*. University of California Press.

Grafton, Anthony. 1992. *New Worlds, Ancient Texts*. Belknap Press of Harvard University Press.

Hall, Sam. 1987. *The Fourth World*. New York: Alfred A. Knopf.

Hapgood, Charles H. 1966. *Maps of the Ancient Sea Kings*. Philadelphia: Chilton Co.

Haugen, Einar. 1942. Voyages *to Vinland*. New York: Alfred A. Knopf.

HNAI = Sturtevant, William C. 1978. *Handbook of North American Indians*. Washington: Smithsonian Institution.

Holand, Hjalmar R. 1958. *Explorations in America Before Columbus*. New York: Twayne Publishers, Inc.

Holmes, George. 1962. *The Later Middle Ages, 1272-1485*. Edinburgh: Thomas Nelson and Sons Ltd.

Horsford, Eben Norton. 1891. *Norse Discovery of America*. Boston: Horsford.

Hubbard-Brown, Janet. 1995. *The Shawnee*. New York: Chelsea House Pub.

Hurt, R. Douglas. 2002. *The Indian Frontier 1763-1846*. Albuquerque: University of New Mexico Press.

Hyde, George E. 1962. *Indians of the Woodlands, from Prehistoric Times to 1725*. Norman, Okla.: University of Oklahoma Press.

Ingstad, Helge. 1966. *Land Under the Pole Star*. New York: St. Martin's Press.

JRAD = *Jesuits: Letters From Missions*. 1959. *The Jesuit Relations and Allied Documents*. New York: St. Martin's Press.

Kent, Rockwell. 1990. *N by E*. Lebanon, N.H.: University Press of New England.

Key, Mary Richie. American Indian Languages before Columbus. In *Across Before Columbus,* ed. Donald Y. Gilmore and Linda S. McElroy, Edgecomb, Maine: NEARA Pub.

Keys, David. 1999. *Catastrophe.* New York: Ballantine Books.

Kopper, Philip. 1986. *The Smithsonian Book of North American Indians.* Washington: Smithsonian Books.

Lee, Thomas E. 1966. *Archaeological Discoveries, Payne Bay Region, Ungava.* Quebec City: Université Lavel.

————. 1970. *Archaeological Investigations of a Longhouse, Pamiok Island, Ungava.* Quebec City: Université Lavel.

Lehane, Brendon. 1981. *The Northwest Passage.* Alexandria, Va.: Time-Life Books.

Llewellyn, Karl N., and E. Adamson Hoebel. 1941. *The Cheyenne Way.* Norman, Okla.: University of Oklahoma Press.

Mackenzie, Sir Alexander. 1966. *Voyages from Montreal on the River, St. Lawrence.* Rutland, Vt.: Tuttle.

Magnusson, Magnus. 2000. *Scotland.* Atlantic Press.

Magnusson, Magnus, and Herman Palsson. 1966. *The Vinland Sagas: The Norse Discovery of America.* New York University Press.

Malaurie, Jean. 1982. *The Last Kings of Thule.* New York: E. P. Dutton, Inc.

Mason, Theodore K. 1982. *Two Against the Ice: Amundsen and Ellsworth.* New York: Dodd, Mead & Company.

McCutchen, David. 1993. The *Red Record: The Wallam Olum, the Oldest Native North American History.* Garden City Park, N.Y.: Pavley Publishing Group Inc.

McKinlay, William Laird. 1976. *Karluk.* New York: St. Martin's Press.

Medicine, Manitonquat. 1994. *The Children of the Morning Light.* Macmillian Publishing Co.

Mowat, Farley. 1952. *People of the Deer. Boston:* Little, Brown, and Co.

————. 1965. *Westviking: The Ancient Norse in Greenland and North America.* Boston: Little, Brown, and Co.

————. 1980. *The World of Farley Mowat.* Atlantic Press.

————. 1989. *Tundra.* Gibbs Smith Books, Pub.

————. 1998/2000. *The Wayfarers.* Hanover, N.H.: Steerforth Press.

————. 2001. *High Latitudes: An Arctic Journey.* Hanover, N.H.: Steerforth Press.Vermont

Newman, Peter C. 1989. *Empire of the Bay.* Viking Studio/Madison Press Books.

Oestreicher, David M. 1994. "Unmasking the Walam Olum." In *Bulletin of The Archaeological Society of New Jersey, 49 & 50*. South Orange, N.J.: The Archaeological Society of New Jersey.

Oleson, Tryggvi J. 1964. *Early Voyages and Northern Approaches, 1000–1632*. McClelland and Stewart Ltd.

O'Meara, Walter. 1960. The *Savage Country*. Boston: Houghton Mifflin Co.

Parkman, Francis. 1983. *France and England in North America. Vol. 1*. Viking Press.

Pearson, Eva Mildred Mykleby. 1998. *They Did Not Have Horns*. Saint Paul, Minn.: Norbakk Press.

Plumet, Patrick. 1982. "De Maisons Longues Dorsetiennies De L'Ungava." In *Geographic Physique et Quaternaire XXXVI*.

──────. 1985. *Archeologie of L'Ungava: Le Site De La Pointe Aux Belougas et les Maisons Longues Dorsetiennes*. L'Université du Quebec a Montreal.

──────. 1994. La *Paleoesquimax dans La Baie du Diana*. Canadian Museum of Civilization.

Pryde, Duncan. 1971. *Nunaga: Ten Years of Eskimo Life*. Walker and Co.

Reman, Edward. 1949. *The Norse Discoveries and Explorations in America*. Berkley: University of California Press.

Riberion, Aileen, and Valerie Cummings. 1989. *The Visual History of Costume*. New York: Drama Brode Publishers.

Rich, E. E. 1961. *The Hudson's Bay Company 1670-1870*. MacMillian Co.

Richardson, Boyce. 1976. *Strangers Devour the Land*. New York: Knopf; distributed by Random House.

Richie, William A. 1969. *The Archaeology of New York State*. Garden City, N.Y.: Natural History Press.

Rosedahl, Else. 1987. The *Vikings*. Penguin Press.

Rousseau, Jacques. 1948. "By Canoe Across the Ungava Peninsula via the Kogaluk and Payne Rivers." In *Arctic*. Montreal.

Saum, Lewis O. 1964. *The Fur Trader and the Indian*. Seattle: University of Washington Press.

Sawyer, Peter. 1997. *The Oxford Illustrated History of the Vikings*. Oxford University Press.

Seaver, Kirsten A. *The Frozen Echo*: *Greenland the Exploration of North America*. Stanford University Press.

Sherwin, Reider T. 1940-56. *The Viking and the Red Man*. Vols. 1-2. New York: Funk

& Wagnalls Co.

Silverberg, Robert. 1968. *Mound Builders of Ancient America*. New York Graphic Society.

Stefansson, Vilhjalmur. 1964. *Discovery*. New York: McGraw Hill Book Co.

Stromsted, Astri A. 1973. *Ancient Pioneers, Early Connections*.

Sturluson, Snorri. 1964. *Heimskringla*. Austin: University of Texas Press.

Thom, Dark Rain. 1994. *The Shawnee: Kohkumthena's Grandchildren*. Indianapolis. Guild Press of Indiana, Inc.

Thomas, Cyrus, and W. J. McGee. 1903. *Indians of North America in Historic Times*. Philadelphia: George Barrie's Sons.

Time-Life. 1992. The *European Challenge*. Alexandria, Va.: Time-Life Books.

Toye, William. 1959. *The St. Lawrence*. Walck.

Trigger, Bruce G. 1978. *Handbook of American Indians. Vol. 15: Northeast*. Washington: Smithsonian Institution.

Underhill, Ruth M. 1971. *Red Man's America*. Chicago: University of Chicago Press.

Vogel, Vigil J. 1972. *This Country Was Ours*. New York: Harper & Row.

Weatherford, Jack. 1988. *Indian Givers*. Crown Publishers, Inc.

Weilager, Clinton A. 1972. The *Delaware Indians: A History*. Rutgers University Press.

Willison, George E. 1945. *Saints and Strangers*. New York: Rynel & Hitchcock.